WHITE KNIGHTS

Book One

Julie Moffett

White Knights is a work of fiction. Names, characters, places, and incidents are products of the author's imagination or are used fictitiously and are not to be construed as real. Any resemblance to actual locales, organizations, events, or persons, living or dead, is entirely coincidental.

White Knights
Copyright © 2017 by Julie Moffett
All rights reserved.

Published by True Airspeed Press
ISBN: 978-1-941787-26-7

Cover art by Earthly Charms
Formatting by Author E.M.S.

Praise for Julie Moffett's
Lexi Carmichael Mystery Series

"The Lexi Carmichael mystery series runs a riveting gamut from hilarious to deadly, and the perfectly paced action in between will have you hanging onto Lexi's every word and breathless for her next geeked-out adventure." ~**USA Today**

"I absolutely, positively loved this book...I found the humor terrific. I couldn't find a single thing I didn't like about this book except it ended." ~**Night Owl Reviews**

"Wow, wow, and wow! I don't know how Julie Moffett does it but every book is better than the last and all of them are awesome. I may have 6 authors in my top five now!" ~**Goodreads Reader**

"Absolutely loved this book! I love the concept of a geek girl getting involved in all kinds of intrigue and, of course, all the men she gets to meet." ~**Book Babe**

"This book can be described in one word. AMAZING! I was intrigued from the beginning to the end. There are so many twists and turns and unexpected agendas that you do not know who's on the good side or who's on the bad side." ~**Once Upon a Twilight**

"Personally for me when authors create a series by book 9 the stories are the same and the characters are turning in circles. Not with Julie Moffett. The Lexi Carmichael series keeps moving forward expanding the world Julie Moffett has created, and I can't get enough of this series!" ~**Book Him Danno Book Reviews**

"Lexi Carmichael has to be the most lovable character I have come across. She is 100 percent geek and has zero street smarts, but she tries to think outside the box while putting herself in dangerous places without knowing how she got there. The author keeps you guessing who might be a double agent and who might want to harm Lexi." ~**Goodreads Reader**

"One could never go wrong with this exciting detective series. Socially awkward Lexi is a hoot, and her character provides comic relief when the mystery becomes too deep and the romance gets too hot. There are bullets flying, intense action, and hunky Navy SEALs! Moffett's ideas and imagination never cease." ~**Romantic Times**

"I love the zany things that Lexi does, she really makes me laugh. My poor husband was roused from a deep sleep because I was laughing so much—I just could not put the book down." ~**Goodreads Reader**

"The Lexi Carmichael mysteries are my go-to books when I'm feeling blue, under the weather, frustrated with life, or just in the mood for an escape." ~**Goodreads Reader**

"I just love this series so much. Julie Moffett is definitely one of my most favourite authors the way she writes the Lexi Carmichael series with such, intelligence, suspense, mystery, adventure and even the perfect mix of romance and humour, these stories always make the perfect read, re-read and re-read again." ~**Goodreads Reader**

"Klutzy, social awkward geek girl Lexi is a fun narrator and I appreciated how she got out of trouble by using her brain." ~**Goodreads**

Books by Julie Moffett

White Knights Mystery/Spy Series

White Knights (Book 1)*
Knight Moves (coming 2018)*
One-Knight Stand (coming 2018)*

The Lexi Carmichael Mystery Series

No One Lives Twice (Book 1)*
No One to Trust (Book 2)*
No Money Down (Book 2.5-novella)
No Place Like Rome (Book 3)
No Biz Like Showbiz (Book 4)
No Test for the Wicked (Book 5)*
No Woman Left Behind (Book 6)*
No Room for Error (Book 7)*
No Strings Attached (Book 8)*
No Living Soul (Book 9)*
No Regrets (Book 10) Release Date 1/2018
No Stone Unturned (Book 11) 1/2019
No Title Yet (Book 12) TBD

*Print versions (available or coming soon)
All titles are available in audiobook, and some on CDs.

DEDICATION

To my sister and best friend, Sandy Moffett Parks.
The first geek girl I knew and admired.

ACKNOWLEDGMENTS

I am grateful for the ever-guiding hand of my sister, Sandy, in getting this book written and to market, my mom, Donna, for proofing all the various versions, my brother, Brad, for his wisdom and excellent brainstorming sessions, my wonderful cover artist, Su at Earthly Charms, my excellent copy editor, Sara Brady, the fantastic formatter Amy Atwell, and last, but in no way least, my extraordinary editor, Alissa Davis. You ALL rock!

CHAPTER ONE

Angel Sinclair

On the 5,802nd day of my existence, my safe virtual life exploded into reality.

I should have seen it coming—I'm smart enough. My name is Angel Sinclair and I'm a geek. For most of my nearly sixteen years, I've lived online, roaming the information highway—hacking, gaming, and manipulating the environment to suit my every whim. The Internet is my world. I control kingdoms and maintain important and critical alliances. I don't need real-life entanglements, friendships with people who will come and go, or a boyfriend so I don't feel alone. I'm never lonely online.

I'm not bragging when I say I'm good at what I do. When I was eleven, I broke into my school's computer system, just to see if I could. At thirteen, I changed the Twitter profile of a well-known gamer to read "Geek Girls Rule" after he posted a particularly sexist and ugly meme about women in the tech field. Later that same year, I hacked into the local police department looking for information on my father. I've hacked a *lot* of places since then, getting better and faster each time. I'm not into cracking—hacking with malicious intent. But I'm not above a hack when I feel it serves the greater good.

My older sister, Gwen, is always getting on my case to go out, hang with people, be social *off* the computer. Why would I? The girls at my school are always talking about guys or taking selfies to make sure they post the best angle of themselves. Who cares how you look while you're eating in the cafeteria? I'd rather connect with the people who *do* matter via my phone or laptop. Online I've got constant access to what and *who* is important, and it is *way* less stressful than a face-to-face conversation.

So, my plan for my senior year of high school was this—survive by keeping my head down, restricting my social life to online, and not making any waves.

Simple, right?

Wrong.

I desired invisibility but would have accepted peaceful coexistence.

Instead, they brought me war...on the very first day.

Usually on the first day of school, the bus is late. I attend high school at the Excalibur Academy for the Technologically Gifted and Talented in Washington, DC, and most days the traffic sucks. But today the bus arrived promptly at my stop and dropped us off early. Grateful for an extra fifteen minutes before school started, I headed to the inner courtyard, which has a fountain featuring an elaborate sword encased in stone. I sat down on the bench, connected to the school Wi-Fi, and started work on my secret project.

The search for my dad.

I was eighteen months old when my dad left. Well, he didn't exactly leave—he vanished. The police never found a body; he never showed up in a hospital with amnesia or appeared years later married to someone else. He was just gone. Never to be seen or heard from again.

No explanations. No clues.

A brilliant mathematician, he worked as security engineering analyst for King's Security. According to the police files, he made a decent living and was happy with his work. He left home for the office one day and never arrived. His car was parked in its usual spot at work, but he didn't make it into the building. His wallet, filled with cash and credit cards, had been placed atop his neatly folded jacket on the passenger seat. The car was locked from the outside, the key tucked underneath the front left tire. There was no evidence of violence, foul play, or robbery. He was on good terms with all his colleagues and had no known enemies. My dad had been considered intelligent, hardworking, and reserved, but was never disliked by anyone. He hadn't withdrawn a large sum of money before his disappearance, his paychecks were all accounted for, and he hadn't taken any extra clothes, personal items, or his passport before he disappeared.

Mom was questioned at length by the police. No, they weren't having marital problems, their finances were in order, and he supposedly loved my older sister and me. No hint of trouble in paradise. Fourteen years later, Mom still wore her wedding ring. I couldn't decide if she was hopeful or delusional.

The police opened a missing-person case, which went nowhere. When I turned thirteen, I found out why. After hacking into a police database and reading the reports on my father's disappearance, I learned the detectives believed it was a voluntary disappearance.

Even though they were unable to discover a motive—no known girlfriend, no trouble at work, and no financial black hole—they came to the unofficial conclusion that my father simply wanted to rid himself of his family and start over.

Maybe they're right. At the time of his disappearance, I was too little to do anything. But now, at almost sixteen and with mad hacking skills, I want to know the truth. I *deserve* to know the truth. So do Gwen and Mom. If he's alive, I'll find him. He owes us an explanation for his desertion—and it'd better be a good one. If he's not alive, I'm not stopping until I know the truth as to what really happened to him. *He* deserves that.

Of course, I didn't let anyone know what I was doing. It made Mom sad to talk about him, and Gwen clammed up whenever I asked her any questions. I think Dad's disappearance was harder on Gwen than me, because she remembered him. While that sucked for her, a part of me was envious that at least she had memories of him.

"Yo, Angel?"

I blinked and looked up from my laptop. Wally Harris, the shortest guy in the senior class and one of three students I work with at an after-school internship at a cybersecurity and intelligence company called X-Corp, stood with one hand on the back of the bench, his brown hair tousled, his thick glasses crooked on his nose.

"Hey, Wally. What's up?"

"Welcome back to school. I've got a question for you. What's the cube root of 0.000216?"

I frowned. I never quite knew what Wally was thinking. Was he testing me? Being competitive? Or was this just a weird stab at friendliness? How was a girl like me to know?

"Why do you want to know, Wally?" I asked.

"Just humor me."

I did the math in my head. "It's 0.06."

Wally smacked me on the shoulder. It almost knocked my laptop, which was perfectly balanced on my knees, out of my hands. "Excellent. Wanted to see if you've got game on the first day of school. Guess you do. Good luck this year."

Well, whatever his reasons for interaction, it was awkward. Nothing new there. Things were usually awkward when they involved me.

He hefted a heavy backpack over his shoulder, heading to the interior school entrance. On the way, he tripped over a discarded Coke bottle, stumbled into the door, and promptly got jostled by two guys on the wrestling team.

Yes, I said wrestling team. While there were certainly smart kids on the wrestling team, there were also lots of students at Excalibur who *weren't* there for their IQ. Politician's kids, children of ambassadors and the offspring of the rich and famous roamed the halls, ruling the school largely unchecked. Private schools, like any school, needed money to run on. That was the price the rest of us had to pay for attendance at an "exclusive" school.

I watched Wally stagger along, shaking my head. Just another HBI—Hulking Barbarian Interaction. Nothing had changed in the eleven years I'd been going to school. Jocks were jocks, pretty girls were cheerleaders or dancers, and even though I was at a school for geeks, we were at the bottom of the social pecking order. Not that I cared much about the pecking order, but since I fell into the geek category, I had to watch my back.

I'm also the youngest senior at the school. I won't turn sixteen until the end of October, but I'd been pushed ahead a year because even the gifted program at

Excalibur was too easy for me. I would have happily (and easily) skipped the last two years of high school. So far, I'm the only student in all of Washington, DC, with an IQ of 153 on the Mensa International test for persons under eighteen. I know because I hacked into Headmistress Swanson's email to read the Mensa report. Apparently, my IQ puts me in rarified company with some of the smartest individuals in history. Unfortunately, it didn't get me out of having to attend Excalibur my senior year.

My mom nixed any idea of skipping more than one grade in high school. She spouted nonsense about social integration and maturity, so here I am. She did compromise, however, and let me take some online computer science courses at Georgetown University to keep me academically engaged. I hope to go there next fall on a full academic scholarship, provided I survive the year.

The warning bell rang. I closed my laptop, sliding it into my backpack. I had three minutes to get to class. I strode to the door and took one step into the hallway before I collided with a brick wall.

What the heck? I rubbed my forehead and took a step back.

Mary Herman glared at me. "Don't you ever watch where you're going, Carrot Top?"

I had to look up to see her face. While everyone else had finished their growth spurts, I was still working on mine. On a good day, I stood five foot three and weighed 105 pounds soaking wet. I have shoulder-length red, not orange, hair—thus, the inaccurate carrot reference—and sky-blue eyes. Blue eyes and red hair is the rarest combo on Earth, which makes me a statistical freak of nature. My pale skin also makes the spray of freckles across my cheeks and nose look more prominent, which I hate.

The collision was no accident. Mary had been waiting for me—she'd probably spotted me in the courtyard and decided that torturing me would be the perfect way to start her final year of high school.

Mary was swim team captain. Her father was a senator, and she'd hated me from the moment she heard I was interning at X-Corp. The internship wasn't the problem. The problem was Mary didn't like the *person* for whom I interned, Lexi Carmichael. Lexi is a female geek kicking it in the tech world as the Director of Infosec at X-Corp. Lexi recently went undercover as a student and saved my high school from a group of terrorists, so I owe her my life. During the incident, Lexi stood up to Mary's jerk of a brother when he would have gotten us all blown sky-high. Mary would be dead without Lexi, but she was either too dumb to realize that or too intent on making someone pay for her brother's stupidity.

Unfortunately, my size and lack of athletic ability made me an easy target. As if I needed more trouble.

Flanked by her swim buddy Susie Manover, Mary gripped the fleshy part of my arm and jerked me across the hallway and into the girls' locker room in a laughably easy gesture. No one in the hallway even paid us a passing glance.

"Feel like going for a swim?" Mary said, pushing me into a locker.

Oh, crap. I *knew* I should have gotten the waterproof cases for my phone and laptop.

She grabbed my arm again, yanking me toward the pool door. I could have shouted for help, but it would have been useless. Gym didn't start until second period, so the pool would be as empty as the locker room. I was on my own. I'd better come up with a plan or I'd be taking a cold morning swim.

Mary was stronger and heavier than me. I couldn't

overpower her, but I could strike a spot on her body that would leave her temporarily disoriented so I could get away. That had to be the plan.

That was the *only* plan.

Susie already stood out in the pool area, conveniently holding the door open for Mary. How to disable her? Where was the best place to strike on the human body?

I gripped a locker handle and managed to shrug out of my backpack, dropping it to the floor. When we jerked to a stop, Mary narrowed her eyes and reached over to pry my fingers loose from the handle.

It was the opening I needed. When her head was close enough, I gave her a hard, openhanded slap to the ear. I'd read somewhere that an open slap to the ear was as effective as a right hook for smashing an opponent's equilibrium. I could only hope that was correct.

As soon as my hand connected with the side of her head, Mary yelped, staggering sideways into a locker. I didn't waste any time. I scrambled to my feet and ran. Snatching my backpack in one hand as I darted past, I burst out of the locker room without a backward glance.

I ran down the now-empty hallway, up the stairs and into my first-period class, Multivariable Calculus, which, to my dismay, had already started. Ms. Horowitz looked at me in surprise as I burst in, my green uniform skirt askew and my hair disheveled. I was breathing like I'd run a marathon.

"Everything okay, Ms. Sinclair?" she asked, raising an eyebrow.

I took a moment to survey the class. There were only six other students, but all of them were staring at me wide-eyed. I smoothed down my hair and refused to think how furious Mary was going to be and what she'd be plotting next. While some part of me itched to tell Ms. Horowitz what had happened, Mary would deny everything. Punishment would then hinge on whom Headmistress Swanson believed. Better for me to handle it on my own.

"I'm good, Ms. Horowitz. I'm sorry I'm late. I was, ah, distracted."

Sighing, she held up a pink tardy slip between her fingers. "I already submitted the attendance form. You'll have to take this to the office and get it straightened out."

I stepped forward reluctantly and took the slip. Great. My senior year was starting off with a bang.

CHAPTER TWO

Angel Sinclair

I stepped into the main office holding the tardy slip. Ms. Eder, the school's administrative assistant, was missing. No one was in the main office at all. I considered leaving the slip on her desk with a note, but I could hear voices coming from the corridor that held Headmistress Swanson and Vice Principal Matthews's offices.

Figuring Ms. Eder was in one of the offices, I started down the corridor. If she wasn't around, I could ask Mr. Matthews to take care of the tardy slip. He was one of the reasons I'd been able to endure Excalibur. In the short time he'd been at the school, he'd seen my boredom and restlessness and had worked together with a few of the teachers to form a couple of independent study projects in math and computer science that made my academic life at Excalibur bearable. I was eternally grateful to him for that.

He was also one of the toughest guys I'd ever met. One rumor I'd heard was he'd single-handedly pulled a kid and his mother from a burning car, kicking in a

10

window and dragging them out seconds before the car exploded. I asked him about it once, and he laughed and told me not to believe everything I heard. But he didn't deny it, either. One day I'd caught him doing one-handed push-ups in his office. I'd stood there quietly in the doorway and counted fifty-seven of them. He didn't take crap from anyone.

That was what I liked best about him.

Sometimes I wished he were my dad. He was fair and listened when you spoke, treating you like a person with valid opinions. He was smart, too. Unlike a lot of adults I knew, he could speak tech and was well versed on many trending subjects in the field. He listened a lot to me, mostly because I had no one else to talk to at school. That was, of course, my choice. I'm a loner and a geek, and proud of it. But combined with the glaring red hair and social awkwardness, it is a lot for one girl to manage.

The voices became louder as I got closer to his office. I could hear Mr. Matthews speaking. He sounded angry, which was surprising, because I'd never heard him lose his temper before. I couldn't make out what he was saying, but his office door was ajar. Someone whose voice I didn't recognize was talking.

"…overreacting about a minor thing."

"I would hardly call this a minor thing," Mr. Matthews said. "This is a serious matter."

I hesitated at the office door, knowing I should walk away. Who could possibly cause Mr. Matthews to lose his cool? I peeked into the small opening and saw he was talking to a man in a dark leather jacket and blue jeans. The man's back was to me and one of his hands was in his rear pocket. There was an unusual oversize ring on the third finger of his right hand.

Mr. Matthews was seated behind his desk, his face flushed a dark red. "You're not listening to me, Vincent."

"I am. You need to calm down. I said I'll look into it."

The man abruptly turned and took two strides to the door. Before I could move, he yanked it all the way open.

Crap.

A frown crossed his face when he saw me standing there guiltily.

"Who are you?" he snapped. The man's dark hair fell over a pair of mirrored sunglasses as he bent toward me. It was unnerving that I couldn't see his eyes.

I took a step back. "Angel Sinclair."

"How long have you been standing there?"

My brain raced through a series of possible answers, none which absolved me from eavesdropping on a conversation that was clearly meant to be private.

"Um, I just got here."

Mr. Matthews joined us in the hallway. "Angel? What are you doing here? Is everything okay?"

I held up my tardy slip. "Ms. Eder wasn't in, so I thought you could sign off on it. I didn't mean to interrupt."

Mr. Matthews glanced at the man. "It's okay. My visitor was leaving."

The guy met Mr. Matthews's eyes and gave him a nod. "Yes, I am. Remember what I said, Ryan." With that, he strode down the empty hallway without a backward glance at us.

Mr. Matthews returned into his office and picked up a pen from his desk. He marked his initials on the slip and handed it back. "Go back to class, Angel."

He didn't even ask me why I'd been late. Usually I had to explain myself at great length. "Thanks, Mr. Matthews. Sorry to have bothered you."

"It's okay." He didn't even look at me, so I turned to leave, worrying that something bad had happened. As I stepped across the threshold, he spoke.

"There is one more thing, however."

I paused and turned around. He smiled at me. "Make it a good year, okay? Especially since it's your last one here."

It sounded like a simple request, but he had no idea how tall an order that was for me. Or maybe he did. That was Mr. Matthews—always encouraging me to reach for the stars.

"Sure. No sweat. I've got that covered." I hoped I sounded confident, because I wasn't so sure I did.

"Yes, you do."

As I left his office, I had no idea just how wrong I was.

CHAPTER THREE

Jim Avers

Cryptosecure Phone

Deputy Director of the Operations Division, National Security Agency
From: Chief, International Surveillance Branch (CISB)
Classification: Secret, No Foreign
0340 GMT

Message Follows:

Urgent! We have been contacted by the avatar Hidden Avenger via an old server. He is requesting a secure method to communicate. He says he has information he'd like to trade. Please advise.

End of Message

Jim Avers stared at the brief text on his agency crypto-secure phone in surprise. It was exactly 10:47 p.m., and he was at his bathroom sink in his pajamas, brushing his teeth. Quickly, he shook the water from his toothbrush before swishing some water around in his mouth and spitting. When he came out of the bathroom, his wife was already in bed reading one of her favorite spy novels.

"Was that your phone?" Lydia asked without lifting her eyes from the book.

"Yes."

"I hope that doesn't mean you have to go in to the office."

He didn't respond. After staring at the screen for a minute, he pressed his finger to the biometric reader and started typing.

> From: DDIR, OPS
> To: CISB
> Classification: Secret, No Foreign
> 0348 GMT
>
> Message Follows:
>
> Are you sure it's him? Any idea why he is contacting us?
>
> End of Message

Jim waited for the answer, worriedly rubbed the balding spot on the top left side of his head. It was a nervous habit, and one he hated, but he couldn't stop himself from doing it. A part of him hoped that one day he'd feel the prickle of new hair growing in, while another part had accepted baldness as an inevitable milestone of growing older. He'd aged a lot in his climb to Deputy Director of Operations at the NSA. It was a coveted position and one he'd worked hard to get. The agency had been through a lot of tough times over the past few decades. Accusations of unlawfully spying on

US citizens, leaks that were damaging to the intelligence community's reputation, as well as serious threats to agents. He'd handled every challenge that had been thrown at him...except one.

The Hidden Avenger remained an unresolved matter at the NSA. Fourteen years ago, the NSA had been able to spy on just about anyone in the world. Using a hidden back door built into the RSA encryption program—the program used by most of the world to transmit secure data—the NSA could open whatever encrypted messages they wanted from *anyone*, anywhere. Along came the Hidden Avenger, who, without warning or public fanfare, slammed the door shut with a patch he called ShadowCrypt. In other words, the hacker hacked the hackers and stole the key to the back door, effectively locking out the NSA.

For the first few weeks after he'd locked them out, it had been chaos at the agency while they tried to get back in. Despite their best efforts, it was futile. They were locked out for good, and there was no trace of the Avenger. Analysts spent hundreds of hours trying to determine if he was a hostile player. Would he sabotage the network? Make public the fact the NSA had the back door in the first place?

The Avenger had done neither. He said only that he took the action because the NSA was illegally spying on US citizens using the back door. He was right, of course, but the action cost American intelligence agencies a lot of leverage in terms of monitoring real-time threats.

The Avenger occasionally surfaced after that, but only to let various US companies or government agencies know they had been compromised by various security holes. To the best of anyone's knowledge, he never took advantage of those security holes, nor did he use the back door into the RSA encryption standard for nefarious purposes. Regardless, the fact that the NSA had never gotten a single lead on the Avenger after fourteen years was a hard pill to swallow.

Jim considered the Avenger an enigma. For one thing, unlike many hackers who enjoyed the notoriety of a high-profile hack, the Avenger preferred to remain invisible and largely unknown to the public. He didn't publish a manifesto or claim to act on behalf of any group or cause. No one knew much about him, even though the NSA had spent considerable time and resources over the years trying to track him down. The fact that he had approached the NSA out of the blue was significant, and perhaps even ominous. If, of course, this individual really *was* the Avenger, and not a copycat or a wannabe.

These days it was hard to be sure.

Jim's phone beeped. He had to reuse his fingerprint reader and reenter his password. One of the hassles of working with classified devices. Scrolling past the message header, he read on.

> He didn't say, sir, only that he had information regarding a matter of national security and many lives were at risk. I'm passing it up the chain to you, as protocol demands.

Jim rubbed his temples, a headache starting to brew behind his eyes. Now it was up to him to determine if the guy was legit or not.

His wife put her book in her lap to study him. "Jim? Everything okay?"

"Yeah, sorry, honey. Everything's fine. Just work." He tapped a return message on his phone.

> What does he want in exchange for this information?

The return message came back quickly.

> I don't know. He didn't say yet. Maybe he wants
> to come in and wonders if we'll offer him a
> deal. The national security part may be a ruse.

Jim stood and paced several times back and forth across the bedroom, wondering how to answer. He wasn't an indecisive man, but at this moment caution seemed the wise choice. This wasn't just any request. He had to be extraordinarily careful in the way he handled this situation. His position at the NSA, and possibly the positions of those who worked for him, could be in danger. If something went wrong, he had no illusions that he would come out of this unscathed.

After considering for another minute, he sat down on a bench at the foot of his king-size bed and logged back in to his phone.

> I've got to do this exactly by the book.

Jim had his own thoughts on how to proceed, but he was always open to fresh insights, so he added another sentence.

> What's your sense of how reliable this guy is
> and whether he has something meaningful for
> us?

Jim watched his phone for several minutes until the response returned.

> Hard to gauge. If he is the Hidden Avenger,
> then I think he's got something. He's one of the
> most revered hackers out there. We've never
> been close to getting a line on him after all
> these years. He has no known partners or

associates, and his reasons for doing what he
does are a mystery. He's so secretive we truly
have no idea what he's working on. He never
broadcasts his successes, and I'm not sure the
FBI could pin any crime on him, even if they
tracked him down. Can they prosecute him for
plugging a hole we weren't supposed to have in
the first place? At the same time, he clearly
doesn't understand the mission of the NSA is
to monitor foreign threats, not domestic ones.
Maybe he's a highly misguided security savant.
We generally only hear of him after he's
privately handed companies information on
their security holes he's identified. No one
knows, of course, if he had already taken
advantage of them before he gave them the
information, but I don't think so. There doesn't
seem to be a pattern of exploitation. The
community assessment is he sees himself as
some kind of avenger, protecting the ordinary
citizen from...us.

Jim frowned and rubbed the top of his head. His
stomach was churning. All he needed was another do-
gooder pretending to be a superhero and interfering in
important government operations. As if his job wasn't
hard enough. This Avenger was a royal pain. That he'd
surfaced now was troublesome. The problem was, there
was more than enough reason to consider him credible,
which meant Jim couldn't just dismiss the potential
intelligence.

You think he may have something?

Hard to say, sir. Seems unlikely he would risk
contact without something to offer...and
something to be gained.

Jim stood. That was going to be the real kicker, wasn't it? What did the Avenger want? What were his demands? He had no choice—it was his duty to follow up. Once he had more confidence this guy was the real deal, he'd take the next step and pass it farther up the chain. If he couldn't get a better feel on his authenticity, then he'd disengage. No harm, no foul.

Ignoring the headache, Jim typed his answer.

> Fine. Let's see what he's got to offer. Set up a channel and we'll talk.

Jim clicked off the phone and sat for a moment with it pressed to his chin. Events were now in motion. There would be no going back. If the Avenger was the real deal, then every step he took from this moment on would face extreme scrutiny.

He only hoped he wouldn't screw it up.

CHAPTER FOUR

Angel Sinclair

My stomach knotted as I changed into my gym uniform. The last class of the day was, by far, my worst. Today for PE, we were headed outside to play softball, one of my least favorite sports. Technically, I'm not a fan of *any* sport, since I have no upper-body strength and zero coordination. Softball was a sport that required a lot of both, so I was looking forward to it as much as I would a root canal.

Ugh.

In my opinion, geek survival in high school is predicated—at minimum—on a thorough understanding of the following five items.

1. Where the local hackerspace is located.
2. How to crack the WEP key on a wireless router.
3. The difference between a comic book and a graphic novel.
4. How to use a proxy server to stay anonymous online.
5. How to endure PE.

Number five is ironclad. Physical education is a geek's worst nightmare. I don't understand the intellectual justification that makes physical education a graduation requirement. Why couldn't it be offered as an optional course, like photography, wood shop, or art?

I'm not ignorant of the benefits of exercise. I'm all for strengthening muscles, especially the heart. I just don't want to do it in front of my peers. I can't think of anything more humiliating than exercising in front of an entire class when you have the ability and coordination of a limp noodle. Don't even get me started on square dancing or the physical fitness exam.

Although I despised every minute of our school's *required* physical education class, I did have to admit the swim facility at Excalibur Academy was cool. No expense had been spared. The pool sat in the middle of the gym, flanked by basketball hoops, movable bleachers, and an arched roof. When the pool was not in use, special motors automatically moved a wooden floor into place over the pool and, voilà, the gym floor was ready for basketball, volleyball, or whatever. An admirable feat of engineering. Today, the pool was open. The swim and water polo teams practice after school, which was why Mary Herman had thought it would be hilarious for me to have a morning swim in my school uniform.

I was tying my shoes on the locker room bench when Mary stalked down the row of lockers toward me. I sighed inwardly. Mary was in my PE class, too? This year was going to suck worse than I expected...and I expected bad things.

Her eyes narrowed as she saw me. I didn't respond because I was sure she wouldn't kill me in a room full of witnesses. Then again, it never hurt to be prepared, so I stood.

Mary was about two feet from me when the girl next

to me, who wasn't paying attention, pulled her T-shirt over her head. Temporarily blinded, she stepped directly into Mary's path. The two collided and Mary stumbled into the lockers. Mary pushed at the girl's chest, shoving her backward.

"Watch where you're going."

The girl's head popped out of the T-shirt. Her hair was jet black and pulled back into a ponytail. "Oh, sorry about that. I didn't see you. I'm new here. Frances Chang."

She stuck out a hand to shake, but Mary slapped it away. "Seriously? Don't get in my way again, fat girl."

Anger bubbled inside me. It was one thing to bully me, but to push around a girl who'd just arrived? Heat surged into my cheeks. "Leave her alone, Mary. It was an accident."

As soon as the words were out of my mouth, I regretted them. Why did I feel a need to stand up for a girl I didn't even know? Fly under the radar, be invisible—that needed to be my mantra for my senior year. I wanted to finish this year alive. Unfortunately, the way things were going on my first day, it wasn't looking good for me.

There were gasps in the locker room at my bold statement. Perhaps even a few gulps. Mary's eyes squeezed into tiny slits. She glared at me with a silent message that clearly said, *you're dead.*

I glared back at her. Anyone who knows me well is aware of the fact I can't control my mouth when I'm angry. Even when I faced down a girl nearly twice my size and weight for the second time in one day.

Unfortunately—or maybe fortunately—Mary wasn't stupid enough to hit me in front of everyone. She leaned over, lowering her voice so only I could hear. "You'd better watch your back, geek." She glanced at the gaggle of girls who were watching us with wide eyes, then stalked past me and disappeared into the pool area, headed toward the door that led out to the baseball field.

I blew out a breath and sat down on the bench. The other students lost interest now that my life wasn't in imminent jeopardy. Frances sat next to me.

"Hey, thanks for sticking up for me," she said. "What's her deal anyway?"

"No deal. She's got it in for me and you were in the way."

"Well, I appreciate it anyway." She stuck out her hand. "My friends call me Frankie. I hear we're playing softball today. Sounds like fun."

She didn't seem unnerved at all by the exchange. Instead, she wiggled her hand, still waiting for me to shake it. I hesitated. Just because I'd stuck up for her didn't mean I wanted to be her friend. Still, I didn't see an out, so I shook it.

"I'm Angel." I clasped her hand, surprised at the firmness of her grip. "Sorry about, you know, that stupid remark Mary made."

Frankie smiled and lifted her shoulders. She had a nice smile, perhaps because I could sense it was genuine. "Don't be. I'm perfectly happy with my weight. My doctor says I'm healthy, so that's good enough for me. Chubbiness runs in my family."

My mouth quirked into a smile of my own. A little one. It wasn't like I was starting to like her or anything. I was just being polite. Still, I surprised myself by continuing the conversation. "Where are you from?"

"Nowhere and everywhere. My dad's in the military. We moved here from California. Before that, we lived in Nebraska, South Dakota, Florida, and Texas. He just got assigned to the Pentagon."

"Wow. That's a lot of places."

"Oh, we move around a lot, but I don't mind, because

I like seeing new places and meeting people. Keeps things fresh, you know?"

Honestly, I didn't. I hated change and couldn't imagine having to move every year or so and being forced to meet new people over and over again. I could barely stand the ones I already knew. I turned to leave the locker room when Frankie stopped me.

"Hey, wait up. Let's go out together, okay? I've got to finish tying my shoes."

I paused, shifting uneasily. I had no desire to give her the impression I was interested in further contact, but I couldn't think of a way to ditch her without being rude. Left without recourse, I waited. She took forever to tie her shoes, mostly because she was talking so much and apparently couldn't do both at the same time. By the time she finished, we were the last ones to leave the locker room.

I led the way through the gym. Frankie oohed and ahhed over the swimming pool, the gym equipment, and the custom-made movable bleachers. She kept up a steady stream of chatter until my head hurt. We'd just slipped between two of the movable bleachers, headed for the outer gym door, when one of them rolled toward us.

Two thoughts immediately crossed my mind. First was calculating the speed we would need to run to cover the distance to slip free of the bleachers before they crushed us. The second was the realization that even if we ran at full speed, we'd never make it in time.

CHAPTER FIVE

Angel Sinclair

I caught a blur of movement from the corner of my eye just as Frankie screamed. A dark shape slipped from behind one of the bleachers and disappeared into the school. I instinctively threw out my hands to hold back the weight of the bleachers, even as I knew it was futile. There was no way the strength in my two puny arms, even with help from Frankie (if she'd stop screaming and help), would have blocked them. Still, I held my breath and braced myself anyway, just as a man stepped between the bleachers.

Vice Principal Matthews.

He stuck his foot right beneath one of the bleachers' huge metal rolling mechanisms. The wheel rolled right up on his foot and...screeched to a stop. I squeezed my eyes into tiny slits, waiting for screams of excruciating pain. But he didn't flinch, cry out, or collapse.

At all.

My eyes widened as I stared at him in shock. He took one look at us and jerked his head toward the tiny opening behind him. "Out. Now."

Frankie and I didn't need to be told twice. We scrambled as fast as we could, scooting our way with our backs against the bleachers, moving toward him as quickly as possible and trying not to bump into anything. We finally slid out from behind him and stood at the pool's edge.

Frankie looked dazed, and I was trembling like a geek who'd gone too many hours without a Mountain Dew. I wrapped my arms around my waist to calm myself as Mr. Matthews managed to remove his foot from beneath the heavy mechanism. The bleachers slammed together with a sickening thud.

It was a sobering sound. If Mr. Matthews hadn't come along, we'd be dead.

How in the world had he done it? Disbelieving, I stared at his foot. He walked toward us without any sign of a limp or pain. Given the inarguable forces of physics, gravity, and weight, he should be screaming in agony, the bones in his foot pulverized. Instead he stood calmly in front of us without a shred of discomfort on his face.

"Are you girls okay?" he asked.

Frankie took a breath and nodded. I didn't answer.

"Angel?"

I slowly raised my eyes from his foot. "I'm okay, Mr. Matthews. Thank you for saving us. But how—" I pointed to his shoe.

He regarded me with amusement. "Superhero powers. What happened?"

He'd sidestepped my question, but I didn't press. Not now. I ran my fingers through my hair and tried to think back calmly. "We were heading out to the field for PE when one of the bleachers started moving and we got trapped between them."

"Where's your teacher and the rest of the class?"

"They're already outside. We were the last ones out of the locker room."

He frowned and took a minute to study the bleachers. "Those locking mechanisms are hard to disengage. I'll have to check all of them now. The gym is off-limits until further notice. I'll let Mrs. Roy know to bring the students back through the front entrance. You girls ready to rejoin your class?"

Honestly, I wanted to go home and call it a day. A *very* bad day. But when Mr. Matthews looked at me with such confidence, it made me feel like I could handle anything. I almost snapped my heels and gave him a salute, but I settled for a half smile instead.

"Sure, I'm good to go, I guess."

"What about you, Ms. Chang?"

Frankie straightened. "I'm okay, too, Mr. Matthews. I just got a little scared. I can handle it."

Mr. Matthews nodded approvingly and patted us both on the back. "That's the spirit. I'll give your parents a call later to let them know what happened. For now, I'll walk you out to the field and talk to Mrs. Roy myself. Let me lock the gym door and we'll go."

After he locked the door to the gym from the inside, we followed him out. I glanced over my shoulder one more time as we exited, but the area remained empty. What had I seen out of the corner of my eye? Was it a person? It couldn't have been Mr. Matthews—he'd come in from the other side. Was it Mary? Did she really hate me enough to try to kill me? Even by bully standards, that was extreme.

There was also the matter of Mr. Matthews not limping or in pain. That was another mystery that needed solving.

So much had already happened on the first day of my last year of high school. I needed a quiet place to think and process the events so I could make sense of it. Too bad the quiet part wasn't going to happen any time soon, because Frankie had started a steady stream of nervous conversation. Plus, I still had to play softball.

This day was getting as bad as a Microsoft security patch, and unfortunately, there wasn't much I could do about it.

CHAPTER SIX

Angel Sinclair

When we got to the field, students were already warming up. Some were swinging bats and others were tossing balls around or looking in a big plastic tub for a glove that fit. Mary was on the mound pitching to a catcher. If she was the one who had unlocked the mechanism on the bleachers' wheels, she would have had to run fast to get out here so quickly. I didn't think it likely, but it wasn't implausible, either. She was a pretty good athlete.

Mrs. Roy looked up from her clipboard and spotted us. She was probably doing attendance. When she saw us trudging her way, relief crossed her face. She strode across the grass and met Mr. Matthews and us outside the metal fence.

"Mr. Matthews? Girls? Is everything okay?" She shaded her eyes from the sun with one hand. "What took so long in the locker room?"

"One of the locking mechanisms on the bleachers disengaged." Mr. Matthews put a hand on my shoulder. "Luckily no one was injured. But until I can get the bleachers checked out, I want you to avoid the gym area. Please bring the class in from the front entrance."

"Of course." She studied me with concern. "That's odd. It's never happened before."

"No, it hasn't." Mr. Matthews met her eyes and then looked away. I could tell he was worried. *Really* worried. "Stop by my office after school, Karen, would you?"

"I will." Mrs. Roy seemed to think we didn't need to hear any more, so she turned and pointed to the field. The whistle around her neck glinted in the sun. "Girls, go warm up. You're both on the batting team."

Ugh!

That meant Mary would be pitching to us. I considered arguing against the assignment, but Mrs. Roy was already deep in conversation with Mr. Matthews. So, as directed, Frankie and I headed toward the dugout.

As we walked, Frankie wiggled her arms as if warming up for batting. "I can't believe I almost got seriously hurt on my first day of school at Excalibur."

"Not hurt, Frankie. We would have been crushed— human pancakes. Those bleachers weigh a ton."

"So how did Mr. Matthews stop them?"

"I don't know." The image of the bleacher rolling onto his foot played over and over again in my head. "Science dictates his foot should have been pulverized. I don't have a logical explanation."

"Well, whatever the reason, he's my hero," Frankie declared.

"He's my hero, too." I looked over my shoulder where he and Mrs. Roy were still talking. "You know, I don't get along with many of the teachers, but Mr. Matthews always has my back."

"I believe that. He seems pretty cool." She tugged on my arm, speeding up. "Come on, Angel, let's try to forget what just happened."

It was good advice, so I trailed her, wishing I could relax as easily as she could. Seeing Mary on the mound, warming up as pitcher, did not help. My mind began sorting through all the possible outcomes that could happen with me holding a bat and Mary pitching.

None were good.

As we walked behind home plate, Mary's smile widened. She smacked the ball in her glove a couple of times. I darted the rest of the way to the dugout, half expecting her to throw the ball at my back. She might have if it hadn't been for so many people watching.

I moved to the farthest corner of the dugout and remained quiet, trying to form a strategy to make it through the game. Frankie, on the other hand, cheerfully chatted it up with one of the guys in the batting circle. She didn't seem to mind talking to people she didn't know, even though it was her first day at a new school and she'd almost been pulverized by huge rolling bleachers. She acted like the day was wonderful and everyone she met was a long-lost friend, including me. That was just strange.

I couldn't worry about that now. I had more pressing matters at hand. If I were lucky, our team would get three quick outs and go onto the field. If the ball came my way, instead of fielding it, I'd drop it or let it roll between my legs so we'd *never* get up to bat again. While I could survive the jeering and exasperation of my teammates, I might not survive being hit with Mary's fastball.

Unfortunately, we had several jocks, both female and male, on our team. The first five batters got hits, driving in three runs. One girl hit a double. I began to think Mary wasn't a very good pitcher. Either that or she was letting everyone get a hit so she'd have an opportunity to pitch to me. As it stood now, only two people stood between the bat and me. No one was encouraging me to step up yet, thank goodness. But Mrs. Roy would notice if the team skipped me. She always noticed things like that.

We needed to get a couple of outs, and fast. I was hopeful. Frankie was up and didn't seem concerned in the least that Mary was pitching. She chatted and smiled the entire way to the plate, oblivious to the fact she was holding the bat wrong, and stood on the plate instead of beside it. Mrs. Roy had to show her how to properly position herself. She got two strikes right away but then miraculously managed to connect with the ball. She got out at first base, but she drove a run home. Respectable performance.

"Angel Sinclair?" Mrs. Roy called out from behind home plate.

Crap.

I cringed in the corner of the dugout and stood perfectly still.

Colt McCarrell poked his head into the dugout. "Hey, Angel, you're up."

I didn't move. It wasn't fair. There were at least two other people who hadn't batted yet.

Colt must have figured out why I wasn't moving. "Ah, come on. You'll do fine."

Easy for him to say. He'd already had his turn, and he'd hit a triple. He was sort of new at our school, having come to Excalibur last October. But he'd quickly become the most popular guy at the school and the best quarterback Excalibur had ever had. I knew that for a fact, since I ran statistics for the football team as extra credit for Mr. Maxwell's AP Statistics class. Colt's good looks and smarts hadn't hurt his climb to the top of the social ladder, either. It was kind of surprising that he even knew my name.

Regardless, I still didn't move. His smile broadened, and a lock of brown hair fell over his forehead. "What's the worst that can happen?" he said. "You strike out. So what? It's a dumb gym class."

Colt's comment made me feel marginally better. On the other hand, he didn't know about Mary and her death wish for me.

Frankie poked her head around Colt's shoulder. "Angel, he's right. You can't stay in there forever. Just go for it."

Great. Now they were ganging up on me. Fine. I wouldn't be a baby about this. I guess I could do it. I summoned my courage and exited the dugout.

Colt gave me a fist bump and a grin. "That's the way. Knock 'em dead. You've got this."

Students started yelling at me to hurry up. I walked toward the plate as slowly as possible, glancing at Mary, who smirked. It seemed crystal clear to me that she'd pitched badly on purpose—letting everyone get hits so it would lead to this exact moment.

Mrs. Roy handed me the batting helmet and the bat before showing me where to stand. The helmet was too big, wobbled on my head, and smelled like sweat. There was no way to fasten it, so it kind of slid around on my head, half covering my eyes. Mrs. Roy gave me a brief rundown of how to swing, which was more even embarrassing and excruciating than striking out. Just because I was terrified of batting didn't mean I didn't know where to stand or understand the mechanics of the swing. I was fine on the physics and timing part. *That* wasn't the problem. The problem was the execution.

Mrs. Roy patted me on the back and stepped away. My hands were slick on the heavy aluminum bat. Mary prepared for the pitch with a long stare. If she was trying to freak me out, it was working. She wasn't looking at the catcher's mitt or the position of home plate as she contemplated her pitch, but directly at my head.

My entire body tensed as she pitched the ball. Everything seemed to move in slow motion. As the ball approached me, I jumped backward and wielded the bat like a sword, slashing at the ball with all my might. My goal wasn't to hit a home run, but simply to deflect it from my head.

Somehow, I missed the ball, and the ball missed my head. But the momentum caused me to spin around. I'm not sure how it was physically possible to trip over my own feet, but I did, spinning like a drunken ballerina. The batting helmet flew off my head and hit Mrs. Roy in the face.

The last thing I remember was falling over the catcher and onto my back. Right before I hit the ground, I completed the final coup de grâce, braining myself with my own bat before I was out cold.

CHAPTER SEVEN

Angel Sinclair

When I woke, Mrs. Roy asked me anxiously, "Angel. Are you all right?"

Something tapped my cheek. Everything was blurry before Mrs. Roy's face came into view. She had a strange red mark on her cheek—a bruise or something. The sky was a vivid blue behind her. For a moment, I had no idea where I was or why Mrs. Roy's head was floating in the sky. Then I saw Frankie peering down at me, and it all came back to me in a horrid rush.

"Oh...God. I must..."

"You must what?" Mrs. Roy asked, her brow knitting together.

"Move to Siberia," I finished.

She let out a breath. "Help her sit up," she said to someone.

I tried to sit up on my own but felt dizzy. My forehead hurt, probably from connecting with the bat. Worse, my pride had been irreparably damaged. Someone helped me sit up. Turning slightly to my left,

I saw it was Colt. Frankie was holding my hand, patting it soothingly. I snatched it away. I didn't want anyone to baby me.

Smothered laughter came from a few meters in front of me. It wasn't going to take long until the entire school knew of my disastrous performance.

"Let's get you to the nurse," Mrs. Roy said. "We need get you up."

Without asking permission, Colt slid his hands under my armpits and lifted me to my feet with almost no effort. I staggered away from him, my face hot from sheer mortification.

"Easy there, slugger," Colt said, putting a hand under my elbow to steady me.

"Come on, class," Mrs. Roy announced. "It's time to go in. The side door is locked, so we'll be going in through the front. No one is to enter the gym area without my permission for the time being."

Since the show was over, everyone started walking toward the school. Mary and a few girls were walking together in front of us, looking back over their shoulders and laughing loudly. I almost wished I'd been squished by the bleachers. Anything would be better than having to live with the shame of what I'd done to myself.

Mrs. Roy, Frankie, and Colt stayed back to walk with me. "I'm sorry about your cheek," I said to my teacher.

"It's just a bruise." She waved her hand dismissively. "I'm fine."

Sure. No worries. I'd only brained myself and injured the PE teacher with one swing. That had to be a school record or something.

As we walked, Frankie kept staring at my shoes. I finally asked her what was up.

She looked at me apologetically. "Okay, I know this isn't a good time to bring this up, but the company that makes that brand of tennis shoes is not environmentally friendly."

I stopped abruptly, bringing everyone who was walking with me up short. I lifted my foot and stared at my unremarkable white shoe. "It's not?"

"No. They use a plant in Ecuador that pollutes the surrounding countryside. You should rethink your choice."

Since I wasn't going to do that at this very moment, I put my foot back down and started walking again. Frankie started chatting about today's lunch with Colt, who seemed amused by her nonstop analysis of what might be the mystery meat in the lasagna.

When we got back inside the school, Mrs. Roy separated me from the other students and personally walked me to the nurse's office. Frankie had a moment to whisper in my ear, "Way to get Colt's attention. He touched your armpits. Lucky you."

I had a coughing fit as Mrs. Roy steered me down the hall. Mrs. Guiley, the nurse, listened as Mrs. Roy told her what happened before checking my eyes and forehead. After learning I'd been knocked out for a short period of time, she insisted on calling my mom at work. While Mrs. Roy got off easy with an ice pack for her cheek, I had to suffer the insult of listening to Mrs. Guiley explain to my mom how I'd injured myself. Even though I insisted I was fine and could take the bus home, the nurse insisted my mom had to leave work early and pick me up. Mrs. Guiley was concerned I had a mild concussion—not to mention an ugly bruise—and needed to be observed for the next few hours. I thought it was overkill. Other than a slight headache, I felt fine. Unfortunately, I still hadn't solved the more pressing problem of how to relocate to Russia.

I refused to lie down on the uncomfortable bed in the nurse's office and instead sat in a chair holding an ice pack to my forehead. While I was waiting for my mom, the release bell rang and the sounds of scuffling feet, slamming lockers, and shouting voices filled the school. A few minutes later, a thin, dark-haired kid with a long, hooked nose, wearing a black T-shirt and jeans, strolled into the nurse's office, backpack slung over his shoulder and holding his right hand protectively against his stomach.

Nic Nerezza.

The bane of my existence. We were rivals in just about everything at Excalibur, especially academics. Not that I cared about his grades, but *he* cared about mine. To say he was completely obsessed with outdoing me would be an understatement. From the moment we'd met and were placed in most of the same classes, he'd made it his life mission to outdo, outscore, and outperform me every chance he could. He wanted to be valedictorian of Excalibur's senior class. He'd made no secret he'd steamroll over me, or anyone else, who got in his way. I disliked him intensely so I sat perfectly still, trying not to draw his attention.

"Nic, what happened?" The nurse walked over to him.

He held out his hand. "I jammed my fingers in my locker. I thought it was a pinch, but they've been swelling."

As she examined his fingers, Nic glanced over and saw me. So much for my plan to hide in plain sight. Dislike flashed in his eyes—one blue and one brown. I didn't like the fact that we were similar in being statistical freaks—he with his heterochromia and me with my rare red hair and blue eyes combo. I didn't want to be linked in any way to him, even if it were just by statistics.

Nic's lips curled into a grin. "Hey, Angel, what happened to you?"

The way he said my name was the same way you might say a food that tasted gross. He was probably annoyed because I'd gotten to the nurse's office before him, as if I'd planned on knocking myself out with a bat so I could be first to have her attention. Nic viewed everything, and I mean *everything*, through the prism of a competition.

Mrs. Guiley glanced at me as she wrapped Nic's fingers, probably wondering why I remained silent. Since Nic and I were good at pretending our relationship was a friendly rivalry, I had to think on my feet.

"Nothing. Just a headache."

He didn't believe me. I figured the first thing he'd do upon leaving the nurse's office was ask around until he found out what had happened. Then he'd discover some way to use it against me in his evil plot to dominate me, as well as the entire senior class.

Wow, this day really sucked.

At that exact moment, my mom rushed in. She still wore her white pharmacist's coat, which was unbuttoned, and her name tag that read Aileen Sinclair. She knelt beside me, brushing my hair over my shoulder, examining the bump and fussing over me like I was dying or something.

"Are you okay, Angel?" Concern was etched on her face as she cupped my cheeks and looked deeply into my eyes. She had red hair like me, but her eyes were hazel instead of blue. Faint lines that she called laugh squints marked the corners of her eyes. She'd never lost her positive outlook, even after her husband disappeared and left her with two little girls to raise. It mystified me.

"How in the world did you hit yourself in the head with a bat?" She shook her head as if she couldn't believe I'd hurt myself...again.

Nic snorted from across the room. I forced myself

not to look at him so I couldn't see the expression on his face.

"It was an accident during PE, Mom. No big deal. I'm fine. Can we go home?" I set aside the ice pack I'd been holding to my forehead and stood.

My mom, however, insisted on talking more with Mrs. Guiley about whether I should go to the hospital. While they were discussing this, Nic held up two bandaged fingers in a mock salute and then pretended to swing a bat.

I rolled my eyes, but it hurt. He left the nurse's office, his laughter echoing off the walls of the hallway.

"Mom? Now?" I tapped my foot impatiently. I wanted to be anywhere but here.

At last she stopped talked to Mrs. Guiley, apparently reassured I wouldn't expire immediately. "Of course." She scooped up her purse after thanking the nurse. "Mrs. Guiley believes you'll be fine with observation for the time being. Gwen is already on her way home, because I have to go back to work."

I blew out a breath. Great. Now I'd have to endure my big sister's lectures on sports safety. Would this day never end?

Mom signed me out in the office. As we headed toward the front entrance, we ran into Mr. Matthews. He saw my mom and his face lit up. "Aileen, how are you?"

Mom pushed her hair from her shoulder, color infusing her cheeks. The amount of blushing surprised me, as did her sudden need to fuss with her hair. "I'm fine, Ryan, thank you. Just a little worried about Angel."

The smile faded from Mr. Matthews's face. His brows knit together. "I'm sorry. I haven't had a chance to call you yet about the incident."

"That's okay. Mrs. Guiley filled me in."

"Mrs. Guiley?" He looked closely at me. It suddenly occurred to him that what *he* was talking about and what *my mom* was talking about were two different things. That happened a lot when I was involved.

"Angel? What happened?" He took a closer look at me, then frowned when he saw the knot on my forehead.

Suppressing a sigh, I filled him in on the events at the softball field. In turn, Mr. Matthews told my mom what happened in the gym with the bleachers. Of course, he left out any mention of how he'd stopped the heavy bleachers by using his foot and didn't seem to have any injury to show for it. I still hadn't figured that one out.

My mom sighed. "Oh, Angel. All of this on the first day of school?"

"Yeah, my senior year is starting out peachy." I raised an eyebrow when neither adult responded. "That was sarcasm, in case you missed it. Just so we're clear, I did tell both of you that high school was not a good fit for me."

They both ignored me. After more pointless chatter and a reassurance of the new safety precautions that would go into effect for the bleachers in the gym, Mr. Matthews promised my mom he'd keep a closer eye on me. Finally, we parted and headed for the parking lot.

I won't lie. I was glad to leave the school after the day from hell.

We climbed into the car, and my mom put the key in the ignition. She didn't turn it and instead sat there quietly.

I held up a hand. "No. I don't want to talk about it. I mean it, Mom. I'm doing the best I can. I'm sticking with it, okay? Let's move on to other more important issues of the world."

She shifted in her seat so she could look at me.

"There is nothing more important in the world to me than you and your sister. I'm trying to make the right decisions, but it isn't always easy."

The guilt card. I should have known. "Don't blame yourself, Mom. You're doing your best and so am I. I got a full scholarship to Excalibur, and I'm academically solid. I don't do drugs and I'm a good kid, if not mind-numbingly boring. It's not your fault I'm clumsy. Nine more months until graduation. I'll survive, okay? Please, let's just go home."

Without another word, she turned the key and backed out of our spot. I knew she was wondering whether her decision to keep me in high school had been the right one. It hadn't, but making her feel bad about it at this point wouldn't make a difference. I'd finish out my high school education, one way or the other.

As we drove through the parking lot, I glanced at Mr. Matthews's gleaming red Corvette parked in the faculty section. It looked like a ruby gem among a sea of ordinary vehicles.

I had no idea it would be last time I ever saw it.

CHAPTER EIGHT

Jim Avers

NSA Headquarters, Fort Meade, Maryland

Jim walked into the NSA, flashing his badge and submitting his palm print before depositing all his personal electronic devices in a secure storage bin where he could retrieve them later, then walked through the metal detector. He strode to the elevator, taking it to the second floor, where the director of the National Security Operations Center waited for him. He endured another security check after he got off the elevator and was escorted into the director's office.

Candace Kim rose to meet him, coming around her desk to shake his hand. She was taller than he and athletically built. He had no doubt she could take him down without trying, even if he were at his physical best, which he wasn't. She wore her long black hair in a tight bun at the back of her neck.

"Jim," she said, shaking his hand. "Nice to see you." Her keen eyes assessed him. She'd been just as intrigued by the surprise contact of the Hidden Avenger as he had.

She had a firm handshake and one of the finest minds he'd ever known. She'd risen in an agency at a time when men hadn't believed women could handle the complexity of intelligence missions. She'd proven them wrong again and again until she finally reached the directorship of NSOC.

He hadn't told her much in his request to speak with her, only that contact had been made, and it had been initiated by the Avenger himself. That was enough to get him in to see her first thing this morning.

Jim sat in a visitor chair while Candace leaned back against her desk, crossing her arms against her beige-and-white jacket. She waited for him to talk, regarding him thoughtfully, even though he knew she was dying to ask him what he knew. Fourteen years ago, both he and Candace had been midlevel agents on the fast track to the top. They'd been caught up in the frenzy the Avenger caused. Now they were at the top and this situation was theirs to handle.

"He initiated and made direct contact with us," Jim finally said. "He claims to have critical national security and potentially life-saving information."

She studied him with a critical eye. "How do you know he's the real deal? Don't we get a half dozen probes like this a week?"

"We do. I'll be honest, I didn't know if it was him. Not at first. Neither did CISB. But the channel he contacted us on was unusual and valid. It was one of our older servers and not well-known. He quickly identified himself as the Avenger and offered this potentially life-saving intelligence. That alone flagged CISB's interest, which is why he passed it to me. However, I didn't intend to bring it to you until I had confidence the individual might indeed be the Avenger."

Candace's eyes gleamed with interest. Jim could almost hear the wheels in her head turning. Bringing in the Avenger would give her a high-profile boost toward her goal of becoming the director of the NSA. Ever since General Norton announced his forthcoming retirement next year, and had offered the stunning news that, for the first time, the position would be open to a civilian, Candace hadn't kept it secret she wanted the job. She was already well positioned to get it, but there were plenty of other people who wanted it, too.

Personally, he thought Candace would be an excellent director. He also liked the idea that if she succeeded, she would become not only the first woman in NSA history to get the position, but the first nonmilitary individual to do so. It also meant there was the possibility she'd bring him along as her deputy.

"What did he offer that's brought you to my office?" she asked.

"Not a lot, but enough. He provided a few minor details as to the intelligence he says he possesses. Homegrown terrorism. I ran the details past Jack Fowler at the CIA, and he said they panned out and jibed with potential information he'd heard."

"That's it?" She looked slightly disappointed. "We weren't able to trace him?"

"We were not."

Candace moved from her perch on the desk and walked over to a small refrigerator, where she pulled out a bottle of water. She offered him one, but he declined. She took off the top and took a swallow.

"So that's all you've got?" she finally asked.

"That's it. At least for now. One thing is sure—he has serious reservations as to whom he can trust at the agency."

"No wonder." She set the water bottle on her desk. "There are a lot of people at the NSA who would like him to hang. What were the hints he gave you that you ran past the CIA?"

"The big one is he says his surveillance indicates one of the terrorist networks is plotting a major attack on US soil in the next six months."

Candace whistled under her breath. She leaned back against the desk and studied him, assessing the validity of the information, as he had already done.

"Yet we still have no idea who this Avenger is?" she asked.

"Other than he's an elite hacker who seems to know us inside and out…no."

"Do we know what he wants in return for this information?"

Jim leaned forward in his chair. "That's the interesting part. He wants immunity from prosecution for himself and his family."

"For what?" Candace frowned. "Plugging the hole? Hacking? Did he do something else we don't know about?"

"That's the problem. I have no idea. He's not giving up the details until we agree to broker a deal."

Candace pushed off from the desk. "That's ridiculous. Even if we knew what he did and who he was, we don't have the authority to make that kind of deal."

"We can take it up the chain. He must know that. But that isn't all. He has other demands."

"More?" She waved a hand, stopping him before he spoke. "Let me guess. He wants money."

"Possibly. Again, he's not saying yet. Only that immunity and protection for his family will not be his only demands."

Candace narrowed her eyes and walked over to the window. She stood there, staring out at the parking lot below, silent. After at least a full minute, she spoke.

"Why do you think he surfaced now?"

"I'm not sure. Maybe he does want to help us by passing on the terrorist info. But honestly, I think he's testing us. First to see if we'll deal. Second to see if we'll deal fairly."

"Do you really think he controls ShadowCrypt?"

"I don't see why he'd come to us otherwise." Jim lifted his shoulders. "He knows we'd require a certain level of authenticity before we'd deal."

"What do you recommend?"

He was flattered she asked. "I recommend we apply the *Washington Post* test. If a major terrorist attack occurred here, and it got out that we had the ability to stop it and didn't, could the agency handle the fallout?"

She sighed and shook her head. "No."

"Exactly. I don't think we can risk that scenario, either. We need to find out what he has and whether it's worth the deal. I'm not high up enough on the food chain to do make that happen, which is why I brought it to you."

Candace turned around from the window, her expression impassive. "All right, then. Let me see what I can do."

CHAPTER NINE

Angel Sinclair

D id no one care I was almost sixteen?

I was perfectly capable of taking care of myself, yet my mom acted like I was a little kid. I wasn't sure what was worse—suffering the humiliation of my sister leaving work to come babysit me or the swelling lump on my forehead from knocking myself out.

At least my sister, Gwen, is sort of cool, even though I'd never admit that to her face. She's six years older than me, but we look alike. She's no slouch in the smarts department, either. She'd gotten a full-ride scholarship to the Massachusetts Institute of Technology, majoring in microbiology. She isn't into math or computers as deeply as I am, but she has a better understanding of biology and technology. Plus, a germ doesn't stand a chance against her.

Gwen now works for ComQuest, a cutting-edge technology firm in Baltimore, as a microbiologist. At first I didn't understand how a microbiologist could work at a company that spent most of its money designing microchips and circuit boards, but apparently, she is very much in demand. Although she isn't permitted to give me many details about her work, she's part of an innovative team studying yeast as a possible engineering design for microchip security. Sounds crazy, I know, but she's super smart. Sometimes she picks my brain to get a better perspective from the computing side of things, which in turn gives me insight into her world.

She has a small efficiency apartment near her work in Baltimore, but she often comes home on the weekends to help Mom and me. We live in Laurel, Maryland, which is nestled between Washington and Baltimore. She's got a cool boyfriend, a total computer geek who is smart as heck and a nice guy to boot. It's not that I want or *need* a boyfriend, but if I ever decide I do, that's the kind of guy I'd want—brilliant, nice, and totally into computers.

When my mom and I arrived at our apartment, Mr. Toodles, our adorable white shih tzu, yapped and ran so many circles around my legs, I almost fell again. Mom insisted I sit on the couch while she fixed me a cup of hot chocolate, accompanied by plate of chocolate chip cookies. Perfect snack for the four-year-old who got a boo-boo.

Sigh.

Mr. Toodles snuggled up next to me on the couch and looked hopefully at the cookies.

"Forget it," I said to him. "Chocolate is a killer for dogs."

Mr. Toodles looked disappointed as I sipped the hot chocolate and nibbled a cookie. I was seriously considering playing the I'm-too-injured-to-go-to-school-tomorrow card when Gwen strolled in.

Her hair was windblown, her cheeks ruddy. A backpack, which probably carried her laptop and some books, was slung over her shoulder. She gave Mom a hug and Mr. Toodles a bunch of kisses before dropping her backpack on the couch and standing in front of me.

She put her hands on her hips and inspected me, looking scarily like Mom. "What happened to you, Angel?"

"Nothing. I'm fine. Got a bump on the head and everyone is acting like it's the end of the world."

"Mom said you knocked yourself unconscious."

"For about ten seconds." Technically, that was a lie. I didn't know exactly how long I'd been out, but I doubted it had been more than a minute or so. I figured I was safe with a little fudging. "It was an accident in PE. Softball. My favorite sport. NOT."

Gwen rolled her eyes. "Seriously? On the first day?"

"Why are you looking at me like that? It's not like I went to school hoping for an opportunity to knock myself out, okay? Let's drop it. Having to relive the experience is making my head hurt worse."

There was no way I was telling her about the bleacher incident, because she'd probably freak out six ways to Sunday. I wanted to unwind and do some online surfing.

When Mom left to go back to work, Gwen went into the kitchen to get herself a snack. As soon as she was gone, I pushed Mr. Toodles aside. The dog wasn't too happy with his displacement and jumped to the floor, padding into the kitchen to see what Gwen was doing. I opened my backpack and slid out my laptop. Time for more research on my dad.

It was times like this, after I'd done yet another hugely dorky and stupid thing, that I missed my father the most. He'd been a math and computer geek like me. Had it been a lonely life for him when he was growing up, or was he more socially adept, like Gwen? Did he leave us on purpose because he couldn't handle the emotional and social demands of a family? Even more important, would I do the same thing to my family?

That last question got to the crux of the matter. How much was I like my father? Would I turn into him one day?

Blowing out a breath, I logged on and resumed reviewing my personnel file on my father. I'd already compiled most of his medical and educational information, including Social Security, passport, and DMV data. I had the complete police report of his disappearance. I also had a document where I'd combined whatever personal data I'd gleaned from Mom over the years. For example, my dad loved praline ice cream, cheese enchiladas, football, puzzles, and lemon-frosted cookies. While that was nice to know, I needed more substantive information, like what he did as a security engineering analyst and was that a normal occupation for a mathematician?

Information was scarce.

Other than a few mementos of Dad that Mom kept in a trunk in her closet, including a favorite tie, his wallet, a pocket watch, his passport, some papers, and a couple of photographs—including one of him holding me shortly after I'd been born—I had no tangible connection to him.

Since his disappearance, I'd been able to confirm no one had used his Social Security number, old addresses, personal information, or any variation of his identification. Today I was expanding my search into the databases of several large physical security companies. I'd already completed an exhaustive—not to mention morbid—search of the profiles of dead John Does that had never been identified. I'd reviewed hundreds of hospital, missing persons, police, and cemetery reports. While many had met the general physical and age profile of my father, none were a match with his dental records. Just because I couldn't find a match, it didn't mean my dad *wasn't* dead. It meant I couldn't confirm it.

Gwen returned to the living room carrying a sandwich on a plate and a white mug that probably contained lemon herbal tea, her favorite. Mr. Toodles padded after her. I closed the window I was working on. She wouldn't approve of my search for Dad. Not that I planned on telling her about it, but if she noticed, we would have words.

For her, the matter with him was over, closed and forgotten. At least that's what she said. Maybe it helped her deal. I didn't begrudge her that.

That wasn't my style, however. I needed answers and information. I was the leave-no-stone-unturned kind of girl. Knowledge was my endgame. Until then, the search for my father would stay on my radar.

My business, my quest.

"What are you doing?" she asked me, sitting on the couch and pulling up her bare feet beneath her. She balanced the plate on her lap and set the tea on the end table with the lamp that was positioned between us. Mr. Toodles sat at her feet, eyeing the sandwich.

I shrugged, tried not to look guilty. "Stuff. I'm fine, you know. I don't need a babysitter."

"I understand." She took a bite of her sandwich. "I'm not worried about that. You have a hard head. And I mean that in more ways than one."

"You're terrible at making jokes."

"It wasn't a joke." She got a thoughtful look on her face.

My stomach tensed. She always got that expression when she was about to launch into a lecture of some kind.

"Look, I know school is hard for you, Angel. Not academically, of course, but socially. It wouldn't kill you to try to be nice to people occasionally." She plucked a piece of turkey from her sandwich and popped it in her mouth. "Stop looking at the world with such a cynical eye."

"I *am* nice to people." I frowned. "To a point. And I'm not cynical. I'm realistic. There's a difference."

Gwen sighed and straightened her legs, resting her ankles on the coffee table. She relocated the plate with her sandwich to her thighs. Mr. Toodles jumped from the floor to her chair, squeezing in beside her and watching the sandwich with great interest.

"I know. But you need to break down your walls a little more. Put yourself out there. Make some friends, go to a party, meet new people. Just show some interest in the human race, okay?"

"I *do* show interest. And I get out enough. I have friends."

"In the real world?"

I shut the lid of my laptop. "I take offense to that term, but I'll answer anyway. Yes. I talk with Wally, Piper, and Brandon all the time at X-Corp."

"About computers and code and stuff no one else in the world understands. Do you ever do anything with them outside the internship?" When I didn't answer, she pressed on. "Do they invite you to parties? To the movies? To a football game?"

I remained silent.

She sighed. "Look, you're a great kid, Angel, and a pretty decent sister." Gwen looked at me sadly, which I hated. I didn't want to be the object of anyone's pity, even my sister's. But I couldn't stop her, so I didn't try. When she was on a roll, there was no stopping her.

"You're funny, clever, and interesting. But the truth is you need friends. It's not because kids don't want to be friends with you—they do—but you don't show any interest or provide any incentive or encouragement."

"Because I don't have any, okay?" My blood pressure

was rising, which might not have been the best medicine for someone who got hit in the head. "Why is my social life, or lack thereof, so interesting? Can't you leave me alone? Maybe I like being by myself."

Her face softened. "I'm not trying to force you into relationships. I want you to be open to them. Like if a friendship or relationship came along, you wouldn't shoot it down before even giving it a chance."

Before I could retort, the landline rang. Gwen put her plate on the coffee table and walked across the room, picking up the receiver.

"Hello?"

She listened for a minute. "Yes, it is. How can I help you?" She paused and then blinked in surprise. "Okay, sure." She walked over to me and held out the phone. "It's for you. It's your *friend* Frankie, from school."

I couldn't help it—I gave her an I-told-you-so look and snatched the phone, even though I was pretty startled myself.

I pressed the receiver to my ear. "Frankie? How did you get this number?"

"Hey, Angel. Wally, of course." Her voice sounded funny and strained, not at all like the chatty, happy girl I'd met today in the locker room. "You forgot to give me your cell number."

I hadn't forgotten. It had never occurred to me to give her, or anyone, my number. What would be the point?

"What's up, Frankie? Why did you call?"

At first I thought maybe she was checking up on me to make sure I'd gotten home safely. That would have been weird since I'd just met her, but Frankie was all about friendliness, and I wasn't an expert on that kind of behavior. How the heck would I know?

"Listen, Angel, I need to tell you something." Her voice wavered. "It's something I thought you would want to know before school tomorrow. Something terrible has happened."

Terrible? How terrible was terrible? What could be worse than knocking myself out with a bat?

I looked up at Gwen and saw she was staring at me. Okay, this *was* sort of a novel situation—me getting a phone call from a friend, even if it was one bearing bad news.

"Tell me already, Frankie. What happened?"

She exhaled audibly. "Well, I had to stay after school today because my mom needed to sign some forms and she wanted to talk with Headmistress Swanson about my transfer. While we were in Ms. Swanson's office, a call came in. It was about Mr. Matthews. He was in a terrible accident. On the way home from school, he hit someone with his car, Angel. A woman. She's in bad shape. And Mr. Matthews…" She let her sentence trail off.

Shock swept through me. Mr. Toodles nudged my ankle with his cold nose and whimpered. "What…happened to him?" I asked. My hand started to shake.

Gwen's expression turned to alarm. Frowning, she put a hand on my shoulder and gave me a questioning look.

"He's alive," Frankie finally said.

I closed my eyes in relief. At the minimum, I could work with that.

"But he's seriously injured," she continued. "Even worse, the police and witnesses told Ms. Swanson the accident is his fault. They're saying he hit her on purpose. He ran her over without stopping."

"*What?*" That did not compute at all. "That's impossible. That's attempted murder. Mr. Matthews wouldn't do that. He doesn't hurt people, he helps them. He *saved* us today."

"I know." Frankie's voice cracked. "It doesn't make any sense."

My thoughts were whirling. "We have to find out what happened. What *really* happened."

"How do we do that? The police—"

"Don't always get the whole story," I interrupted. "So we better make sure we do."

CHAPTER TEN

Angel Sinclair

I t had been a long time since I *wanted* to go to school, but the next morning I couldn't wait to get out of bed and get dressed. The swelling on my forehead had gone down and I was left with a little bump and a purple bruise. Thankfully, I had no headache and no significant aches or pains. To keep things that way, I planned to pop a couple of ibuprofen with breakfast.

Last night after telling Gwen and my mom all I knew about Mr. Matthews's accident, I'd pretended to be tired and gone to bed early. I wanted time alone to do some hacking, starting with a search of the DC police department. Unfortunately, the police had yet to file an official report—at least not an electronic one. There was a brief mention of a traffic accident involving a female pedestrian, but there were no further details. Since I had the address of the accident, it didn't take me long to figure out where the closest hospital was located.

Unfortunately, the hospital had a decent IT team, because it took me a lot longer to hack. Once in, I discovered Mr. Matthews was in intensive care being treated for multiple injuries, including internal ones. That was about all I could understand. The rest was all medical jargon that was beyond my understanding.

Gwen had already left for work by the time I got up. Mom was dressed and in the kitchen making french toast. Her white pharmacist's coat lay over the back of her chair. When she saw me, she gave me a kiss on the cheek and brushed the hair off my forehead, checking my bump.

"It looks better. How do you feel?"

"Great." I sat down at the table and picked up the glass of orange juice, guzzling it.

"You can stay home today if you want." She walked to the stove and brought over some french toast, sliding it onto my plate with a spatula. "You could use another day of rest."

"No, I'm good." I picked up the syrup and squeezed some on the toast. "Ready to go to school."

My mom sat down across from me. "Angel, I know you're worried about Mr. Matthews. But he's a fighter. I'm sure he'll pull through. I have friends who work at the hospital where he's being treated. I'll ask around about his condition."

I downed a glass of juice and stabbed at my french toast. I'd lost my appetite. I planned on gathering as much information as I could about the accident, but if my mom wanted to check her sources, too, I wouldn't turn away information.

"You like Mr. Matthews, don't you, Mom?"

She reached over to grab my empty glass. "Of course I like him."

"I mean as more than a friend."

Mom froze. "Excuse me?"

I could have changed the subject, mumbled something different, but I didn't. I put my elbows on the table and forged ahead. "I can tell when you talk to him. You play with your hair and your cheeks get pink. You like him."

As if to confirm my suspicions, she blushed and set my glass carefully on the table. "What do you expect me to say, Angel? That Mr. Matthews is an attractive man? He is. Do we have similar interests? We do. Yes, I've noticed sometimes he looks at me little longer than normal. I'll be honest—I don't mind. Despite being your mother, I'm also a woman. Sometimes I get lonely. But I'm a married woman, and my heart remains with your father. I assure you my concern for Mr. Matthews is purely platonic."

"Dad is gone, Mom." My throat felt tight. "Why don't you just go for it?"

She stiffened. "Your father is *not* dead. He's missing."

"For fourteen years! If he's not dead, he might as well be. He's dead to us—to you. What are you doing?"

I shouldn't have raised my voice. My mom didn't deserve that, but I couldn't help myself.

Mom didn't respond angrily. Instead, she reached over and touched my forearm. "I feel your frustration. I know it's not easy growing up without your father. I understand that in the short time he's been at the school, Mr. Matthews has helped you in ways your father might have done had he been around. Now he's hurt. It's painful for you to realize that he, too, might disappear from your life."

"Mom!" My face heated. "This isn't about me."

"Isn't it?" She pushed the hair off her forehead, her eyes sad. "Angel, you need to know your father isn't dead to me. He won't *ever* be dead to me. Okay? And Mr. Matthews's accident...it's all going to work itself out. You can't worry yourself sick over it."

I closed my eyes, not knowing how to respond. Not sure if I should. Finally, I spoke. "Mom, I'm sorry I said that about Dad."

"It's okay, honey. It's been a stressful start to the school year for you." She leaned over and kissed me on the top of my head. "Finish your toast and I'll drop you off at the bus stop."

We didn't say anything else about Dad or Mr. Matthews on the way. Unfortunately, the kids on the bus were as noisy and obnoxious as ever, which didn't help my mood. Usually I tuned it out, but I was having a hard time doing that today.

I swarmed into school with everyone else, but instead of going to my locker, I went straight to the office. Ms. Eder wasn't at her desk, so I walked down the corridor, past Mr. Matthews's dark office and stopped at the headmistress's door. I raised my hand and knocked.

After a moment, Ms. Eder opened the door. "Angel? What's wrong?"

"Nothing. Could I have a moment to speak with Ms. Swanson?"

Ms. Eder looked over her shoulder at the headmistress, who sat behind her desk. Ms. Swanson waved her hand. "Sure, Angel. Come on in and sit down. We'll talk later, Marge."

"Of course." The secretary shut the door behind her when she left.

The headmistress regarded me as I sat and tried not to fidget in the chair. She was pretty, with golden-blond hair that reached to her shoulders and curled a bit on the ends. In my opinion, she was kind of young to be a headmistress—barely thirty, by my best guess. Of course, I'd heard that her grandfather owned the school, which certainly would have aided her in the job department. Still, I don't think she needed the help. The diploma hanging on the wall indicated that she had a PhD in education. Nepotism aside, she was well qualified. Personally, I liked her. She was a no-nonsense kind of person and, more importantly, fair.

I leaned forward in my chair. "I heard about Mr. Matthews's accident. Do you know what happened?"

"I'm going to make an announcement today, Angel."

"I figured you would. But he's okay, right?"

"He's stable for the moment. I was there when he pulled through the surgery last night. He isn't awake yet. I spoke with the medical staff on the phone not ten minutes ago."

"But he might get worse?"

"I recommend you defer any questions until after morning announcements. I'll let the students and staff know what I know."

"The police think the accident is his fault," I blurted out.

Surprise played across her face. "How do you know that?"

"I'm not at liberty to say."

"Let me guess. The new girl, Frances Chang?"

I didn't answer, instead pressing my point. "He didn't hurt that woman on purpose. You know that."

A pained expressed crossed her face. She threaded her fingers in front of her, placing them on the desk, probably trying to figure out how much to tell me. "Why do you say that?"

"Because he's always helping people."

Her eyes softened. "I know, Angel. But sometimes people have secrets."

I thought about his foot and how nothing had happened when the heavy bleacher wheel rolled on top of it. Then I thought of the man who had been in his office just hours before the accident warning him he would take care of something. "Did he have problems?"

"I'm afraid that's none of your concern. It's not up to us to figure out what happened. That's the responsibility of the authorities. There are witnesses who saw what happened, professionals who will conduct an accident reconstruction, and mechanics who will examine the car. We will certainly support him in every way we can. But ultimately he has to be responsible for his actions."

It seemed unfair to me that she was not taking Mr. Matthews's side. "If he's guilty, he could lose his job," I protested. "He could go to jail."

The headmistress was silent as she rose. She came around the desk and perched on the side, crossing her arms against her chest. "This concludes our discussion. I'm sorry, there's nothing else I can tell you."

I swallowed my frustration as I picked up my backpack, slinging it over my shoulder. "I understand. But so we're clear, I think he's innocent, and I'm going to prove it."

CHAPTER ELEVEN

Angel Sinclair

Frankie was waiting for me by my locker. What the heck? Was she stalking me?

Today her hair was in a long braid tied with green and white ribbons—school colors. Her white uniform polo shirt was only half tucked into her skirt. Her knee socks were uneven. She looked like she'd just rolled out of bed, but somehow, she pulled it off.

"How did you know this was my locker?" I spun the combination dial and jerked it open before setting my backpack between my legs and pulling out some books. Crankiness swept through me, despite my effort to squash it.

"I asked Wally. We're friends now."

"You are?"

"We are. I hadn't even been at school for an hour before he signed me up for the homecoming dance committee."

"Wally is on the homecoming dance committee?"

Frankie nodded. "He said he signed up via the student council to chair the committee in hopes of meeting girls. The problem is that no one else joined, including girls, and now he's stuck doing it alone. Until I said I'd help him out."

"Wow. That was really...*nice* of you." I was going to say foolish, but stopped myself in the nick of time.

"Good morning, ladies. Are you talking about me again?" Wally sauntered up, carrying too many books in the crook of his arm while adjusting his glasses with his other hand. "I distinctly heard my name. You can always come straight to the source for more information, you know. No need to speculate on what makes me tick. I'd be happy to tell you. The two—or three—of us alone, a bucket of popcorn, a dark room would totally work for me."

I rolled my eyes. "Give it up, Wally."

"Never." He grinned before leaning over and lowering his voice. "Did you hear what happened to Mr. Matthews?"

"Yeah. Frankie was in her office when the police called Headmistress Swanson."

"The police are saying it's his fault." He lowered his voice, speaking in a hushed whisper. "He supposedly pressed on the gas as he approached the stoplight and mowed down a woman. I guess as fast as he was going, it's a miracle she's still alive."

"He didn't do it," I protested. "It's not true."

To my relief, Wally agreed. "Of course it's not true." He shifted his books to his other hand. "This is Mr. Matthews we're talking about. I'm saying that's what the witnesses are reporting."

"How do you know what the witnesses are reporting?"

"I may or may not have seen the police report, if you know what I mean." He grinned, proud of himself.

"Wait. It's been filed? It wasn't in there last night."

Wally stared at me suspiciously. "How do *you* know it wasn't filed last night?"

"I may or may not have taken my own look." Now it was my turn to grin.

"Whoa." Frankie held up a hand. "Time out. You *both* hacked into the police department?"

Tensing, I squeezed Frankie's shoulder. "Sure, go ahead and announce it to the entire world, why don't you? Keep it down."

"Is nothing sacred anymore?" She narrowed her eyes at us.

"Sacred, yes. Private, no." I shrugged and turned back to Wally. "What else did the report say?"

"Based on an absence of a criminal record for Mr. Matthews, they are focusing on a problem with the car. But it isn't looking good for him."

"Why not?"

"The car has no history of malfunction with either the gas or braking system. Before you ask, yes, I checked that out myself. The police report says he's had the car for four years. Of course, it could be a problem it recently developed. The police ordered a toxicology report to rule out drinking and drugs."

I personally couldn't imagine Mr. Matthews drinking or taking drugs. He'd seemed perfectly normal when my mom and I had talked to him after school. No dilated pupils or slurred speech. Nothing was adding up. I needed to look at that police report myself, but unfortunately, I had to go to math class.

I slammed my locker shut, then paused to take a closer look at Wally. I'd been working with him at X-Corp after school and during the summer weeks. He had excellent hacking skills and he'd been nice to me when I came onboard with the internship. Now he seemed genuinely interested in helping Mr. Matthews. As much as I didn't like asking for help, it might be useful to have Wally available to lend a hacking hand, as well as a set of wheels.

I forced myself to ask. "Hey, Wally, are you in for helping Mr. Matthews?"

"Of course. Why do you ask?" He studied me for a moment. He was probably wondering what I had in mind, considering what I might say.

No sense in beating around the bush. "I have a plan."

"What kind of plan?"

"I may have some, um, investigation requests for you...if you get my drift."

Oh, he got it, all right. I was familiar with the gleam in his eyes, the one hackers got when offered a potential challenge.

"May I say that hearing those words from your lips excites me in ways I cannot express in public?"

"Focus, Wally." I tried not to smile.

He laughed. "Your request is my command, geek girl." He bowed with an exaggerated arm flourish. "What do you need?"

"You've got a car, right?"

"Right."

"Will you take me to see Mr. Matthews at the hospital after school today? It's not easily accessible by either bus or metro, and I want to get home in time to have a better look at that police report on my own."

"Wait. I'm supposed to help by serving as your chauffeur?"

"For now."

"I thought you wanted me for my mad hacking skills and stellar good looks."

"Um...mad hacking skills, yes. But first I need a ride, and you have a car."

He crossed his arms against his chest and tapped a finger on his chin. "Okay, chauffeur duties are accepted, but in return for a favor."

"Favor?"

"Yes. Join my homecoming dance committee."

"Are you out of your mind? I don't do dances or committees. Find someone else."

"Come on, Angel," Frankie cut in. "I'm going to put my artist skills to work on posters, name tags, and decorations. It'll be fun."

"Fun? You said the same thing about the softball game, and look what happened."

Wally crossed his arms against his chest. "Sorry, but my offer is nonnegotiable. After you join my committee, we will have three members, including me. Obviously, I need your help. Lucky for me, you need mine. Seems like a match made in heaven."

"Come on, Wally," I said. "Can't it be anything else?"

"Nope. That's the price for a round-trip visit to the hospital and my assistance on the keyboard as required. Might I add, I truly look forward to joining minds?"

I blew out a frustrated breath. "Fine. I'll join your committee. But I have conditions. No dancing. No speeches. No excessive talking to people. What else can I do for the committee that doesn't involve any of that?"

His smile widened. "I'll find something that will suit your skills perfectly. No worries." He held out a hand, and I shook it. "Despite the tragedy that has brought us together, this is turning into good day. I got two new committee members *and* I'm going to have a girl in my car."

"Make that two girls," Frankie said. "I want to help Mr. Matthews, too."

Annoyance swept through me. I didn't need any more people involved in this situation. Two people were already one too many. "Whoa. No, Frankie. This isn't a party."

Frankie frowned. "I'm not signing up for a party, although that would be fun. I'm not stupid, Angel. I get that this is important."

"I didn't say you were stupid." My face heated. I was

handling this all wrong. "I just don't need any more help."

She pressed her lips together and turned away. I'd hurt her feelings. Ugh. Why was talking to people so hard for me?

Wally slung an arm around Frankie's shoulder, his voice light. "My car, so my vote is Frankie's on the team."

Exasperated, I looked at him. "Really?"

"Really."

I studied his face. He wasn't backing down, and I needed his help.

"Okay." I sighed. "Frankie's on the team."

A smile crossed Frankie's face. "Yay!" She gave Wally a high five.

"So, what's the plan of action, oh fearless leader?" Wally asked.

"Ugh. Don't call me that. I'm hoping that if Mr. Matthews can talk to us, he'll give us some insight as to what happened so we can help him clear his name."

"What if he's still unconscious?" Frankie asked.

"We have to risk it. It's important to try."

Wally studied me for a moment and then shrugged. "Okay." He slapped me on the shoulder as the bell rang. "Meet both of you in the parking lot after school. See you later."

He took off without looking back. I stood there awkwardly with Frankie, not sure what to say.

She studied me. "I really can help, Angel. I think it's nice that you're trying to help Mr. Matthews. You're a good person. I'll see you later."

I should have said something—corrected her impression of me or apologized for trying to freeze her out—but instead, I said nothing.

She strode off, her socks still mismatched in height. I almost yelled at her to fix them, but I managed to restrain myself. I was still a bit surprised how easily I'd let myself be maneuvered into being on a homecoming committee and in charge of a trio of kids trying to save their vice principal.

I just hoped everyone understood this was a onetime deal. I preferred to work alone, and this arrangement wasn't going to change that.

Ever.

CHAPTER TWELVE

Angel Sinclair

Everyone at school was talking about Mr. Matthews's accident. After Headmistress Swanson's morning announcement, telling the students in the most generic way possible what had happened, his name was spoken constantly. It was in the whispers and murmurs of conversation as I walked down the hallway, between students at lunch, and in classrooms before the lessons started. The only silver lining was that Mr. Matthews's accident overshadowed everything else, including my spectacular self-knockout.

Once again, I owed him.

I headed toward my next class, a cybersecurity course called Red Teaming and Security II. Piper, Brandon, and Wally were in my class along with one other student, Wen Hai Chan. It was advanced material.

It was my favorite class.

Mr. Franklin was our teacher. He was about thirty years old and cool. He'd studied computer science and technology at Virginia Tech. Unlike the other computer science teachers I'd had, he was plugged in to what was new and interesting in the field. He challenged us and didn't seem to mind if sometimes we knew more than he did.

I sat next to Piper, and she gave me a fist bump. She was the daughter of the Irish ambassador to the US and she, along with Lexi, Brandon, and Wally, had played a critical role last year in saving our high school from terrorists who had tried to take it over. Until recently, I had considered Piper my closest friend at school, even though we'd never really done anything together other than intern at X-Corp. After the past day of interaction with Frankie and Wally, I began to see the difference between an acquaintance and a friend. I wasn't sure what it meant in the scope of things, but I'd started mentally collecting data.

After we were all seated, Mr. Franklin told us to close our books and pull out our notebooks.

"Today I'm going to throw the curriculum to the wind and introduce a new subject that has recently been in the news and that I personally find fascinating. I'm talking about the role of AI, or artificial intelligence, in cybersecurity."

The classroom fell silent. All five of us were riveted on his every word, just as he knew we would be.

Mr. Franklin smiled as he started walking and speaking. "Some of you may be aware that several new advances in the field have more tightly intertwined artificial intelligence and computer security. Some people refer to this growing phenomenon as machine learning. Have any of you heard that phrase before?"

I immediately raised my hand. "From what I've read, machine learning is similar to how our brains operate in terms of memory recall and knowledge storage. The artificial intelligence of, say, a computer has the same ability as a human brain. It can learn from data and improve function over time. Or to put it simpler, it can get smarter."

Mr. Franklin nodded in approval. "Yes, Angel, that's an excellent explanation. Now, how does that tie into cybersecurity?"

While I was thinking, Piper raised her hand, and Mr. Franklin called on her. "I suppose it could be useful if those of us working in cybersecurity could train artificial intelligence systems to detect threats," she offered.

"Excellent, Piper." Mr. Franklin beamed. "But how would that work?"

We all considered the question for a moment. It was so quiet that I could hear the tick of the clock as we tried to figure out the answer.

"If AI systems could detect irregularities that were actual threats, they might be able to weed out the regular irregularities," Wally suggested. "It would be a start, anyway."

"Yeah, I see where you are going with that," Wen Hai added. "If you could train an army of AI systems, you could eliminate the need for humans and still have more brains working to protect critical information. More brains equals more protection. At least that's the theory, right?"

"Right. That's the theory. But now that's becoming a reality. It just so happens a couple of cyberscientists working with an AI group in Paris have made interesting advances into this exact field. Gustav Monteray and Omar Haider, the two leading experts in this field, have said it should soon be possible for AI systems to replace dozens of humans who are monitoring networks and firewalls."

"Computers replacing humans?" Brandon scoffed. "Didn't I already see a movie or six about this? Look how well that turned out."

Piper smacked him on the shoulder as Brandon grinned and gave Mr. Franklin an innocent look.

"Mr. Franklin, are you saying we're going to be out of a job in a couple of years?" Wally asked.

"I think your jobs will be safe for the time being," Mr. Franklin replied. "The problem the scientists and bioengineers are having is that so far AI is unable to accurately utilize situational and environmental awareness as well as humans can. Since cyberthreats change and evolve so quickly, it's hard for the AI to assess the right course of action based only on established methods."

"No gut feeling," I murmured.

"What's that, Angel?" Mr. Franklin asked me.

I considered the best way to explain my thinking. "Well, an AI system isn't going to get a gut feeling. I've found that sometimes the best hacks can happen when you go with a gut feeling. It's like being able to put yourself in your opponent's shoes and figure out that if it were you, what would you do next? Then, of course, you have to apply a Red Team strategy to make sure you aren't doing what your opponent actually wants you to do."

Everyone was looking at me, wide-eyed. Wally's right eye twitched nervously. I backpedaled quickly. "I'm, ah, speaking hypothetically, of course. Not that I've hacked…much…or anything."

I could tell by the way Mr. Franklin was looking at me he knew better, but at least he didn't push me on it.

"Man, you guys realize where we're headed with this, right?" Wally's eyes lit up excitedly. "AI systems will be hacking our brains. And we think we are so smart."

"That's crazy," Brandon scoffed. "It's not going to happen. Regardless of the advances, AI is *not* organic like a brain."

"No, it's better," Piper said. "The gut feeling may be missing, but the processing capability would, by far, make up for that, in my opinion. Research indicates the human brain is capable of juggling about three to five variables at any given time while deciding. AI can account for hundreds of variables at the same time and then process them in a span of mere seconds. It's tough to beat that, even without a gut feeling."

Mr. Franklin seemed happy with our discussion as he perched on the corner of his desk and listened to our theories. We went on for a bit more until we started getting out there and Mr. Franklin stopped us.

"The reason I brought this up is that there is a meeting on this very topic coming up in Washington, so I thought it an interesting subject to bring to your attention," he said. "All of this means your homework for the next couple days is to learn more about it, read about the conference and what the scientists are trying to accomplish. We'll discuss it further in class."

We spent the rest of the class working out of our textbook, but my mind wandered back to Mr. Matthews and how he was doing. I was still thinking about him as I walked toward AP Chemistry. Chemistry was way too easy for me, but that was cool. I could do the minimum and still pass with an A. Just the way I liked it.

Someone stepped into my way shortly before I was about to enter the classroom. I looked up in surprise at Mary Herman. Oh, for crying out loud. Could I never escape her?

"How's your forehead?" she asked and snickered.

The bump had hardly crossed my mind all day, thank goodness. But the shame hadn't, and apparently Mary wasn't going to let me forget it.

"I'm good. Thanks for asking." I tried to move past her, but she blocked me.

"I heard you almost got smashed by some bleachers.

Sorry they missed you. Now they've closed the gym until they inspect all of them. We've got to go to another school for swim practice. Way to go, loser."

"I'm the loser?" I should have kept my mouth shut, but the heat crept up my neck to my face. "People could have died, and you're upset because you're *inconvenienced*? You're the loser."

A teacher walked by, giving us an interested look— probably because of my raised voice—so I slipped past Mary while she was looking. I walked into class, tossed my backpack under an empty table, and perched on a lab stool. A glance out the window indicated it was a sunny, pretty day. Unfortunately, the weather didn't cheer me up. I was mad at Mary and stressed out about Mr. Matthews, fighting for his life.

"Anyone sitting here?"

I looked up as Colt McCarrell slid onto the stool next to me.

For a smart girl, it was baffling how quickly I lost the ability to form coherent thought. "As in the chair next to me?" I blurted out.

He smiled. "That would be the one."

"No one is sitting there. Go ahead. If you're sure…you know, you want to sit there and nowhere else." I glanced over my shoulder. There were plenty of empty stools left, including one next to Patty Trent, one of the prettiest girls in school. She looked disappointed when Colt shrugged out of his backpack and pulled out his book, notebook, and a few pencils, putting them on the table.

My face heated as kids behind us started whispering. I knew they were gossiping about me. Why would the most popular guy in school want to sit next to me when he had a lot of better options? I didn't know if Colt could hear them or not, but he didn't seem worried or concerned about it. His athletic frame filled up his half of the table. He had large hands and long fingers, excellent for football and pitching, I supposed.

I tried to ignore him and tried to sit on the very edge of my stool, as close to the window as possible, so I didn't invade his space in any way.

He leaned over toward me, lowering his voice. "Hey, Angel, what do you think happened to Mr. Matthews?"

"I'm not sure...yet."

"He's a good guy. My dad is friends with him. Do you think he'll be okay?"

I wasn't sure how much he knew, especially since Headmistress Swanson hadn't given students much insight during her announcement today—she'd left out the fact that he was under criminal investigation. "I don't know. I hope so."

Colt looked at me, and I mean *really* looked at me. "I hope so, too, Angel, because this school needs him."

CHAPTER THIRTEEN

Angel Sinclair

Any further conversation was interrupted by the start of class. Unfortunately, Colt and I didn't have another chance to talk. As soon as the bell rang, Sam Garrison started talking to him about football practice. No way was I waiting around like some kind of groupie, so I slipped toward the locker room for PE and my last class of the day.

Somehow I survived PE, even with Mary glaring at me every chance she had. We played softball again—God forbid. Mrs. Roy hovered, which made me nervous, and Frankie, apparently thinking I needed to be distracted from my nervousness, didn't stop talking for the entire hour. It got so bad I had visions of duct-taping her mouth shut. By the end of class—during which I thankfully hadn't had to bat—my head hurt. It wasn't from my injury.

As soon class was over, Frankie and I changed out of our gym clothes. I still hadn't figured out a way to apologize for my insistence she not come with us, so I did what any self-respecting introvert would do—

I ignored the issue.

Together we hurried to the parking lot, where we found Wally waiting for us next to a beat-up gray Honda.

"*This* is your car?" Frankie glanced over the hood and windows.

"What?" Wally shrugged. "You were expecting a Lamborghini?"

"That would be nice."

I elbowed Frankie in the side, and she glared at me. "Just kidding. It's a great car, Wally. Really. Loads of character."

"Yeah, loads," I agreed with too much enthusiasm. "Let's go."

Wally held open the passenger door on the driver's side. "Okay, who goes in the back and who goes next to me? Don't fight over me, ladies."

"I'll get in the back." Frankie slid in quickly before I could protest. "Angel can navigate. I'm terrible with directions."

"I could navigate fine from the back seat," I grumbled. But since she was already buckled in, there was no sense in arguing. I walked around to the passenger seat and got in. The car was clean inside. Worn, but functional.

I gave Wally the address for the hospital, and he punched it in on his phone's GPS before turning the key in the ignition. I ran my hand over the leather armrest. "The car is in good shape, Wally."

"Yeah. I take care of her. I paid for this baby after working for two summers." Wally backed up and pulled out of the parking lot. "We've got some history."

"I'm impressed." I'd always had a difficult time saving money. I typically sank it into my computer and/or the latest software.

Frankie leaned forward between the seats. "What are you guys thinking in terms of Mr. Matthews? Do you think he has a secret that caused him to go all psycho?"

I thought about the bleacher mechanism rolling up on his foot and the way he hadn't even flinched. I had a feeling Frankie was thinking the same thing. Mr. Matthews had a secret, all right, but what was it?

"Going psycho doesn't make sense," I said. "Even if Mr. Matthews had a secret or was despondent over something, he'd never hurt anyone else. He's not that kind of person."

"Agreed," Wally said without hesitation.

"But what if he's taking medication or something?" Frankie persisted. "Sometimes drugs, even prescribed ones, can make people do weird things."

Wally and I fell silent, because she had a point. If he were strung out on drugs, it might account for the fact that he didn't feel the pain in his foot when the bleacher rolled on top of it. But it didn't add up. Not that I was an expert on drugs, but his eyes and expression had been clear and sharp. He certainly hadn't seemed strung out when he'd been talking to my mom and me. Still, I couldn't be sure, which was why we were going to try to talk to him.

"I do know he's not married and he doesn't have a girlfriend," Frankie offered.

I twisted around in my seat. "Really? How do you know that?"

"Headmistress Swanson said so when my mom asked if she was going to call Mr. Matthews's wife."

"Is he divorced? Have kids?" Wally asked. "Family?"

"I don't know," Frankie said, lifting her hands. "The conversation didn't go that far. Do you know, Angel?"

I didn't. It suddenly occurred to me how sad it would be if Mr. Matthews didn't have anyone to visit him in the hospital, even though Headmistress Swanson said she'd been there last night. I mean, having a visit from your boss was okay, but I don't think it was the warm, fuzzy kind of visitor that made people get well faster. While we weren't Mr. Matthews's family, exactly, we were still his students. Maybe that was the next best thing to a family. I was glad we were going.

We reached the hospital seventeen minutes later and drove around for another five until a spot opened in the underground parking lot. We climbed out of the car and headed for the elevator. After we wandered around for a bit, a nice orderly directed us to a nurses' station. The nurse located Mr. Matthews's room for us.

"He's in the intensive care unit," the nurse told us. "Are you family?"

Before anyone could answer, I piped up. "I'm his niece."

She studied me for a moment and then looked at Frankie and Wally. "And they are...?"

"My friends."

She looked at our school uniforms.

"We go to Excalibur Academy High School," I offered.

"Nice school. Do you have any ID?"

"Will a student ID work?"

She nodded, so I handed mine over, and she typed some information into her computer. Finally, she stood and motioned for us to follow. We took the elevator up a couple floors, and she led us to a waiting room with plastic chairs and the smell of bad coffee permeating the air. A middle-aged woman knitting was the only person in the room.

"Wait here," the nurse instructed and disappeared.

Wally wandered over to the vending machine, and Frankie went to the bathroom. I sat in the corner, as far away as I could get from the woman who was knitting. I had no desire for small talk.

"Hello, young lady," she said anyway.

Crap.

"Uh, hi."

"How are you?"

I was in a hospital, which should have been a clue as to how my day was going, but all I said was, "I'm okay."

She didn't respond. Maybe I had handled that badly. Remembering Gwen's advice to be nice, I tried again. "That's a cool hat you're making."

"Thank you. It's for my fourth grandson. He's due in two weeks." Her knitting needles clicked so quickly, I could barely figure out what she was doing. "What brings you to the intensive care?"

"I'm here to see my...ah, uncle. He was in an accident." I started to rise and join Frankie in the bathroom. No offense to her, but talking to strangers—well, *anyone*—was not my thing.

The knitting needles kept their steady clicking. "Oh, I'm so sorry for you. Terrible thing. It's been kind of lonely here in the waiting room. It's nice to have someone to talk to."

I sat back down. Looked like escape was not in my cards. "Why are you here?"

"My daughter was hit by a car last night. She's in surgery now."

I swallowed hard. Was this woman's daughter the pedestrian hit by Mr. Matthews? A lot of people were hit by cars every day, but I couldn't discount the fact that there was a significantly higher statistical chance she'd have been brought to this hospital along with Mr. Matthews. Then another horrible thought occurred to me.

"This isn't the pregnant daughter, right?"

"No, thankfully." She stopped her knitting and looked at me. "Her younger sister."

"I'm sorry. I hope she's going to be okay."

"Oh, don't you worry. She's a fighter, my Anna. She's going to pull through."

"I sincerely hope so."

Wally wandered over and plopped down in a seat next to me, holding a bag of chips. "You're his niece? That's the best you could come up with on a moment's notice?"

I jerked my head toward the knitting lady and narrowed my eyes, silently urging him to be quiet. He got the message, but rolled his eyes and opened the bag with a single pop.

Frankie returned from the bathroom and sat next to Wally. Without missing a beat, she immediately struck up a conversation about knitting with the lady, who seemed delighted by Frankie's knowledge. They chatted animatedly while I watched in wonder. I had no idea how or *why* Frankie would ever want to strike up a conversation with a complete stranger on purpose, and then enjoy it, but apparently, she did.

The mysteries of life—especially those involving interacting with people—confused me.

After a few minutes, the nurse returned and walked right up to me. "Your uncle is not awake, but I'll take you in for a moment if you still want to see him."

Disappointment swept through me, but I nodded. "Yes, please."

"Your friends must wait here. It's family only."

"Okay. I understand."

I made eye contact with Wally, who nodded slightly before I followed the nurse. We walked down the corridor to the next to the last door on the right side. She peeked in and then motioned for me to enter.

I took a couple of unsteady steps toward the bed. Mr. Matthews lay still, with his hands resting on his stomach. He was hooked up to a bunch of machines. There were wires in his arms, on his fingers, and snaking beneath his hospital gown. The constant hum of the machines sounded like a hive of bees. The room was cool, and the air smelled like antiseptic and bleach. He seemed a lot smaller in the bed than he did in real life. His eyes were closed, dark stubble covered his cheeks, and his eyes were shrouded in dark, bruised circles.

"Is he…" I cleared my throat. "Is he going to make it?"

She patted me on the shoulder. "He's not giving up. I understand he's a tough guy. That works in his favor. Plus, he's in good hands here."

I nodded, wanting to believe her. I took a step closer to the bed and stared at him for a long moment, willing him to open his eyes. He didn't. I touched his hand, and it was cold.

"Hey, Mr. Matthews, it's me, Angel," I whispered.

The nurse glanced at me puzzled. "You call your uncle Mr. Matthews?"

Oh, snap. What was I thinking?

"Uh, yeah, we're, ah, formal like that."

She looked at me like I was certifiable but didn't say anything else. We stood for another minute staring at Mr. Matthews, but he didn't move.

"Are you ready to go?" The nurse touched my shoulder. Her eyes were full of sympathy. I didn't know how she and other nurses did it day in and day out. Taking care of people who were sick, injured, or dying and keeping a smile on your face while you did it. There had to be a special place in heaven for them.

I was about to nod when some objects leaning against the wall on the other side of the bed caught my eye. The room was dim, so I couldn't make them out clearly, but they looked odd.

"What's that?" I asked, pointing at the objects.

She followed my gaze and walked over. I followed close behind. She unplugged one of the objects and lifted it up as I gasped and took a step back.

"That's…a leg," I managed to get out.

"Legs, to be exact. They're your uncle's prostheses."

84

CHAPTER FOURTEEN

Angel Sinclair

Wally and Frankie took one look at my face when I came out of Mr. Matthews's room and didn't say anything. I waited until we were in the parking lot before I spoke.

"You aren't going to believe this," I finally said.

Wally put a hand on my arm. "The expression on your face is killing me. Was it that terrible? Is he going to die?"

"No." I closed my eyes, took a breath. "I mean, I *hope* he doesn't die. He had so many tubes and machines hooked up to him, it's hard to tell. He's badly banged up, but the nurse said even though he's unconscious, he's not giving up. But that's not the issue. I saw his legs."

Frankie clapped a hand over her mouth. "OMG! Were they crushed?"

"No. They were plugged into the wall."

"*What?*" Frankie and Wally exclaimed at the same time.

"He has prostheses," I explained. "Two legs, to be exact."

85

"Oh, no! He lost both legs in the accident?" Wally's expression was horrified.

"No." I shook my head. "I think he's had them for some time."

Frankie looked at me, stunned. "Mr. Matthews has fake legs?"

"Yes. But these are remarkably lifelike legs and feet." I ran my fingers through my hair and started pacing behind the car. "That's why he didn't feel the bleacher when it rolled up on his foot."

"A bleacher rolled on his foot?" Wally asked. He looked between me and Frankie in bewilderment. "What don't I know?"

"I'll tell you about it later. I need to think for a moment." My mind was racing. I needed to rationalize, put everything in order. "I didn't get a chance to examine the prostheses thoroughly, but from what I did see, they were highly advanced. Not like a lump of plastic or a metal contraption. It was simulated skin that looked totally real. The limbs appeared fluid, bendable. They're rechargeable. I had no idea he had them. His walk was normal, not stiff or jerky at all. He drove a Corvette, for crying out loud."

Wally still looked stunned, but after a moment he nodded. "Do you think he was in the military?"

"There's only one way to know for sure."

Wally met my gaze over the trunk of his car. He understood exactly what I was getting at. "Time to get hacking."

"Yeah," I agreed. "The sooner the better."

Since Wally and Frankie had their laptops in their backpacks, we decided to go to my apartment. We had three hours before my mom came home from work, so we could focus in peace without interruption. Plus, I had excellent Wi-Fi speed.

On the way, Frankie and I caught Wally up on the incident with the bleachers. Then I told them about the mysterious man in Mr. Matthews's office the day of the accident.

"You and Frankie almost became bleacher pancakes?" Wally said. "Are you kidding me?"

"I wish I were. Even worse, I don't think it was an accident," I said. "Someone slipped out from behind those bleachers."

Frankie shuddered. "If it hadn't been for Mr. Matthews, we wouldn't even be having this conversation."

Wally took a right at the next corner, then slid a thoughtful glance at me. "Do you think it was the guy in Mr. Matthews's office?"

"Why would he try to hurt me?"

"Maybe you weren't the target. Maybe Mr. Matthews was."

That hadn't crossed my mind, mostly because he hadn't been between the bleachers when they started to close. But what if someone had figured he might step in to save us? It was hard to say. People didn't go around trying to murder high school kids and teachers.

Or did they?

All of this meant we didn't have answers, only more questions. Questions we needed to start finding answers to before anyone else got hurt.

When we got to my apartment, Mr. Toodles started yipping like a maniac. Fierce guard dog that he was, he made instant friends with Frankie. She volunteered to take him out for a short walk while Wally and I set up the computers on the dining room table. I crawled under the table connecting everyone and making sure we were all logged in to the Wi-Fi.

"I like your place," Frankie declared after returning from the walk. She held Mr. Toodles in her arms, and he licked her chin. She didn't seem to mind. "Do you have any snacks?"

"Check the kitchen," I said from under the table. "Coke and water bottles in the fridge and potato chips in the cabinet to the top right of the sink."

Frankie set Mr. Toodles down, to his great disappointment, and went in search of snacks. He followed her into the kitchen. Once we had fuel and drinks, we got to work. After less than twenty minutes, I shot Frankie a couple documents for review that I'd been able to obtain after two laughably quick hacks. Wally said he'd work on the Department of Defense connection because he had an established method in. I didn't ask how or why. I wanted to review the latest report from the police station and see what I could find, if anything.

We worked steadily for two hours, stopping only for bathroom breaks and more snacks. Frankie and Wally made a lot of notes on the pads of paper next to their laptops, but other than some random calculations, I kept everything in my head. Finally, I glanced at the time on my computer and called a stop.

Standing up, I stretched my arms above my head. "Let's compare what we've found so far, guys. My mom should be home soon, and I don't want her to know what we're doing."

Frankie stopped typing and looked up from the keyboard. Mr. Toodles snored softly from her lap and she petted him lightly. "I take it she doesn't approve of you hacking."

"She doesn't *know* I'm hacking. But in case you were wondering, there is an important distinction to be made here. What I'm doing is hacking, not cracking. Cracking involves malicious intent. I'm what people in the industry call a white hat. I'm just looking. Not changing anything, not stealing anything, not hurting anyone."

"It's still an invasion of privacy," she pointed out.

"True, but this is a desperate situation. We're trying to help Mr. Matthews, clear his name. He'd probably give us his information if we were trying to help him, right?"

She nodded reluctantly. "I guess so."

Wally pushed back his chair and stood, rolling his neck. "Well, I think there's nothing more exciting than a good hack. Do I go first in reporting my findings?"

"Sure. Fire away." I lifted the water bottle to my mouth and drained it. After wiping my mouth with the back of my hand, I screwed the top back on. "Did you find anything in the DoD database?"

"I did. Ryan Matthews enlisted in the marine corps when he was eighteen years old with both legs intact." Wally picked up his notebook and referred to his notes. "He went to boot camp and graduated at the top of his class. After that he went SOI, which stands for School of Infantry. After an exemplary performance, he was picked up for the marines' security forces and went through special training. He had a couple of years stateside in various positions before he received his first overseas duty assignment—Iraq."

"No wonder he's so tough." I picked up another water bottle. "He was in the Special Forces. Continue."

"He was given the designation of a critical skill operator, or CSO. I guess the CSO guys are tough as nails and multitalented. These guys are trained to execute different kinds of missions, so Mr. Matthews would be considered well rounded in terms of expertise with weapons, hand-to-hand combat, and evasion. Without being an expert on the exact differences, I would say it's kind of comparable to what the Navy SEALs do."

"Mr. Matthews is a stud." Frankie picked up a chip. "Not like we didn't know that already. Still, how extraordinary. To think that after all that amazing training, he ended up at our high school. I hope he's not too disappointed with us."

Wally took a swig of his Coke and continued. "Mr. Matthews served three tours in Iraq. During his last tour and on a trip between two of the bases, his Humvee was ambushed and the vehicle disabled. The driver was shot and killed. According to the report, Mr. Matthews, Private Rick Johnson—a working-dog handler—and his dog, Ruby, escaped and notified others of the attack. They were eventually rescued. On the way back to the base, Ruby alerted them of a suspected improvised explosive device, or IED. When the team dispersed to determine a safe route, Private Johnson stepped on an undiscovered IED. Private Johnson was killed instantly, Ruby was badly injured, and Mr. Matthews, who was standing next to Private Johnson, lost both legs."

He paused. The room had become deadly quiet. Tears shimmered in Frankie's eyes. I understood what she was feeling, because I was dangerously close to tears myself, and I *never* cried.

Wally cleared his throat and continued. "Anyway, Mr. Matthews was given an honorable discharge. He spent the next three years in medical recovery, much of it at Walter Reed medical center in Bethesda."

"Three years?" Frankie gasped.

Wally nodded, pressing his lips together. Adjusting his glasses on his nose, he continued reading. "About the same time, he took online courses and eventually got a bachelor's degree in education. He taught four years at an elementary school in Bethesda while getting a master's degree. His next job was to get hired as the vice principal of Excalibur Academy."

The heavy weight that had settled on my chest did

not let up. A lot more things were making sense now, but it didn't make it any easier to know the difficulties Mr. Matthews had been through.

"Can you shoot me a summary of that when you get a chance?" I asked Wally.

"Sure." He sat back down in the chair and grabbed the potato chip bag, emptying some more into his bowl. He looked paler than usual. This search into Mr. Matthews's life was taking a toll on all of us.

I glanced at Frankie, who still looked like she was trying to pull herself together. To her credit, when she saw me looking her way, she straightened. "Okay, I guess I'm next up. I first went through the rental agreement you sent me. Mr. Matthews lives in Silver Spring in a one-bedroom apartment on the first floor. He lives alone and does not list any extended family—no ex-wife, kids, or parents—on the agreement. Ms. Eder, our school secretary, is named as emergency contact. The emergency contact number is the main number for Excalibur."

"That's sad even by my standards," Wally commented. "Who would want Ms. Eder as an emergency contact?"

Frankie pursed her lips at him and he shrugged, stuffing more chips in his mouth.

"Apparently, he pays his rent on time, has never had a complaint lodged against him, and has few to no visitors, according to the comments on his tenant sheet written by the rental manager," she continued. "He uses the facility gym regularly and has one assigned parking spot, which is included in his rent."

"Thanks, Frankie," I said. "Anything else?"

"Well, according the DMV, he has no outstanding tickets. He received a speeding ticket two years ago in his Corvette, but he paid it promptly without going to court. He was going seventy-three miles per hour in a sixty-five-miles-per-hour zone on the highway. Prior to yesterday, he'd never been in an accident, let alone one that caused injuries to others."

"One measly ticket," Wally said. "He did *not* run over that woman on purpose."

"Agreed," I said. "What did you get from his school phone and email list that I sent you, Frankie?"

"Well, naturally, he has the emails of all the kids and parents at Excalibur, not to mention his own contacts. When I cross-referenced the name Vincent—the name you heard Mr. Matthews call that guy in his office—I got nine hits. Four of the Vincents appear to be fathers or guardians of Excalibur students. One Vincent has the designation *BL* next to his name, and the three others don't have any description, just a phone number."

"We are going to have to run those down," I said. "Good work. It's definitely a thread to pull." I put my water bottle down and perched on a corner of the table.

"Okay, my turn. But before I go, what I'm going to say stays between the three of us, okay? This is not for public consumption. I guess it's because I'm not even sure Mr. Matthews would have shared it with us to clear his name. It's highly confidential. But as it's in the police report and it could be important to our investigation, I'm going to share it with you."

I had deeply conflicting feelings about revealing this information, even though I trusted Wally and Frankie to keep it quiet. But what if they didn't? My hack could ruin his life, and that would totally be on me. Could I live with that?

I decided I didn't have a choice. I needed to trust someone. Mr. Matthews's life was as good as ruined anyway if we couldn't clear his name.

"Can I have your promise that this stays between us only?" I asked.

Wally and Frankie nodded, serious expressions on their faces. I supposed short of a signed declaration—which wouldn't be legal anyway—that would have to be enough.

I took a deep breath. "I hope you're ready, because you are going to see Mr. Matthews like you've never seen him before."

CHAPTER FIFTEEN

Candace Kim

Crypto-Secure Phone

> From: Executive Director, Research Directorate
> ED/RD
> To: DIR NSOC
> Classification: Top Secret, No Foreign
> 2320 GMT
>
> Message Follows:
>
> What's this I hear about the Avenger offering
> us info on a terrorist group via a back door into
> ShadowCrypt?
>
> End of Message

Candace Kim was getting out of her car in front of her house when her secure phone dinged. Her Secret Service tail, the one that always followed her around for her protection like she was the president, pulled up to the curb beside her house and turned off the engine. She was in for the night, so this team would take the first shift. She couldn't imagine a more boring job.

She fumbled in her purse, pulling out the phone and pressing her finger to the scanner. After typing in her password, she read the text, seeing it was from Isaac Remington, the executive director of the NSA's Research Directorate. She didn't know Isaac well, but what she knew was that he was exceptionally tight-lipped and ambitious. In terms of seniority, they were on the same level, which meant she'd be required by professional courtesy to share at least some of the information she'd gleaned so far. She'd been poised to contact him tomorrow, but since he'd asked, she'd bring him up to speed now.

She considered a response before typing.

How did you find out?

She watched the phone until the message came.

Norton's deputy asked me if the Research Directorate was aware the Avenger had contacted us.

Candace walked to the front door, unlocking the door and turning off the alarm. Norton's deputy was a busybody. How he'd risen to the rank of deputy director was another of the NSA's greatest mysteries. Once inside the house, she set her purse on a small table in the foyer and reset her alarm before typing an answer.

He has. We've done what we could so far to verify it's him, and it looks like it is.

Isaac's response was almost instantaneous.

What does he have, and what does he want?

Candace sat down at the kitchen table and took off her shoes. She wiggled her toes with a sigh. It felt good to be barefoot. Setting her phone on the table, she tapped out a reply.

> He says he has information on plans for a terrorist attack. Says he intercepted encrypted messages from the group and uncovered the plot. I had to get authorization from the director to set up a mutually agreed upon method of secure communication so we can get a couple of files from him. We're still in the process of working that out. The Avenger also apparently has an unusual list of demands—and we don't know all of them. But one of them does include immunity.

> From what?

> I don't know. Hacking, presumably. That's yet to be determined. He also wants protection for his family. There has been another interesting development. I was going contact you about it tomorrow, but since we're talking...it was brought to my attention today that one of our own may be the rogue Avenger. Someone who used to be in the Research Directorate. Have you ever heard of a man named Ethan Sinclair?

Candace pressed Send and waited, curious to see how he responded. When told, she'd been stunned. How was it that this had never been mentioned to anyone before? Now she wanted to see how Isaac would react, especially because the suspected individual had once been in his division.

When she received no immediate response, she went to the fridge and pulled out a Lean Cuisine and a bottle of wine. After pouring herself a glass of merlot and putting the frozen dinner in the microwave, she sat back down. There still wasn't an answer to her text. She was checking to make sure her phone was still connected when a response abruptly showed up.

Who told you that?

Does it matter?

Maybe.

She didn't offer up her source and instead waited. Again, there was a longer than usual delay before his response arrived. She wondered what it meant that Isaac was taking so long to answer.

I've always wondered, from looking at his code, if Ethan was the Avenger.

Candace angrily blew out a breath. Isaac had suspected, too? She tapped a little too hard on the screen.

Why on earth didn't you voice your concerns?

Why would I? Accuse one of our own without proof? This is speculation only.

Leaning over her phone, she tempered her frustration and typed another text.

Can you get me his file?

She took a sip of her wine while she waited for his answer. When her phone dinged, she picked it up.

I can. But in return, I want in on this investigation. If Ethan is the Avenger, I deserve to be in on this. I knew him. Not well, but he was in my division. This investigation is as much mine as yours now.

Candace swallowed her annoyance at Isaac's blatant muscling in. However, seeing as he was her equal in terms of position, she couldn't ignore or refuse him. Diplomacy would be the best approach.

The investigation is mine, but I'll share what I can.

He apparently didn't like her answer.

It's going to have to be more than that. You'll need me. I'll be your best resource in finding him, so keep that in mind.

It wasn't quite a threat, but the implication was there. Not that he was the first man to try to intimidate her. She'd taken on a lot more powerful and ambitious people than him and come out on top. But this was going to be a delicate operation, and Isaac was right that she might need him. She'd have to play this carefully.

I appreciate your offer and am looking forward to having the file on my desk in the morning. I'll let you know if I have anything else I need you to do.

There was at least a minute's pause before another message appeared.

I'll remain available.

Without responding, she clicked off her phone. The hunt for the Avenger was heating up.

CHAPTER SIXTEEN

Angel Sinclair

I looked at the earnest faces of Wally and Frankie and hoped I was doing the right thing by revealing highly personal information about Mr. Matthews. The truth was, I needed them to know. We all had to know so we could help him.

I pushed aside any feelings of guilt. "I'm going to start with the police report, which was updated about three hours ago," I said. "The mechanics could not find anything wrong with his car. But they are still investigating that avenue of possibility."

"That's going to be a tough one to go his way," Wally said. "But you're right. It's not impossible there could be something wrong with his car."

"Let's hope. Now here's the personal stuff. The toxicology report has not been returned yet, and it looks like it could be another week before it's back. The police report, however, indicates a search of his apartment turned up no illegal drugs. That's a good thing. However, one prescribed drug was found in his medicine cabinet. It's called Prazosin."

"What's that?" Frankie asked.

"According to the Internet, it reduces nightmares. I can't vouch for the accuracy of the information—it's from WebMD."

"There's a medicine for nightmares?" Frankie asked.

"I guess. It says it's used primarily for people suffering from post-traumatic stress disorder."

"Oh, wow," Frankie whispered. "PTSD. Mr. Matthews? That's heartbreaking."

"Yeah." I imagined Mr. Matthews waking up alone from nightmares in his apartment. Sadness swamped me. I knew he wouldn't want my pity, and the truth was, I didn't pity him. I only wanted to help him. We had to clear his name so he could resume his regularly scheduled life. He deserved that for his service to his country, and we needed him back at school.

"Other than over-the-counter medicine, that's it in terms of prescribed medications found at his apartment," I continued. "From what I can tell—based on the contents of his medicine cabinet as listed by the police report—he wasn't suffering from depression, hallucinations, or anything like that."

"That's good, right?" Frankie asked.

"I'm not a doctor, but I think the fact that no illegal drugs, or illegally prescribed drugs, were found in his place is a good thing."

"Find anything else?" Wally asked.

"Yeah. The woman he hit is recovering. Her name is Anna di Polo. Looks like she is going to pull through, which is excellent news for Mr. Matthews. We met her mother in the waiting room a few hours ago."

Frankie shifted, and Mr. Toodles woke up. "The nice woman who was knitting?"

"Yes."

Wally popped a couple chips in his mouth and munched. "Well, if Anna di Polo survives, at least they can't charge Mr. Matthews with manslaughter."

"What does that even mean?" Frankie asked.

"It means he watches *Law & Order*," I said.

Wally grinned. "Hey, it's a thought-provoking show. But you can't charge someone with manslaughter if the victim is still alive. At least the police have found no connection whatsoever between Anna di Polo and Mr. Matthews. No premeditation. It looks like she was in the wrong place at the wrong time."

"Are they still insisting Mr. Matthews accelerated through the light?" Frankie asked.

"Unfortunately, yes. That's the determination of the police report, based on witness reports and the accident investigation. That's all I've got so far. The other stuff is a bit more interesting."

"What other stuff?" Wally asked.

"I did some digging on his prostheses. There are several companies that are experimenting with cutting-edge prosthetic devices that are remarkably natural looking and can act as fully functioning limbs."

"That might explain why no one even knew he had prosthetics," Wally said.

"Right." I tucked my hair behind my ears. "It gets a bit more interesting from here. The technology uses something called implantable myoelectric sensors, or IMES."

"Translate, please," Frankie said.

"IMES is a new technology that allows veterans to use their own muscles to control their limbs with their minds."

"Is that even possible?" Frankie asked.

Wally had crashed on the couch when I started talking, but now he sat up and leaned forward, his eyes flashing with interest. I liked that he got as excited about technology as I did.

"Yeah, give us details," he said.

"Well, this is how it was laid out in the article I read. Electromagnetic sensors are implanted in the patient and provide control signals for each limb. Most of the explanation was over my head, but the bottom line is sensors are implanted in what is left of the patient's muscle mass in the limb. The sensors are so tiny they don't interfere with normal muscle movement. In turn, soft tissue holds the sensors in place without the need for big or bulky machines. The sensors are wirelessly powered and can send the electromyography, or EMG, a signal, as needed."

"Wait." Wally held up a hand, trying to process. "The brain itself actually triggers the muscle in the limb and the EMG sensors take it from there?"

"Exactly."

"What are you getting at?" Wally asked. "Are you thinking someone made Mr. Matthews stomp on the gas using his prosthesis?"

"It would be a great theory, but how? The sensors are implanted in the patient and respond directly to the patient's brain. No one can control someone else's brain. That's science fiction."

"Agreed. How does the IMES tech work?"

"Well, it permits the limb to have multiple degrees of freedom. In the old days, amputees could only do one thing at a time—for example, grasp a plate and then release it. A single simple function. The new IMES technology allows people to have multiple movements— like being able to rotate a wrist while grasping. It is definitely amazing."

Frankie held up her hands in a time-out signal. The movement caused Mr. Toodles to jump to the floor. "Mr. Matthews has this IMES technology?"

"That's what it looks like." I rolled my shoulders to try to release the tension stored there. "There's still a lot more to learn about this, but my mom is coming home soon, so we should close up for now."

We were packing up our laptops when my mom waked in. I was under the table, so I greeted her as I crawled out holding a couple of cords. She was so surprised to see kids in the apartment with me, she almost tripped over the rug.

Happiness bloomed across her face. It was painful to see, especially because I hoped she wasn't getting the wrong idea. This was *not* going to be a regular occurrence. "What's going on?" she asked.

"We're studying. Meet Frankie and Wally. They're kids from school."

"Oh, how wonderful. You invited friends home."

My cheeks heated. "They're not friends. Not exactly."

My mom gave me a look that said I was being rude, so I clamped my mouth shut and we all endured an awkward moment until Frankie and her abilities to be nice to *anyone* at *any time* saved the day.

"It's nice to meet you, Mrs. Sinclair. I'm Frankie—that's short for Frances. You have such a nice apartment. I adore Mr. Toodles, too. What a sweet dog. Thank you for letting us use your apartment to study." Mr. Toodles, hearing his name, started yipping and circling around Frankie's feet.

My mom beamed. "Oh, it's so nice to meet you, Frankie. I love that nickname. And you are…?" She turned to Wally.

"Wally Harris, ma'am." He politely shook her hand, too.

"Would you kids like to stay for dinner?" my mom blurted out.

"Wait. What?" I stared at her in disbelief. My mother was inviting people to dinner on my behalf? Did she think I was ten years old? Could my mortification get any deeper?

103

"What are you having?" Wally asked.

"Chicken casserole with green beans," my mom replied. "Interested?"

"It happens to be my favorite."

"Sounds delicious," Frankie said happily. "I'd love to."

"It's settled, then." My mom laid her pharmacist coat over the back of the couch. "Check with your folks, and if they are okay with it, you're welcome to stay. Angel, can I see you in the kitchen for a moment?"

Blowing out a breath, I followed her into the kitchen. As soon we were out of earshot, she turned to me and lowered her voice. "Why are you being rude?"

"Me? I'm not being rude. You invited kids I barely know to dinner. Could you make things just a little more awkward?"

"What's awkward about inviting someone to dinner?"

"I know what you're doing. I can make my own friends."

"I'm sure you can. In the meantime, maybe you could start with these two. Luckily, they are willing to stay, despite your rudeness."

I started to retort but was smart enough to know I wasn't going to win this argument. "Fine, they can stay."

After Frankie and Wally got the okay from their parents, we helped my mom in the kitchen. Within minutes, Frankie and my mom were new best friends. Wally made major points of his own by cheerfully chopping the beans.

"Where are you from?" my mom asked Frankie as she put the casserole in the oven.

"We're a military family, so we've lived all over the world. We recently came to Washington. We rarely live in one place longer than two years, but my dad has promised to let me finish my senior year here."

"Oh, dear. All that moving around. It must be hard."

"Not really. I like traveling and meeting new people. Angel is my first friend here. She stood up to a bully for me on my first day."

Mom looked over in surprise at me where I was grating the cheese. "Angel did?"

"She's exaggerating." I shook the grater until the cheese fell out. "It was nothing."

"Nothing is *not* a six-foot athletic girl," Frankie said. "Angel was very brave."

My mom put her hand on her hip and stared at me. Uh, oh. Mama bear mode had moved to the on position. "Angel, do I need to talk to Headmistress Swanson about this?"

I was beyond horrified at the thought. But I couldn't overreact or she'd be all over it. "No. Mom, it's okay. Really."

My mom met my eyes for a long time before nodding. "I'll drop it for now. But if I get wind of anything else like this, I'm going to speak with her."

"It's completely over. There's nothing to be worried about."

Thankfully, she moved on. Dinner turned out to be surprisingly fun. Frankie got the brilliant idea to ask us *Jeopardy!*-style trivia questions on topics ranging from world geography to movie lines to help us get to know each other better. Wally charmed my mother with dumb jokes, and Frankie was Frankie. After watching her chat about every possible topic under the sun, I was certain there wasn't a person alive she couldn't get to like her.

We all helped my mom clear the table and do the dishes before Wally and Frankie left. My mom looked happier than she had in a long time.

"Those two kids are nice. They would be great friends to have, if you decide to keep them."

I appreciated the fact that she at least conceded the choice was mine. "They're okay." I sounded a bit crabby, but it was the best I could muster. "Don't get all excited. They probably won't come over again."

"You can have them over as often as you like. They're good for you. It's nice to have friends. To put yourself out there."

"Now you sound like Gwen."

"We happen to be related, you know. I do occasionally know what I'm talking about."

"Occasionally."

I acted annoyed, but when I went to sleep later that night, I might have had a little smile on my face.

CHAPTER SEVENTEEN

Angel Sinclair

I intended to get up early to do more research on IMES technology. Unfortunately, I must have hit the snooze button on my alarm twelve times. I only woke up after my mom yelled at me to come get breakfast. I quickly pulled on my uniform polo shirt and skirt, then yanked on my socks, hopping on one foot at a time. I shoved my laptop into my backpack and carried it and my shoes out of my room and dumped them by the front door. After yesterday's view of Frankie's socks, I made sure mine were even before running my fingers through my hair as an alternative to combing it.

Mom had already fixed me a couple pieces of toast and some orange juice. I slid into my chair and took a bite of the toast. Mom brought her coffee to the table and sat in her seat.

"After you went to bed, I called my friend who works at the hospital." She blew on her coffee and then sipped it. "Mr. Matthews is still in the intensive care unit. But he's improving. He actually awoke and was lucid for a short time last night."

My toast dropped to my plate. "Really?"

"Really. Naturally, the police were summoned. He spoke with them for a few minutes before he had to be sedated again."

"What did he say?"

"I have no idea. But I *do* know Ryan. I'm sure everything will get straightened out."

"Mom, how *well* do you know Mr. Matthews?"

"We've socialized outside the school. You know we're friends."

"Did you know he got hurt in Iraq? He doesn't have any legs."

"Of course I know. But his prosthetic legs are so natural, you can't tell."

My eyes widened. "You *knew*? All this time? Why didn't you tell me?"

"Why would I? It wouldn't be my place. If Mr. Matthews wanted you to know, he'd tell you. Speaking of that, how did you find out?"

"I went with a couple of students to the hospital to visit him. That's when we found out."

"That was a nice gesture. Was he able to accept visitors?"

"No, he was still unconscious. But that's how we found out about the prostheses. No one at the school knew. I mean the kids, at least."

"Exactly." She took another sip of her coffee and rose. Walking to the sink, she rinsed her mug and put it in the dishwasher. "It wasn't my secret to tell. Come on, I'll drop you at the bus stop."

During the bus ride to school, I kept thinking about what my mom had said. Mr. Matthews hadn't wanted the students to know about his legs. Still, I figured if my mom knew, then Headmistress Swanson must have known, too. Maybe all the teachers knew.

When the bus dropped me off, I headed for my

locker. Today there was no Wally or Frankie. It was strange, but I had started to expect them. I was pulling books out of my backpack when a hand slapped against the locker next to mine. Nic stood there, a smug look on his face.

"Ready for the quiz today in Latin?" he asked.

Oh, shoot. I knew there was something I'd forgotten to do.

I shrugged, faking nonchalance. "Of course I'm ready. You worried I'll show you up?"

"Not in the slightest, because I happen know you didn't pick up the study guide."

"Ew, Nic. Are you stalking me? Because that's seriously creepy."

"Just putting you on notice. Get ready to fall behind me."

"You need to get a life. Seriously."

"I've got one. Admit it, you hate that I'm smarter than you."

"To be perfectly honest, I don't even give you a passing thought."

He sneered. "Be careful. Mr. Matthews isn't around anymore to protect you."

I turned to face him, disgusted. "You're unbelievable. Mr. Matthews is in the hospital and you're acting like this?"

Nic shrugged. "Like what? He never did anything for me. I'm sick of his constant lectures about kindness, sensitivity, and crap like that. Blah, blah, blah. He's soft. He should show more backbone."

He was pushing my buttons, but I couldn't stop myself from replying. "He's better than any ten of you. I hope you flunk."

He grinned. "Yeah, I bet you do. But I won't. I'm looking forward to stepping on you on my way to the top."

He sauntered off. I started to slam my locker shut, but grabbed my Latin book at the last second. I might be able to do a quick review before the test in math class.

I managed to get a lot of studying done in math, so I felt prepared for the test. Nic smirked at me as I turned in my paper. I ignored him. He wasn't worth my anger or attention.

Wally and Frankie joined me at the lunch table. I was used to eating alone, but this was the second day in a row they'd sat with me. It was odd, but at the same time, I kind of didn't mind.

"Well, it's official," Wally said, placing his lunch tray on the table and sitting beside me.

"What's official?" Frankie opened her milk and stuck a straw in. I slid a little bit away from her. Today her hair was in a bun with what looked like black chopsticks sticking out of it. I didn't want to sit too close to her in case she turned her head suddenly and poked out my eye.

"I'm going to spearhead a fund-raiser for Mr. Matthews," Wally announced.

"You're doing *what?*" I looked at him in astonishment, setting down the sandwich I'd just lifted to my lips.

"I asked Headmistress Swanson this morning if I could lead a fund-raiser to help Mr. Matthews with his legal bills. I figure if we can raise even a few hundred dollars, it will help."

"Wally, I'm beyond impressed." I had a new appreciation for him. "That's really nice."

"I'm glad you feel that way, because I told her you and Frankie were helping me."

"*What?*" I pushed my tray to the side and leaned my elbows on the table. "You're joking, right? Now you want me to serve on *two* committees?"

He took a bite of a hamburger that looked like

someone had stepped on it. Watery ketchup dribbled off one side. "Yep. You didn't think I could do this on my own, did you?"

I sighed in exasperation, searching for ways to get out of it. I couldn't see a clear exit strategy. Somehow, it had happened again. Dang it. I'd been dragged into another social thing. Even if it was for a good cause, committees were not my thing. When had I lost control of my life?

"What do you have in mind?" I asked carefully. Unfortunately, the conversation had completely ruined my appetite, not that it was solely Wally's fault. The limp french fries on my tray looked soggy and gross.

"The Medieval Melee."

I stared at him, waiting for him to burst out laughing. He didn't. "No way."

"Way. Not kidding in the slightest."

"What's the Medieval Melee?" Frankie placed a couple of fries on top of her hamburger before smashing the bun on and taking a bite.

"It's a part of the Medieval Fair Excalibur Academy holds every spring," I explained. "The fair is the school's most lucrative fund-raiser. Everyone dresses in period garb and pays a fee to play a wide variety of games and eat food inspired by that time. Excalibur Academy, get it?"

"I get it. Sounds like fun," Frankie said. "I'll have to start thinking of my costume. Plus, the food sounds yummy."

"It is if you like chicken legs, porridge, honey cakes, and that kind of thing," I confirmed. "But the best part is the games. In addition to the melee, there's an archery game, a climbing tower, a Test o' Strength game, and a bunch of others."

"I can't wait."

"The most popular event, by far, is the Medieval

Melee, however." Wally placed his forearms on the table and leaned forward. "If we're going to earn decent money for Mr. Matthews, this is how we do it."

I had to give it to Wally. It was a sound strategy. If there were one thing Excalibur students loved, it was the melee. "It's good thinking, Wally. I can't believe Headmistress Swanson agreed."

"I can be persuasive when I have to." Wally grinned. "Plus, she likes Mr. Matthews. I fully leveraged that. But we're on our own. She's letting us conduct the game on the football field since the actual season doesn't start until next week. We can also use the props, but this is a wholly student-led activity. By that, I mean the three of us."

"Figures," I grumbled.

"What do you have to do for this Medieval Melee?" Frankie asked.

I pushed my tray aside and grabbed the salt and pepper shakers. "It's played on the football field and is a variation of paintball without the paint or the balls."

"Okay, that made no sense at all." Frankie speared a canned peach with her fork and nibbled a corner of it.

"That's because I'm not finished explaining. The goal is to capture a fake sword embedded in a cardboard stone at opposing end zones." I placed the saltshaker at one end of the table and the pepper at the other to demonstrate.

"Oh, a sword in the stone reference." Frankie grinned. "Excalibur. Medieval. I get it."

"Exactly. The field is covered with obstacles and objects for players to hide behind as they advance to capture the sword. Each team has ten players. Everyone wears a white T-shirt and is given a marshmallow popper."

"What's a marshmallow popper?" Frankie asked.

"It's like a paint gun, but it's not gun shaped," Wally

explained. "The school was clear about the no-gun thing—not even toy guns—so we compromised. The popper is a long plastic tube with a spring inside connected to a lever on top to launch the projectile. But instead of marshmallows, we use powdered sugar."

"Powdered sugar balls?" Frankie's eyes widened. "That sounds cool."

"It *is* cool," I agreed. "Each team has a specific color of sugar. If you are hit with the opposing team's powder, you are out. You freeze in your spot."

"Okay, so, who plays?" Frankie asked.

"Usually the jocks play each other," Wally said. "But since I'm in charge this time around, I'm changing things up a bit."

I raised an eyebrow. "How do you intend to do that?"

"I'm going to have two teams, the Brains and the Trains—or in layman's language, the geeks versus the jocks."

"*What?*" I frowned at Wally. "Are you nuts? The geeks will get crushed."

"Please. I do have a strategy. We're going to get Colt McCarrell to agree to be on the Brains' team. With him as the Brains' leader, and likely the best shooter, the geeks might stand a chance."

"That sounds good in theory, but how exactly are we going to get Colt and the geeks to sign up for this?"

Wally pointed at me. "You'll take care of Colt. I'll take care of the geeks."

I looked at him incredulously. "*Me?*"

He plucked a pickle from beneath the hamburger bun and popped it in his mouth. "Don't act all shocked. I heard from Michelle Knot who heard from Lucy Shoemaker that Colt sat next to you in AP Chemistry. You could have told me you had a thing going on." Ketchup was smeared across his chin.

"There is no *thing* going on." I threw a napkin at him. "Besides, how does Colt sitting next to me in AP Chemistry translate into me getting him to front the Brains for the melee?"

"You'll have the perfect opportunity to talk to him. Just ask him with a pretty flutter of your eyelashes. Or if that fails, promise to do his homework or something."

My cranky meter was rising at an exponential rate. "I am *not* asking Colt to do anything. He doesn't need me to do his homework. He's smart enough to do it himself." I crossed my arms against my chest.

"Don't care. It's up to you how you ask." Wally dabbed at his chin. "But you're our only hope. If Colt is involved, the entire school will come. The athletes will come to challenge him. The geeks will sign up to play because they might have a prayer to win if he's their captain. If the jocks show, the girls will come—and that includes the cheerleaders. If girls in short skirts are there, the geek guys will be, too."

"As long as the geek guys don't act like entitled jerks toward the girls in short skirts. Trust me, that's been my Comic-Con experience in the past."

Wally narrowed his eyes. "No one will bother the girls on my watch. Anyway, the bottom line is, we'll have the entire school in one place, ready to empty their pockets for a good cause. It's a win-win scenario."

Frankie pointed her straw at me. "He's got a point, Angel. It could bring the entire school out—geeks and jocks—for Mr. Matthews."

I tried to think of a way to get out of it. "Look, I'll be honest. I don't know Colt well enough to ask him to do something like that."

"It's easy," Wally said. "Open your mouth and say *please*. He likes you well enough to sit next to you in chemistry. That has to mean something."

"It means there was an open seat next to me," I countered.

"That's enough for me." Wally popped the rest of his hamburger in his mouth and swallowed it with a drink of milk. "You're elected."

"Okay, so we get the jocks and brains to agree to play each other," Frankie interrupted. "That's great, but more importantly, how do we get the students to empty their pockets?"

"There has to be a fee to play in the melee," Wally answered. "Let's say ten bucks a person. We can ask for a donation from spectators as they enter the rally. Since it's a fund-raiser and not an official school activity, we can't require payment for entrance. But I think most kids would give something anyway."

"I think you overestimate the generosity of the human race at Excalibur," I muttered. I picked up the apple from my tray and started to take a bite.

"Wait. Don't eat that," Frankie warned me.

I froze with my open mouth a millimeter from the skin. Slowly I lowered the apple. "Why not?"

"Excalibur buys the apples from FarmBites Ltd."

"So?"

"So, FarmBites is under investigation for human rights violations of its workers. By eating that apple, you will be supporting a company that is showing blatant disregard for the human condition. I notified Headmistress Swanson of this grievous fact yesterday, and she promised to look into it. However, until then, I urge you to reconsider eating that."

"You told the headmistress not to buy apples on your second day at a new school?"

"Of course."

I set the apple down and picked up my tray, emptying the entire thing into the trash just as the bell rang, signaling an end to our lunch.

"Are we getting together again after school?" Frankie asked hopefully.

"I don't think so," I said. "I've got a chemistry quiz to study for, a four-page essay to write for African history, and some computer science homework for my Georgetown course. I also want to do some more research on the things we discussed yesterday." I looked over my shoulder. No one was paying me any attention, thankfully, but I lowered my voice anyway. "You know on what."

Wally nodded. "Okay, I'll do some more poking around, too. Keep in mind, the melee is scheduled for next Wednesday evening, so we don't have a lot of time."

"I'll get started right away on the fund-raiser posters and graphics for social media." Frankie stood holding her tray and stepped past me toward the trash. "Someone has to advertise this, right?"

Wally patted her on the back. "You're great, Frankie. Best volunteer I've ever had."

"The *only* volunteer you've ever had," I corrected, but they ignored me.

We parted ways, and the rest of the day was unremarkable except for AP Chemistry. I sat in the same spot as the previous two days. Shortly after I entered, Colt came in and sat down right next to me.

That made three times in a row. Wally was right. That couldn't be random. He deliberately chose to sit next to me…for reasons unknown.

"Hey, Angel," Colt said, dropping his backpack to the floor. "How's it going?" His brown hair fell over his forehead as he gave me a smile.

"How's it going? With me? It's going. Time, that is. Because time goes along whether we want it to or not. It's fluid like that."

I clamped my mouth shut, wishing for anything to put me out of my dorky misery.

Colt looked confused now, not to mention sorry he asked. He pulled out his chemistry book and notebook, getting ready for the lab. I wanted to give myself a bracing head slap but didn't see how that would make me any less of a moron.

For most of the class, Colt and I didn't talk. Instead we dutifully filled out the study guide for the quiz and listened to Mr. Jackson tell us what things would be on it. At the end of the period, Mr. Jackson informed us we'd have to choose lab partners.

Luckily, that did not include me, so I exhaled a breath of relief. Last year, Ms. Merriam let me off the hook in terms of a lab partner because I was working on complicated experiments under her direct supervision. I assumed Mr. Jackson would do the same. No lab partner required for me.

Colt turned his head. "Would you like to be my lab partner, Angel?"

"Sure," I said without one second of hesitation.

Holy freaking crap. I had no idea what had happened to the girl who never wanted to work with a lab partner. Suddenly I was thrilled with the prospect of working with a partner on what were sure to be way-too-easy experiments.

Colt gave me a smile—a dazzling smile—and closed his book. "That's great. I'll let Mr. Jackson know. By the way, are you interested in studying together for the quiz tonight?"

"You want to study with me? Tonight?"

What the heck was even happening right now? Was I in the twilight zone or something?

"You're my lab partner, right?" he said.

I gulped. "Right."

"Great. Where do you live?"

"Laurel, Maryland."

"That's not too far from me. We could meet

somewhere neutral like the library closest to you, if you want."

"Or you could come to my place." What the heck was I doing?

Something flashed in his eyes. Caution, maybe wariness. It was hard to say, especially because I had exactly zero experience in setting up a study date. Maybe that had been a dumb thing to say. Maybe he thought I wanted to do more than study. How was I supposed to know, with zero experience? I started to clarify, but I wasn't sure what I could say that wouldn't make things worse.

My face heated and I knew Colt could see it, because when I get embarrassed, my face turns into a freaking red beacon.

Mortifying seconds ticked past. There was a thoughtful expression on his face as he stared out the window over my shoulder. "When do your mom and dad get home?" he finally asked.

"My mom gets home about six thirty. My dad...he doesn't live with us."

"Do you think your mom would mind if I came about eight? That would give you guys time for dinner, but not be too late for us to study."

Truthfully, I had no idea what my mom would think, because until yesterday no one had *ever* come over to my house before. Now, on two consecutive days, I'd have different people over. I had a feeling she was going to completely lose it. By that, I meant she would totally misunderstand the situation and be so happy she'd pass out or giggle herself silly.

I did *not* look forward to that.

"I don't think she'd mind," I said.

"Then it's set." He slid my notebook toward him and scribbled a number on the top. "Text me your address later, would you? See you tonight."

Just like that, he grabbed his backpack and went to the front of the room, presumably to tell Mr. Jackson that we were now lab partners. I had a pretty clear idea what Mr. Jackson would think of that. I sighed and stuck my book and notebook in my backpack before standing up. Patty Trent passed by, giving me a cold, snooty look.

"Loser," she mouthed.

I raised my chin, smiled. "Really? Because Colt asked me to be his lab partner. Who did you get?"

Surprise bloomed across her face. I'd never stood up for myself before, and she hadn't been prepared for it.

Her upper lip curled into a disdainful snarl. "We'll see how long that lasts."

I shrugged, but my smile widened. "Guess we will."

CHAPTER EIGHTEEN

Angel Sinclair

After I got home, I walked Mr. Toodles and texted Colt my address. As I pushed the Send button, I thought I should probably mark it as a social milestone or something. I'd texted a guy who wasn't Wally. Wow.

I finished my math homework, wrote a persuasive essay for my English class, and logged on to my account at Georgetown University to respond to a couple of discussion board questions and submit my homework. As I logged out of that, I figured I might have time to clean my room, help Mom get an early jump on dinner, and take a shower before the study date. Not that it was a *date* date, but still…I wanted to be clean and reasonably prepared for all contingencies. Although there was no way I could truly be prepared, because I couldn't even think of a *single* contingency. I had no framework, no reference. What did people do on study dates? Study, yes, but did other stuff happen, too?

Stop overthinking, Sinclair. It's just chemistry.

My heart was beating anxiously. My palms were sweaty. I needed to get a grip on myself before I freaked out completely.

I was headed to the kitchen when my cell rang. I fished it out of my pocket. "Hello?"

"Hey, Angel, it's Frankie."

"Frankie? How did you get my cell number?"

"Wally, of course."

"What's up?"

"Well, while putting the info for the Medieval Melee on my social media, I came across something on my Twitter feed."

"What?"

"I'm not going to explain it. Go check out this website, would you? I'll hold on. It's called nothingbutthetruth.com."

"What is it? Some political site?" I darted back to my computer and sat down.

"I wish."

It took me a few seconds to pull the website up. It was formatted to look like a newspaper. The headline screamed, *Excalibur Academy's Vice Principal Mows Down Innocent Pedestrian.*

I quickly scanned the article, my heart sinking. It was a horrible mix of a few basic facts and a lot of false information—all of it brutally skewed against Mr. Matthews.

Fake news at its worst.

"Who would write this?" Frankie asked, clearly distressed. "It's awful."

I didn't answer. I was already checking out the specs on the website. It had gone up a few hours earlier. "I need time to check this out, Frankie. I'll call you back later."

I spent the next hour doing a probe of the website. Unfortunately, it was well protected and I didn't have time for a lengthy hack. The front door opened, and my mom called out to me. Ugh. I hadn't even cleaned my room, taken a shower, or gotten dinner under way.

I logged off, stuffed all my dirty clothes in the closet, and made my bed. A glance around indicated the room seemed reasonably neat. I ran down the hall to meet my mom. She was already in the kitchen pulling chicken breasts out of the freezer.

"Hey, honey," she said when she saw me. She turned on the water in the sink, dipping her hand in to ensure the water was hot, and then placed the breasts beneath the stream. "How was your day?"

"Okay. Um, I'm going to have a friend over later to study for a chemistry test tomorrow."

Mom grinned. "Frankie or Wally?"

I cleared my throat. "Colt."

"Colt?" My mom turned off the water. "Who's he?"

"My lab partner in chemistry."

"A boy?" Leave it to my mom to obsess over the littlest thing.

"Yes. A boy. It's no big deal, okay? We're going to study for a quiz."

"You didn't need a lab partner last year," she noted.

She *would* have to remember that. My cheeks heated despite a supreme effort to act nonchalant. "Well, this year things are different."

"They are." She turned the water back on to thaw the chicken breasts. "I'll take care of dinner. You go get ready."

The words *get ready* terrified me because, for the first time, I wasn't dressing for school. I hightailed it out of the kitchen. Twenty minutes later I was clad in a pair of jeans and a short white blouse, which I hoped equaled ready. My hair, which was looking more orange than red tonight, was dry, straight, and loose. I wished Gwen still lived with us, because I might have borrowed some of her makeup to hide my freckles. But as I stared at myself in the mirror, I decided makeup for a study date was overkill. Colt was observant and would notice. As it was, I was still indecisive about leaving my hair straight instead of pulled back in a ponytail. In the end, I left it down.

Mom had our dinner ready, and we ate it sitting at the kitchen table, like we usually did, talking about our days. I didn't have much of an appetite. Thankfully, my mom didn't bring up Mr. Matthews, my dad, or the upcoming study session. I carefully steered the conversation to safe things.

I was drying the last of the dinner dishes when the doorbell rang. I glanced up at the clock. It was precisely eight. Colt was punctual. I liked that.

Mr. Toodles went nuts yipping at the door as my mom went to answer it. I stepped out of the kitchen just as Colt came in. He stood nearly a half foot taller than my mom but immediately bent down to one knee to pet Mr. Toodles. I was certain Mr. Toodles liked getting petted by those long, strong fingers. I started to think I wouldn't mind that, either.

When Colt saw me, he straightened. "Hey, Angel. Ready to study?"

"I sure am."

Mom closed the front door behind him. While his back was to her, she gave me an enthusiastic thumbs-up. I tried not to blush but wasn't sure I entirely succeeded.

"It's been lovely to meet you, Colt," she said. "I'm off to my bedroom now to watch my favorite show in peace. Let me know if you need snacks or anything."

"We can get our own snacks, Mom."

"Yes, you can. Have fun."

"Thanks, Mrs. Sinclair. Nice to meet you."

Even though my mom had the wrong idea about the study date, I could not remember the last time she'd glowed with this much happiness. I hoped she didn't get used to people coming over, because I hated to burst her bubble—I had no intention of doing this on a regular basis.

After she left, Colt and I stood facing each other awkwardly. I had no idea what came next. But since he wasn't saying anything, either, I figured it was up to me to speak. "Are you ready to study?"

"Of course. Dining room table?"

"Yeah, that's great."

He shrugged out of his backpack and pulled his chemistry book and notebook out, placing them on the table. I retrieved my book and notes from my bedroom and joined him.

After we organized our study guides, he leaned forward on the table. "Thanks for studying with me, Angel. I appreciate it."

He had such nice brown eyes and a genuinely warm smile. Now that I thought about it, I could see how girls might obsess over him. Maybe a little.

We went through the guide in about twenty minutes. Thankfully, he was bright and seemed to know as much as I did about chemistry. That made me happy, because his intelligence meant I might still be able to do some of the advanced experiments.

When we finished, he sat back in his chair and studied me. "It's true what they say about you."

I looked up in surprise. "Who is *they* and what do they say about me?"

"Some kids at school. They say you're different from other girls."

My face burned hot. "Okay, so, what?" My voice came out more miserable than defiant, as I'd intended.

He leaned across the table. "Angel, I mean that in a good way. You're one of the smartest girls in school. That's something to be proud of."

"It is?" I looked up at him, unsure.

"It is. Tell me the truth—you didn't even look at this material before tonight, did you? You know, we didn't cover about half of this stuff in class."

"I thought that's what tonight's study session was for."

"Exactly." He laughed. "No question chemistry is your thing."

"It's not my *thing*. It's in the genes, I guess. My mom is a pharmacist and my older sister is a microbiologist. My dad...he was a mathematician and engineer. Science and math kind of run in the family."

"Your dad isn't in the picture anymore?"

I stiffened and hoped he didn't notice. "No. He left when I was eighteen months old."

"Oh." Colt was silent for a moment. "Sorry. You only have one sister?"

"Yeah, Gwen. She works as a microbiologist at a high-tech company in Baltimore. How about you? Do you have any brothers or sisters?"

"No." For some reason, he looked sad. "I'm an only child."

"Well, at least you have a lot of friends at Excalibur, which is cool, considering you just got here last year."

He sighed. "Yeah, right. Lots of friends." He looked at me for a moment. "Hey, you have blue eyes. I just noticed. Red hair and blue eyes. That's unusual, right?"

"It's a statistical anomaly. I'm a freak of nature."

For a moment, he looked startled and then smiled. "Wow. Me, too." He laughed, looking surprisingly happy.

"No way. You're the most popular guy in school."

"Maybe. You know, Angel, I think I'm going to enjoy being your lab partner." He started picking up his papers and book and putting them in his backpack. The study session was ending faster than I'd expected. It also reminded me I hadn't asked him about the melee yet.

Nervously, I cleared my throat. "Um, Colt. Before you go, can I ask you a question?"

"Sure." His tone was easy, but his smile faded. There was a new wariness in his eyes. As the most popular kid at school, I bet he got asked for a lot of favors.

I summoned my courage anyway and plunged ahead. "You know Wally Harris, right? He's a senior and I intern with him once a week after school at this cyberintelligence company. Anyway, he's putting on a fund-raiser for Mr. Matthews. We're trying to help him with his medical and legal bills. You remember the Medieval Melee from last spring, right?" When he nodded, I continued. "We're going to do a benefit game next Wednesday evening at the school to raise money for him and…" I let my sentence trail off, trying to figure the best way to say it.

"You want me to play in it?" he offered.

"Yes." I looked up in relief. "But on the weaker team."

He shook his head, puzzled. "What weaker team?"

"Wally has this idea to pit the jocks against the geeks. But the geeks are going to get killed without a little extra help. That's where you come in. We'd like you to be captain of the geeks. The pairing is bound to draw a lot of interest among the student body and will hopefully help us raise more money for Mr. Matthews."

He seemed kind of surprised. But at least he hadn't said no right away.

"Let me get this straight." He folded his hands on the table and leaned forward. "You want me to be the captain of the geek squad for a special melee exhibition game to raise money for Mr. Matthews."

"That's correct," I said.

He started laughing. I watched him, unsure as to whether this was a positive development or not. He laughed so hard, I couldn't help but laugh a little with him, all the while feeling a bit apprehensive as to what he was thinking.

After a minute, he wiped an eye and grinned at me. "I'd be honored, but I have an important question first."

I tried not to get too excited by the honored part, but initial relief swept through me anyway. "Okay, shoot."

"This would be just for Excalibur students, right?" he asked. "We're not inviting other schools to participate?"

I thought it an odd question, but if his participation depended on it, I would answer it as honestly as possible. "As far as I know, only Excalibur students will play in the melee. It will be just one exhibition game. I'm sure we'll be able to drum up enough people to play on each team, especially if you are onboard. Of course, we can't exclude people from other schools from attending in the audience. That's good, in my opinion. The more people, the better chance we have of raising lots of cash. But, between you and me, I can't see why anyone other than Excalibur students would even want to come."

Colt considered and then nodded. "Fair enough." Standing, he swung his backpack over his shoulder. "I'm in."

"You are? That's great, Colt. Thank you so much."

I walked him to the door, and suddenly we stood together in a moment of supreme awkwardness. If he liked me, maybe this was the moment when he would kiss me. I had no idea if people kissed after study dates. Maybe not on the first one. Maybe never. How would I know, since I'd never been kissed before?

"You're really tall," I blurted out.

"You're really short," he countered, grinning and giving me a fist bump. "Thanks, Angel. I'm glad you agreed to be my lab partner."

He opened the door and left me standing there happy but confused. Were we study partners? Friends? Something else? Maybe that was to be determined.

I was picking up my chemistry papers from the dining room table when my cell rang. I pulled it out of my pocket and answered it.

"Angel?"

"Wally?" His voice sounded panicked, which made me instantly anxious. "Are you okay? What's wrong?"

There was a long pause. "I hate to be the bearer of bad news, but the assistant district attorney has decided to charge Mr. Matthews with assault with a deadly weapon."

CHAPTER NINETEEN

Angel Sinclair

"**W***hat?*"

"It's in the report. Go read it." Wally hung up.

I raced to my computer. I didn't believe it, *couldn't* believe it, until I hacked into the police department and read the report for myself.

It was true. All of it.

I felt like throwing up, although that would solve zip. I needed to go to the police station and tell them everything. Although I couldn't prove any of the events were connected, the police needed to know about the bleacher incident and the mysterious person in Mr. Matthews's office the day of the accident, just in case. If I could get Frankie to come, she would help me corroborate the bleacher story. I had no idea if they were related, but I didn't want any information to be left out. I also wanted the police to know the nothingbutthetruth.com website was full of lies and misinformation.

My phone dinged, signaling a text. It was from Wally.

Angel, what are we going to do?

We need to talk to the police tomorrow. We should tell them everything we know.

Agreed. I'm not stopping the fund-raiser. He needs us more than ever now.

I know.

I spent most of the night trying to hack in to the evil website, but whoever was running it was capable. Security was surprisingly top-notch and I was too tired to form an innovative or effective strategy. I fell into bed discouraged and frustrated. We had to do something and quick or Mr. Matthews was toast.

The next day at school was a blur. The bus was late, so I didn't see Wally and Frankie at my locker. I didn't even have the chance to tell them Colt was onboard to help us with the fund-raiser. When I was finally able to tell them, at lunch, they were excited and, not surprisingly, more determined than ever to proceed with the fund-raiser.

Although I'd completely forgotten to study for an AP English quiz, I only missed two questions. Nic, the jerk, was in a surprisingly good mood. He probably got a perfect score. I ignored the satisfied glances he threw my way.

I cared even less about the chemistry quiz and went into full autopilot mode while taking it. My mind was on a million other things. When the quiz was done, I couldn't remember a single question or tell Colt in any coherent way how I thought I did on it. I'm sure he noticed I was preoccupied, but he was nice enough not to ask why. I envied him the ignorance of knowing that Mr. Matthews was about to be charged with assault. I just hoped it wasn't too late to change the police's mind. I wanted the day to be over as quickly as possible, so Wally, Frankie, and I could go to the station and bring them up-to-date on what we knew.

When the final bell rang, Frankie and I headed out to the parking lot together. Wally was already waiting by his car. I climbed in the front passenger seat without even arguing with Frankie about it.

Wally held up his phone. "I've got the station address programmed into my phone. Are you sure you want to do this?"

"Unless you've got another plan, I'm sure." I adjusted my backpack between my legs and fastened my seat belt. "They're going to bring charges against Mr. Matthews. As he doesn't appear to have any family to stand for him, it's up to us."

"That is *so* sweet, Angel," Frankie sighed. "You have such a soft heart."

"I do not." I turned around in my seat and glared at her. "This is about justice and what's fair. There is nothing soft about it."

"So she says." Frankie waved a hand dismissively.

I was about to argue when I saw her hairstyle. I'm not sure how I hadn't noticed it all day. I guess I *had* been preoccupied. "Frankie, what's up...with your hair?"

She beamed. "I thought you'd never notice. It's my wavy asymmetric look with streaks of red highlights. I got a lot comments on it today."

"I bet." I didn't even know what that meant. I wasn't sure how she got away with it given the school's strict dress code, but I hadn't read the section on hair or accessories because, frankly, I didn't care about that stuff. I guess so long as it didn't contain a political or offensive statement, the school was okay with it.

We made a quick stop for gas, during which Wally and I endured a lecture from Frankie on how the gas company violated several international environmental standards. A few minutes after we left the gas station, we pulled into the police station. Wally circled the parking lot twice before someone pulled out and we took the vacated space. We walked to the entrance and tried to go in, but the door was locked.

"State the nature of your business," a gruff voice said.

I looked up at the security camera and voice box. "I'm Angel Sinclair and these are my friends Wally Harris and Frances Chang. We'd like to talk to Detective Martin Barnett about the accident investigation involving Excalibur Academy's vice principal, Ryan Matthews."

There was silence, and then a loud buzzer sounded. Wally yanked the door open and we walked inside, straight ahead to a circular desk where a burly, uniformed man with large biceps and a bald head sat.

"What do you kids want?" he asked. "Spell it out for me again." He didn't seem the chatty type.

"We need to talk to Detective Barnett about an accident he is investigating." I cleared my throat. "We have some information for him."

He stared at me for a long moment. "Do you have an appointment?"

"No. You have to make an appointment with the police?"

He didn't answer. Keeping an eye on us, he picked up the phone, punching in a number. After a moment, he spoke. "Yeah, this is Miller at the front desk. I got three kids out here who want to see you about an accident involving their vice principal."

He listened for a moment and then said, "Understood." He hung up and narrowed his eyes at us. "See that waiting area? Go sit there. Do not move, do not go to the bathroom, do not talk to anyone. The detective will be right out."

"Thank you," I said.

We all followed Wally to the blue plastic chairs and sat down. They were beyond uncomfortable, but easy to clean, which I deduced was the idea. The room smelled like sweat, stale coffee, and disinfectant. There was no one else waiting but us. A large-screen television hanging from one corner of the room was on the weather channel with the volume turned off. A documentary about tornadoes was playing. I watched as a barn was lifted into the air, spun around, and tossed as if it were a toy.

"I have to go to the bathroom," Frankie whispered to me.

"He just said we can't go to the bathroom." I glanced over my shoulder. Sure enough, Miller was watching. He looked at me and pointed his fingers from his eyes to all of us. I got the message loud and clear.

"I didn't have to go until he said that." Frankie wiggled on the chair. "Power of suggestion. Plus, I'm nervous. I've never been in a police station before."

"You're not in trouble. We are helping the police. We are the good guys."

"I still have to pee."

"Cross your legs and hold it."

Before she could argue further, a thin man in a white shirt, black slacks, and a red tie walked over to us. His shirt was rolled to the forearms and his tie askew, as if he'd fussed with it, trying to loosen it. His blond hair was thinning on the top, but he had sideburns that looked like swatches cut from a shag rug. He stood with his hands on his hips and regarded us for a moment.

"I'm Detective Barnett. I understand you're here to see me."

I jumped to my feet. "I'm Angel Sinclair, a senior at the Excalibur Academy for the Technologically Gifted. We're here on behalf of our vice principal, Mr. Matthews. We have information that is pertinent to your investigation of him."

The detective considered for a moment, then sat down next to Wally, leaning forward with his hands between his legs. He laced his fingers together as he studied us. "Is that so?"

When he sat, I returned to my seat. I thought maybe we'd go back to his office, but since no one else was around, this was going to be as far as we got. It was kind of awkward, because now we were all sitting in the same row next to each other on those hard, plastic seats. I shifted in mine so I partially faced him.

"We heard that criminal charges are going to be brought against Mr. Matthews. That's not right. He wouldn't hurt anyone on purpose."

The detective leaned back in his chair and crossed his arms against his chest. "How do you know about the charges?"

Crap. For a girl with a high IQ, that had been a dumb mistake. I shrugged. "I have excellent sources."

The detective stared at me for a long moment. "Why do you think Mr. Matthews wouldn't hurt anyone?"

"He's not that kind of man. You don't know him like we do. He's helped us a lot. He even saved Frankie and me on the day of the accident."

Detective Barnett's eyebrow raised. "Saved you?"

I gave him a brief accounting of the bleacher malfunction, how we didn't know at that point about Mr. Matthews's prostheses, and the dark figure leaving the gym after it happened. Frankie nodded and corroborated parts of the story as I told it.

"You don't know who the figure was?" the detective asked me.

"No, I was too far away and focused on the giant bleacher about to squash me."

"It could have been a kid passing through the gym."

"Possibly, but why wouldn't they have tried to help us or at least gone for help?"

He turned to Frankie. "And you are?"

"Frances Chang. I just moved to Washington. My dad is in the military. By the way, this happened on my very first day at Excalibur."

"Interesting. Did you see the dark figure, too?"

"No. I was too busy screaming my head off. But I believe Angel."

"Did she tell you about this figure after Mr. Matthews saved you?"

Frankie considered for a moment. "Not right away, but we had PE right afterward—we were playing softball—and that's when she knocked herself out with a bat, so we didn't discuss it until later."

Thank God he didn't ask for further details about the bat incident. Instead, he leaned back at his seat and looked between Frankie and me. "Angel didn't tell you until after Mr. Matthews's accident?"

I held up a hand. "Wait a minute. Why does it matter when I told her?"

"It might not matter at all. I'm trying to make sure I have a clear timeline of events." He paused for a moment before asking me the next question. "Did Mr. Matthews see the figure?"

"I don't know. I didn't ask him. We were pretty shaken up. I guess at that moment, we thought it was an accident. I was upset from the near-death experience and the fact that he hadn't screamed in agony when the bleacher rolled on his foot. It seemed kind of surreal."

"Do you know why Mr. Matthews was in the gym at that moment?"

I thought about it. "No. But why shouldn't he be? He's in charge of the school. He's allowed to be everywhere."

"Fair enough."

"Hey, aren't you going to take notes?" Wally interrupted. "All the detectives on television always take extensive notes when taking witness reports."

"Are you a witness?"

"Well, not exactly. But I'm an excellent character reference for Mr. Matthews."

Detective Barnett smiled and tapped his temple. "I don't need notes. I have a mind like a steel trap. And your name is?"

"Wally Harris. Senior. I wasn't in the gym at the time of the bleacher accident, but I do know Mr. Matthews. Cool dude. American hero. Not someone who hurts unarmed pedestrians."

"Thank you for that succinct analysis, Mr. Harris."

"You're welcome."

Detective Barnett turned his cool blue eyes on me. "Any reason why someone would want to hurt you?"

"Me?"

"There's this girl Mary who has it in for Angel," Frankie interjected. "There was a bit of a, um, disagreement in the locker room right before we headed into the gym."

"Is that so? Why?"

"Because she's a first-class bully, that's why." Frankie launched into a breathless account of the altercation, exaggerating my role a little but essentially covering the basics.

"So you think Mary did it?" He asked me the question.

"I don't know," I admitted. "It's possible, but unlikely. She was already warming up as a pitcher by the time we got out to the baseball field. She would have had to move fast. But she could have done it, I guess. She's is a capable athlete—captain of the swim team. But trying to kill us is extreme, even for a bully."

"Does this Mary have a last name?"

"Herman."

"Okay. Anything else I should know?"

"Yes." I lowered my voice. "Mr. Matthews had a visitor at school on the day of the accident."

Detective Barnett frowned. "Really? And you know that how?"

"I saw him. I was tardy for my first class, so I went to the office to get my slip signed. Ms. Eder wasn't at her desk, so I went to see if Mr. Matthews would sign off on it. He was in his office talking to someone—a man. His office door was ajar and Mr. Matthews's voice was raised, which was unusual because I'd never heard him raise his voice before."

"Did you hear what they were saying?"

"Only that Mr. Matthews was concerned about something. He said it was a serious issue, but the other guy said he was overreacting and he'd take care of it."

"Did you get a decent look at the guy?"

"Yes. Mr. Matthews called him Vincent. They both caught me listening at the door. This Vincent guy was tall with dark hair. He wore a leather jacket and he had a ring on the third finger of his right hand. The ring was silver with a black stone."

Detective Barnett was silent for a moment. "You're quite observant, Miss Sinclair. Did anyone else, other than Mr. Matthews, see Vincent?"

"I don't know. Mrs. Eder wasn't in the office and Headmistress Swanson wasn't around."

"Okay. What happened next?"

"Nothing. Vincent left and Mr. Matthews signed off on my tardy slip and told me to go back to class."

"Anything else?"

"Isn't that enough? Are you going to try to find him?"

"I will definitely follow up on your information."

The way he said that had me wondering if he would. "There's also this matter of a website that is attacking Mr. Matthews's character," I said. "It's full of lies and disinformation."

"Would you be referring to nothingbutthetruth.com?"

"You've heard of it?" I said in surprise.

He lifted an eyebrow. "I am a detective, after all."

"Well, don't believe anything on that site. I don't know who is running it, but it's lies and disinformation."

"Is that your personal assessment?"

"It is. What do you think about it?"

"I think freedom of the press is a protected right in our country. Mr. Matthews is, of course, free to press defamation charges, if he so chooses, once he recovers. At this point, however, all it means is that someone has a view opposite yours. Just so you know, you aren't the only students who have been here."

"What? We're not?" I said in surprise. "Who else came?"

"Someone who doesn't have as high an opinion of Mr. Matthews as you do." He stood up. "Thank you for stopping by. I appreciate the information."

Panic rose in my throat. "You're not going to charge him, right?"

"It's not up to me, but if it were, I'd charge him. The accident investigation showed that Mr. Matthews intentionally accelerated into the woman. There was no evidence of tampering or malfunction with the car. Regardless, even if the evidence pointed elsewhere, it wouldn't matter at this point. We'd still charge him."

I gazed at him flabbergasted. "Why?"

"Because he woke up a couple hours ago. He remembers everything and has admitted to pressing on the gas moments before he hit the woman."

CHAPTER TWENTY

Angel Sinclair

We must have looked stunned, because the detective put a hand on my shoulder, his voice softening. "I know you're disappointed, kids. But leave this in the hands of the authorities, okay? We'll get to the truth. I promise."

He reached into his back pocket and pulled out his wallet. He withdrew a business card and handed it to me. "If you think of anything else, here's my number. You don't have to make a trip next time. Just call, okay?"

Without another word, he strode away, leaving us all standing there with open mouths.

"Well, that didn't go as well as expected," Frankie finally said. "Maybe we should have brought him cookies."

"Who would come down to the station to talk trash about Mr. Matthews?" Wally said angrily. "Everyone likes him."

Dejected, we left the station and piled into the car. "Now what?" Wally asked as he backed out of the parking spot.

"If we aren't going to get help from the police, we take matters into our own hands," I said firmly. "Starting with finding the mysterious Vincent."

The mood in the car was decidedly somber, so none of us spoke, not even Frankie. Wally dropped me off, then drove Frankie home. I had a lot to do. Despite my earlier comments to Nic, I desperately needed to study and catch up on homework. But now that I was home alone and highly motivated, I wanted to do some hacking first.

I started with the prostheses. There had to be a finite list of companies that made prostheses like Mr. Matthews's pair. Once I narrowed down the companies, I could cross-reference them for a client named Ryan Matthews. It seemed logical to me if someone had visited Mr. Matthews at his office, they would likely be in the Washington metropolitan area, or at least have a branch office.

Unfortunately, unlike the police department, tech companies usually had decent IT staffs. That meant my hacks would take longer and be harder. I would need both Wally and me working on it. But it was another thread to pull, at least.

For now, no hacking. I started with public sources. What companies in the area with offices—or branch offices—made prostheses with IMES software and hardware?

It was a quick search. Only four companies popped, most of them, not surprisingly, located near the Walter Reed medical center in Bethesda, Maryland, where many injured servicemen and -women were treated. DuoMed, Flex Force Ltd., BioLimbs, and Kinetic Bio.

I did an online search of the company websites to see if any employees were named Vincent. Unfortunately, all four websites listed the CEOs only, and none were named Vincent. I hadn't thought it likely that a CEO would travel to a high school to assure a patient things would be okay, but I thought it was worth a shot.

Next I got online to LinkedIn to see what happened when I cross-referenced the four companies with employees named Vincent. Bingo. Thirty-six hits. I was going through them one by one when my mom got home. I logged off and went out to meet her.

She kissed me on the top of the head. "How was your day?" She shrugged out of her pharmacist's coat, placing it over the back of the couch. "Everything okay?"

I hadn't planned on telling her, but it came rushing out before I could stop it. "Mr. Matthews is going to be charged with assault with a deadly weapon for hitting the pedestrian."

"What?" A shocked expression crossed her face. "How do you know this?"

I told her everything, including going to the police station, but minus any hacking information.

Mom listened intently. "I'm going to find out what's going on," she said firmly. "Charges or not, I'm going to see Ryan. If it's true—that he's going to be charged—he's going to need to see all the friendly faces he can."

"How will you do that?"

"I'll start by talking to him. That should help me figure out what he needs and what we can do to help."

"You're going to go see him at the hospital?"

"I'm going to try. Are you kids going forward with the fund-raiser?"

"Absolutely." I nodded. "Wally is determined."

"I really like that boy."

"Yeah, me, too."

We started fixing dinner, both of us quiet with our thoughts. I was chopping carrots when my mom took off her wedding ring and set it on the counter while she washed a head of lettuce. Although I'd seen her do it a hundred times before, given my reflective mood, it prompted a question.

"Mom, why do you still wear your wedding ring?"

Mom stilled, then turned off the water. She shook the lettuce once and set it on a paper towel. "I know it must seem silly to you, Angel. But I still feel married. It's hard for me to accept your father is not with us when he remains so close here." She tapped her chest.

I set the knife down and pushed the carrots to the side. "Why didn't you get a death certificate?"

She blinked in surprise. "Because I have no evidence he's dead."

"Maybe the fact that he hasn't been around for fourteen years is as good a reason as any."

Mom pulled off a paper towel and wiped her hands. I knew her well enough to see she was trying to measure her response. When she spoke, her voice was calm but firm. "Angel, the reasons I have for holding out hope for your father are mine alone. We haven't talked a lot about this, but your father loved you very much and provided well for our family. He created college funds for both you girls before he disappeared. Our savings accounts were solid. When he vanished, he didn't leave any problems behind, including debt."

"So he gets a medal for deserting his family because he left us in excellent financial shape?"

"Angel." My mom's voice was hard now. "Stop it."

"Then why don't you enlighten me? You never talk about him. You've never even told me if you think he left of his own will or if he was…murdered." My breath hitched, garbling the last word. For the first time, I understood why Gwen never wanted to talk about Dad. It was painful beyond belief. But I pushed ahead anyway.

My mom flinched as if I'd slapped her. Reaching out

a hand, she steadied herself against the counter. But when she spoke, she said something I didn't expect.

"Does it matter?" She spoke quietly, her face pale. "The results are the same. He's not here with us."

My mouth dropped open. "It matters to me, Mom. If you know something, tell me. Please."

"Your father was a good man. Brilliant, heroic, tender, and kind. He loved me, you, and your sister with all his heart. If he left of his own free will, there was an important reason. Nothing anyone can say would change my mind about that. That's all you need to know."

"I'm sorry, but it's not. I'm going to find out what happened to him, Mom. I mean it."

My mom smiled. "You remind me a lot of him, you know. Passionate, committed, obsessed with the truth. It meant everything to him. Your father also considered himself a loner, although he was the most charming and gracious man I'd ever met. But sometimes...I saw a sadness in his eyes." She looked off at the wall above my shoulder, clearly lost in a thought. "Leave this alone, Angel. Please."

"I can't, Mom. I *won't*. I'm not going to lie to you. I won't give up until I know what happened to him."

She blew out a breath and pushed a strand of hair out of her eyes. "You know who else you remind me of? Your aunt Dorothy. She's the most dogged person I know, next to you, of course. Once she gets her mind set on something, there is no dissuading her."

Just like that, the tension dissolved. It was hard to be mad at the only parent you had, especially when she was suffering as much as you were.

I mustered a smile. "Hey, I'm not dogged. I'm invested. There's a big difference. Besides, how can you possibly compare me to Aunt Dorothy? She still thinks I'm ten years old. She gave me a Hello Kitty bra last

Christmas. That isn't normal."

Mom chuckled. "I forgot about the bra. She's always in bigger sister mode with me and now with you two girls."

"Well, it's embarrassing."

"She loves you. She's a bit quirky. Go easy on her."

"I always do."

We grinned at each other before I walked across the kitchen and wrapped my arms around her waist. She hugged me back. We stood there for a bit without talking.

"I love you, Angel." She tucked a stray strand of hair behind my ear.

"I love you, too, Mom. But I'm not giving up on finding Dad, and I'm not giving up on Mr. Matthews, either. I'll figure things out. I promise."

My mom twirled a strand of my hair around her finger. "No matter how hard you try, some mysteries may never be solved. Are you prepared for that?"

Before I could respond, my phone rang. I dug it out of my pocket. Wally was calling.

I pressed the phone to my ear. "Hey, Wally. What's up?"

"Are you alone?"

I looked over my shoulder at where my mom had resumed washing the lettuce. "Give me a minute." I walked out of the kitchen toward my room. "I'm clear. What happened?"

"Detective Barnett updated the police report."

"Again?" I went into my room and closed the door. "What is it this time?"

There was a long silence. "I'm sorry, Angel, but I don't think you're going to like what he wrote."

CHAPTER TWENTY-ONE

Angel Sinclair

I went to my room and sat down in front of my computer. "Give it to me straight, Wally."

He was silent for a long moment.

"Wally?" I said.

"Just read it, Angel. Then call me back, okay?"

Wally's voice sounded different. Strained. Distant. Something was wrong.

My fingers shook on the keyboard as I hacked in. As I read the new entry to the report, a fist tightened around my throat. Words floated across the screen.

Troubled young woman...wishful thinking...transference... misguided.

Detective Barnett didn't believe me. Since no one except me had seen the mysterious Vincent, my information was to be considered suspect. He'd interviewed both Ms. Eder and Headmistress Swanson, and neither had reported seeing a dark-haired stranger. Vincent hadn't signed in on the office clipboard, which made sense, since Mrs. Eder hadn't been there to ensure he did.

But the report went on. While the detective concluded it was not impossible I saw someone, he feared I might have exaggerated the exchange in a misguided effort to help Mr. Matthews. He supported his conclusion about me by saying he believed I was transferring the loss of my father onto Mr. Matthews. He'd done his research on me—which shouldn't have surprised me, since he was a detective—but it still stung. I wasn't the suspect here. He'd even attached the seven emails (none of which had ever been answered) I'd sent to the police department over the past few years, regarding possible leads to my father's disappearance.

Humiliation swamped me as I pressed my hand against my mouth. *They didn't believe me.* All those emails to the police department, leads to finding my dad—they didn't care. They thought I was a nutcase, completely unbalanced because I'd never given up hope of finding my father. Now Wally had read the report, so he knew everything…about me and my father.

How could I face Wally now? What if he told people? I'd become the laughingstock of the entire high school.

My phone beeped. I looked down. I had a text from Wally.

Call me?

I ignored the text and stuck my phone in my pocket just as my mom called out that dinner was ready. I shut down my laptop, took a couple of deep breaths, and went out to dinner. There was no way I was going to tell her of this development.

Until I could figure out what to do next, I was on my own.

CHAPTER TWENTY-TWO

Isaac Remington

Executive Director, Research Directorate ED/RD, NSA

I saac stopped by a nearby Target on the way home from his work at the NSA. He hated going into stores; it was so…pedestrian. He preferred ordering everything online because it was cleaner, solitary, and noninvasive. Children were too loud in stores, germs were everywhere, and the unpleasant smells of cheap perfume, sweat, and bad breath bothered him. Unfortunately, however, some items were best purchased in store and for cash.

Now was one of those times.

Keeping his head down, Isaac put on a pair of thin black gloves and quickly grabbed five burner phones, going rapidly through the express line.

When he got home, Isaac hung up his coat, set his briefcase down next to the table in precisely the same spot he put it every day, and perched on a corner of his couch. It took him three minutes to activate one of the new phones. As soon as it was ready, he dialed the number.

"Hello?" a male voice answered.

"It's me. We have a problem. The Hidden Avenger made contact with the NSA. Candace Kim is in charge of the investigation at this point. Someone on the inside raised the possibility that it's Ethan Sinclair. It's only a matter of time before they confirm it. I was forced to hand over his file to her."

"Who identified him?"

"I don't know. She wouldn't say and I couldn't press further without looking suspicious. Right now, it's a rolling ball I'm trying to keep in front of. I'm maneuvering to be a part of the investigation so I can keep an eye on things."

There was silence before the person on the other end responded. "Why has he surfaced now?"

"I'm not sure. My guess is the retirement announcement of General Norton may have prompted him to speak out."

"Oh. He knows you're angling for the directorship."

Isaac shrugged. "Or he may want to come in, so he's offering what he has in hopes they'll give him immunity.

"From what?"

"Hacking, I assume. He's offering them information on a terrorist plot he obtained by hacking into their networks using ShadowCrypt."

"Brazen."

"Yes. But it may be the break we've been looking for in terms of finding him."

"As long as they don't bring him in before we do."

"They won't," Isaac said confidently. "We've got people where we need them. We've patiently waited fourteen years to get a lead on him. Now we've got it, all we need to do is follow up. Let me be clear. If we want to ensure our agenda is implemented, I must be in the director's seat. That means we need to find the

Avenger before they do. We can't have him blabbing or raising any questions about me."

"Does he want anything else other than immunity?"

"Protection for his family." Isaac stood and walked into the kitchen, opening the refrigerator and pulling out a bottle of water. He took a swig of the water and wiped his brow.

There was a soft chuckle. "From who? Us?"

"I would suspect that is correct. So far, the Avenger has only agreed to a secure method of communication. I want to be there when the virtual exchange goes down, so I can find out what he really wants."

"What do you want me to do?"

"Since protection for his family is foremost on his mind, start there. Observe, monitor, and report on them. I don't care what you do, or how you do it, so long as you get a lead on his whereabouts."

"We've monitored his family before and got nothing. He's careful."

"That was then. This is now. It's hard out in the cold. He wants to come in, get his old life back. We need to leverage that."

"You think he's in the vicinity? Near enough to be watching his family?"

"That's exactly what I think. We need to exploit that. Take whatever steps are necessary. Get started right away."

There was a long pause. "You do know you're not going to get official permission to wiretap. They're US citizens on US soil."

Surely he couldn't be so stupid. "Do I have to spell everything out for you? Do what you need to do. I don't care *how* you do it. Are we clear?"

"Crystal. Do you want me to bring in anyone else?"

"No. Let's keep this information tight to the core group. I'll give you what I can when I'm able."

"Understood. One more question. What do we do if we find him first?"

"What we've always needed to do. Eliminate him."

CHAPTER TWENTY-THREE

Angel Sinclair

The next morning, I skipped going to my locker and went straight to math class since I already had my book. I'd ignored three more text messages from Wally last night and one this morning. I ran into Frankie in the hall and she tried to talk to me, but I told her I was in a hurry and ran off. It wasn't until lunch that Wally cornered me.

I was planning on skipping lunch and going outside, but he caught me at my locker even though I'd waited until lunch had already started.

"Angel, we have to talk."

I yanked my locker open and shoved in my books. "About what?"

"You know what."

"What's there to talk about? The police think I'm crazy. End of story."

"Are you?"

I slammed the locker shut. "What kind of question is that?"

"A simple one. Are you delusional or not?"

I hadn't expected that, so I crossed my arms against my chest and studied him. "Do you think I am?"

He lowered his voice. "Look, calm down, okay? We're not enemies. And, since you asked, no, I don't think you're crazy. I didn't tell Frankie, either."

I blew out a breath, leaning back against the lockers. I closed my eyes and tried to do what Wally asked me to do—calm down. My anxiety was sky-high. None of that would help Mr. Matthews—or me, for that matter.

"They aren't doing anything to find my father. They think he disappeared on purpose."

"I'm not judging, Angel, but the evidence I read is compelling for that scenario. However, further research indicates to me it's not the whole story. There's something not right there."

"You read my father's file, too?"

A slight bit of color touched his cheeks. "I didn't intend to pry. But I want to help Mr. Matthews. I needed to know if you're solid."

I was torn between extreme mortification and outrage. "And your diagnosis, Dr. Harris?" I was an exceptionally private person, and the revelation that he now knew more about my life than even my mother was agonizing.

He shrugged. "You're good in my book, Angel. Truth is, if I'd been in your shoes, I'd have done the exact same thing. Let's move on and get back to helping Mr. Matthews. We can't expect much, if any, help from the police."

I stared at him. "That's it? Just like that."

"Yeah, just like that."

I swallowed. I appreciated his vote of confidence more than he would ever know. In fact, I was so dangerously close to tears it scared me. I'd cried like five times in my life.

I raised my chin, pretended all was cool. "Thanks, Wally. I'll see you after school at X-Corp."

I started to walk away when he reached out and grabbed my arm.

"Hey, I'll give you a ride to X-Corp. It'll save you from having to take the Metro. I should have offered you a ride a long time before this."

I pulled my arm from his grasp. "Don't feel sorry for me. I feel bad enough having you drive me around town as it is."

"I'm doing this of my own free will. You're not making me do anything. And I don't feel sorry for you. Trust me, if I didn't want to drive you, I wouldn't. It's simple logistics—we're going to the same place at the same time. Meet me at my car and we'll go together. Okay?"

I let out a breath. "Okay, thanks."

"And Angel?"

"Yeah?"

"I think it's time to bring Lexi onboard to help. Maybe even Piper and Brandon, too. Not the stuff with your father—that's between us—but if you saw some guy named Vincent in Mr. Matthews's office, and I believe you did, then we need to find him regardless of whether the police believe you or not. That's got to be a priority."

"I agree. I'll talk to Lexi today."

"Great." He gave me a light punch on the arm. "Are you going to have lunch with us now? Frankie is wondering what's wrong with you today. I told her it was your time of the month."

"*Wally!*"

He laughed and pushed his glasses up on his nose. "Just kidding. Come on, let's eat and assure Frankie we still love her."

I hesitated and then followed him. All of this was so

foreign to me. I hadn't expected this level of support. He could have laughed, agreed I was a total nutcase, or worse—told everyone. Instead, he'd learned one of my deepest secrets and shrugged it off like it was no big deal.

At that exact moment, it occurred to me perhaps what I'd been afraid of with my peers was being *understood*, rather than *misunderstood*. Now that Wally understood me and accepted me anyway, what did it mean?

I pondered the question. I didn't have answers, but I had a feeling I was going to find out.

CHAPTER TWENTY-FOUR

Isaac Remington

NSA Headquarters, Fort Meade, Maryland

Isaac couldn't keep the grin off his face as he strode into the conference room where the team was assembling the first consistent line of communication with the Avenger. He knew he'd pissed off Candace Kim by insisting on being part of information exchange. He didn't understand why she was resisting his help. She acted all high and mighty, as if her position outranked his. It didn't.

Needling her wasn't necessary, but it amused him to put that angry glint in her eye. If only she knew how much more he intended to do as the investigation continued.

A technician climbed out from beneath the table and typed something on a laptop. He raised a hand in greeting to Isaac when he saw him.

"Just in time. We're ready to go. We've installed the email host software on the target server and established the account there as requested. The laptop has been triple wiped to make sure that it contains nothing other than the required software. It's completely isolated from our internal network and SIPRNET, and has access to the Internet."

Candace was already seated at the table with a notepad in front of her and pen in hand. She looked surprisingly relaxed given what they were about to do. Jim Avers, the deputy director of operations, sat next to her. He looked a lot more nervous.

Candace waved Isaac to the chair in front of the laptop without greeting him. "Have a seat, Isaac. You're going to be the one corresponding with the Avenger today."

He hadn't seen that one coming. "*What?* You set this up for *me* to talk to the Avenger?"

"Sure. Why not? Of all of us, you're the one who knew him best."

"I didn't *know* him. We worked in the same division on a couple of the same projects."

"That's more of a connection than anyone else here has. Sit down, Isaac. Don't worry, we'll tell you what to say. You don't have to give him your name—we just want your take on his questions and answers."

Isaac took the seat, his fury building. How *dare* she order him about like a subordinate. They were equals in terms of position and she thought she could demean him? His first action as director would be to get rid of her. He took a breath to calm himself. For all her show, she'd given him exactly what he wanted—a front seat to the exchange.

"What do you want me to say?" Isaac asked.

"Tell him we need to know his demands before we can deal fairly." She glanced at Jim. "Can you proof his message before he sends?"

Isaac bristled at the suggestion he needed oversight for one sentence. He almost rose out of his chair to confront her but with supreme effort remained seated.

His jaw was clenched so tightly, he couldn't speak.

After Isaac finished typing, he leaned back so that Jim could proof it. Jim leaned forward and nodded his approval. Isaac hit the Enter key with more force than required.

"It's been sent," he said. "I hope our adversary is paying attention."

Candace studied Isaac. "Adversary? You think he's our adversary?"

Isaac stared back at her in surprise. Could she really be that stupid?

"Have you forgotten that he terminated the access to the back door we were using to monitor terrorists worldwide? No telling how many lives were lost in terrorist attacks since then that might have been prevented."

"That's only partially true." Candace spoke lightly, as if she didn't have a care in the world. "We were also using it for a lot of other unauthorized activities."

"All in the name of national security," he shot back.

"That's fine, when it's approved by Congress. What was going on was largely unregulated. There is a reason this country has checks and balances."

"Those checks and balances are useless." Seriously? Was she really that naive? The woman who wanted to be the director of the NSA?

Candace raised an eyebrow. "Isaac, I'm astonished you feel that way."

Isaac clamped his mouth shut. He had no idea why she was baiting him, but he wasn't going to accommodate her any longer. As of this moment, his first act as director of the NSA would be to find a way to fire her.

Jim stood, walking around the room while swinging his arms back and forth in a stretch. "I'm having a hard time wrapping my mind around the Avenger. He's puzzling, to say the least. We know he's identified dozens of security holes worldwide that could have been compromised, but he doesn't take advantage of them. He doesn't appear to be working for a foreign entity or tied to any specific cause. Now he's offering us information to stop what he claims could be a potentially devastating terrorist attack. He certainly doesn't fit the profile of a hacker who does it for attention or fame. What's his deal?"

"His deal is that he's a criminal and a traitor," Isaac said. "By all definitions. Just the fact that he's asking for immunity implies he's conducted criminal activity."

"True," Jim conceded. Still, he looked troubled at the suggestion. "However, he's not another Edward Snowden. He didn't provide direct intelligence to our adversaries. He didn't spill any beans on the NSA, either, at least as far as we know. He just shut the door."

"We don't know what he *has* or *hasn't* done," Isaac snarled. "Don't make him out to be a hero. He cut us off. We *needed* that access."

"We also *need* those innovative tools from the research and development shop you promised were on the way at the last agency budget presentation," Candace said mildly.

Isaac glared at her, but she didn't seem to care. He was thinking of an appropriate response when the laptop dinged.

"We have a response," the technician said.

Isaac opened the email and read the message aloud.

"'Before I list my requests, I offer to you, in good faith, the most current information on the terrorist plot. It can be found in the file labeled 'Initial Downpayment.doc.' It will reside there for precisely three more minutes, and then it will be deleted. It contains names, email addresses, and phone numbers, as well as IP addresses and a synopsis of the planned attack. They intend to target the large crowds celebrating in the streets following the Super Bowl when most of the security precautions will be relaxed. A so-called soft target. The file also contains the IP address of the next server through which we will communicate using the same process as this. This is proof of my good intentions and capability.'"

"Get me that file," Candace said coolly, pointing at the technician. "I want a transcript of his message as well." He nodded and got to work on his laptop.

Isaac continued reading aloud.

"'In exchange, my requests are simple. Federal protection for myself and my family for at least two years, with an agreement in writing by the Department of Justice and the FBI that I will not be investigated, prosecuted, or convicted of any crimes related to my hacking or online activities, to include the real or accidental disclosure of classified information. Finally, I would like to have a personal one-on-one meeting with the director to discuss a personal matter I would like him to consider investigating.'"

"He's deluded," Isaac muttered.

"Keep reading," Candace instructed him.

"'By the time you have read this, you probably have less than two minutes to finish the download of the file. We will communicate again in exactly one month, via this account, as I know you will need time to discuss my offer. I will also consider the possibility of providing the key to ShadowCrypt to the NSA under certain conditions. In the meantime, do not try to contact me or track me down or this offer becomes invalid. Trust me, I'll know. Be fully prepared to address all of my requests in one month's time.'"

Candace turned to the technician. "Do we have the file yet?"

"Yes, ma'am. I'm reviewing it now to ensure it's

legitimate. It looks good. We also have a backup of the email itself."

"Excellent." She turned her attention to Isaac. "Tell him we agree to his terms and will speak with him in one month."

Isaac typed the message and after Jim gave him the thumbs-up, he pressed Send. They waited for a response, but one never came.

"He's gone, ma'am," the technician said.

Candace breathed out a breath. "At least we got the file. Send it up to the director right away."

"Will do."

Isaac leaned back in the chair, his brain on overdrive. What game was the Avenger playing? What did he want to talk about with the director?

"Thoughts, anyone?" Candace's question snapped Isaac from his reverie.

"Did you notice he didn't make demands?" Jim said. "Just requests. That seems odd for someone of his reputation."

"So it matters that he's a polite criminal?" Isaac snapped.

Candace didn't respond. Instead she was looking at the wall, deep in thought. After a bit, she turned to Isaac. "Why do you think he wants to talk to the director?"

"He probably has delusions of grandeur. No one with his record would be granted such high access to the NSA. It would be a dangerous—not to mention stupid—precedent to set."

"That's a strange thing to ask for," Jim observed. "It does lend credence to the fact that he might be one of our own. If so, what would he want to talk about that would be for the director's ears only?"

Candace nodded. "I agree that everything we've seen so far implies he is one of ours. I'm leaning strongly toward your theory, Isaac, that this is, indeed, Ethan Sinclair. What I want to know more about is who he was connected to, what he did at King's Security, and whether he had a specific insight to an operation. We're going to have to dig deep to see what we can find out about him."

"What about bringing in the FBI to help track him down?" Isaac asked. "We could use the help in finding his physical location."

"You think he's in the US?" Candace asked.

"I do. Just a gut feeling."

She picked up a coffee mug and took a sip. "Well, I met with the FBI, and their response was complicated. They were obviously very concerned and, naturally, wanted any information on the terrorist attack. That was their top priority. But they were less interested in investing any resources to try to track down the Hidden Avenger. Without proof of criminal activity, and given the lack of information on him, they could not justify the resources. They recommended that we continue to negotiate with him and get the information we need on the terrorists that way."

"Are they willing to grant him immunity?"

"They don't have the power to do that. It depends on the Justice Department. I'm meeting soon with a contact over there to see for how they feel about something like this. I'll be honest—I'm not sure how well this will be received, especially when I can't provide information on what the immunity would be for."

"I don't get why he's making this so hard," Jim said.

"I don't think he trusts us," Candace said. "And we have to find out why."

"I'll take the lead on that angle," Isaac offered. "I knew him the best, which wasn't much, but it probably means we probably have contacts in common somewhere. If there is anything to find on him, I'll find it."

Candace and Jim both dipped their heads in agreement.

"Okay, Isaac," she said. "The ball is in your court. Just get that information to me as soon as possible."

"I'm on it," he said.

But not in the way they expected.

CHAPTER TWENTY-FIVE

Angel Sinclair

I loved my internship at X-Corp. I'd only been working there since early June, but it was beyond prime. Wally, Piper, and Brandon had been interning a bit longer—since last February—but we all knew we had it good and appreciated every moment under Lexi Carmichael's excellent tutelage.

Lexi had been on my radar ever since she'd saved the school last winter. She was one of the few female tech heads I'd ever met and was, by far, the smartest.

I'd first met Lexi last May, just before she and my sister left on a trip to Egypt. That chance meeting afforded me the opportunity to help Lexi and her boyfriend, Slash, with an important mission. Slash is tall, dark, and Italian, and he works for the government in one of the intelligence agencies. He is hotness to the max and a wizard, which is what we hackers call a true god at the keyboard. I wish Lexi would tell me how she managed to find him and if he has a younger brother available. However, I seriously doubted she'd tell me. Lexi hates talking about her personal life even more than I do.

Just then, Lexi strolled into the cubicle area where we were working. She wore black slacks and a plain white sweater. Her long brown hair was pulled back into a ponytail, and she was devoid of makeup or jewelry. A pair of black computer glasses hung from the front of her sweater.

"Hey, guys. How's it going?"

Wally looked up and lifted a hand. "Great. Piper and Brandon located the test firewall. Angel penetrated the device, and I'm running programs to determine what hosts are behind the filter—a router, packet filtering, or a redirection application. And that's in the first ten minutes."

Lexi patted Wally's shoulder. "Right on schedule. Carry on."

I stood nervously. "Hey, Lexi. Can I talk to you for a minute? Privately?"

"Sure." She waved an arm at me. "Let's go into my office."

I followed her into a prime corner office. A long, sleek desk with a laptop and several monitors was flanked by bookshelves, and another corner featured a couple of laptops side by side, probably running algorithms or detection software. There were ceiling-to-floor windows and a coffee mug that read *I'm Not Bossy, I'm the Boss*. Lexi was twenty-six years old and she had shattered—no, obliterated—the glass ceiling in her corner of a heavily male-dominated tech industry. My hero—correction, heroine—indeed.

Instead of sitting behind her desk, Lexi perched on the arm of one of the visitor chairs while I sat in the chair adjacent to her. Even so, I couldn't believe how nervous I was. What if she thought I was crazy, like the police did? I wasn't sure I could handle that from her.

"So, Angel, what's up?" Her eyes seemed interested and kind.

It took me a few moments, but I took a deep breath and told her. I started with the events from the very first day of school and brought it forward. I told her everything that had happened, omitting only the mention of my questionable mental state in the police report.

Lexi listened carefully, not interrupting me once. When I was finished, my hands were shaking. I held my breath, practically cringing, waiting for her response.

She looked at me thoughtfully and then stood, reaching across to her desk and plucking off a pen and pad of paper. "What are the names of the four prosthetics companies you came up with?"

That was it. No disbelief, no thinking I was a loon. Just straight to the facts. My estimation and appreciation of her rose another notch.

"DuoMed, Flex Force Ltd., BioLimbs, and Kinetic Bio," I said. "I went through the company websites, but no executives named Vincent are listed for any of them. I started looking through LinkedIn to match employee profiles named Vincent, but I haven't got far yet."

"But you saw him, so you can identify him."

"Yes, that's why I was hoping to see a profile listed on LinkedIn."

She tapped the pen against her chest and looked off above my shoulder, thinking. "You could be going about this all wrong. He might not be connected to any of the prosthesis companies."

"He might not," I agreed. "I'm going on nothing more than a gut feeling."

"I trust gut feelings." She slipped on her computer glasses and went to her desk. I remained quiet while she typed something in. A minute later she looked up at me.

"One of those companies you just named hired X-Corp about three weeks ago to investigate a suspected cyberpenetration. I couldn't work directly on it as I was focused on something else at the time, but my staff researched it exhaustively and found no evidence of a break-in. I remembered thinking something seemed off, but I couldn't put my finger on it. Now that you bring this up, my hackles are raised."

"Which company was it, if you're permitted to say?"

"You're an intern here, so you can legitimately be informed. It's BioLimbs."

"Wait." My mind raced through information. "One of the Vincents in Mr. Matthews's contact list at school was a Vincent with the letters *BL* after it. It might be completely unrelated, but I'm not a big believer in coincidences."

"Neither am I. Do I want to know how you got hold of Mr. Matthews's contact list?"

I gulped. "Nope."

"That's what I thought."

She fell quiet until I asked, "What should we do, Lexi?"

She gazed at her screen and then back at me. "As my intern, I may assign you to take a closer look at the situation with BioLimbs, under my careful guidance, of course."

My eyes lit up. "Really?"

She smiled. "Really. Come sit next to me, Angel. Let's see what we can find out about this mysterious Vincent."

CHAPTER TWENTY-SIX

Isaac Remington

As soon as Isaac Remington left the NSA compound for the day, he activated another one of his burner phones and called his contact.

"I received your message. Do you have something for me?"

"I do, but it's not what you may be expecting. It just so happened that a report from the National Security Operations Center crossed my desk today. They've traced a series of hacks coming out of the target's house."

"What? He's in the house?"

"No. It's not him. Here's the interesting part. It's the daughter. She's a minigenius. Hacking, math, and science are her things. She goes to a special school for science and math in DC. I've been watching her work, and she's good. Very good. We've been monitoring all communications coming in and out of the house, but she bypassed our monitoring without even knowing we were there."

"Interesting. So she takes after her father. What's she hacking?"

"Once we figured out how she was bypassing our

monitoring, we adjusted and began tracking her activity. So far, her searches appear focused on one person—Ryan Matthews, a former marine sergeant. Matthews was wounded in action in Iraq, honorably and medically discharged. He's her school vice principal and was recently involved in a vehicular accident involving the serious injury of a female pedestrian. He is under local police investigation for deliberately targeting the woman."

"Other than the fact that he's her vice principal, why does the daughter care about him?"

"I don't know."

"Does he have any connection to her father?"

"None that I could find. Maybe it's not related. So far, she's easily broken into the local police department on multiple occasions. She's read the police report on his accident multiple times. She's also hacked into the company that owns the apartment complex where he lives. Not sure what she was looking to find. All hacks appear to have the same goal—information on Matthews. The investigator I hired reports she and two classmates—their dossiers were sent to you an hour ago—also visited the police department in person to plead the case for the vice principal. Apparently, the daughter strongly believes him to be innocent of charges. I followed her tracks into the police department and downloaded the police report. It notes that Matthews admitted to willfully running over the female pedestrian, but currently has no known motive. There is one anomaly in her searching that I am not sure is significant. She has spent significant time probing a website called nothingbutthetruth.com. I researched it myself, and it appears to be an amateur effort, consisting of fake news culled from the subject's school. I am guessing it's a peer effort, but I can't guess its purpose or her interest. The IP address has been noted, traced, and sent to you. It does not appear her focus on this website is connected to the disappearance of her father, but we can investigate further, as desired. Clearly, she is exceptionally capable of managing high-profile hacks and inciting collusion."

"Collusion?"

"Yeah. She apparently incited a classmate to penetrate a DoD human resources database to obtain information on Matthews's military records."

Isaac swore. "How did we track her in the first place if our monitoring wasn't picking her up?"

"From the DoD hack. It took place from her apartment. I don't know all the details. But I'm adjusting my methods to accommodate her expertise."

"You'd better. What's NSOC going to do about the hacking?"

"At this point, nothing. I told them to pass the information to you as part of the investigation. You should see that on your desk shortly."

"Good. Continue to observe her and report. This is an intriguing development. Maybe there is some way to use the daughter to our advantage."

"How?"

"Let's set up a honeypot. Create a site inside our firewall and populate it with junk and some selective information on her father. Drop some bread crumbs about how to get in and see if she will take the bait. Maybe if we give her some information on her father, she'll lead us to him. If she's that invested in her vice principal, imagine what she might do to find her father. If the IT guys give you a problem about granting her a broken window into our system, have them contact me for authorization."

"What? You can't be serious. She's not even sixteen yet. Do you think she can find her father when we haven't been able to?"

"If he knows she's looking for him, he may come to her. If he does, we'll be ready."

"You're calling the shots. Understood."

"Let me know when you are ready to go with the honeypot. And for God's sake, have someone review and patch the security hole on the DoD site ASAP."

"Already done, sir."

CHAPTER TWENTY-SEVEN

Angel Sinclair

I sat in front of a laptop, my hands itching to start typing. "What are we going to hack first?" I couldn't keep the eagerness out of my voice.

"We're not hacking anything." Still, she smiled at my undisguised enthusiasm. "I still have access to the BioLimbs system."

I was disappointed. "Oh, man. No hacking?"

"None needed." Lexi smiled as her hands flew over the keyboard of her laptop. "We should be able to quickly determine if they have any employees named Vincent. Are you sure that's his name?"

"That's what Mr. Matthews called him."

"Okay, then let's see what we've got." She pulled up a document called "Staff Directory" and started scrolling. "Bingo. There are two Vincents. A Vincent Dodayev and a Vincent Kars."

"Any photos of them?"

"Not in the directory, but now that we have names, let's look on LinkedIn."

She opened another window and pulled up LinkedIn.

Vincent Dodayev had a profile that identified him as working at BioLimbs and a photo. He wasn't the man in Mr. Matthews's office.

Vincent Kars didn't have a profile.

Frustration swept through me. "Figures. Maybe we can hack into the DMV to get a look at him."

"Not from X-Corp." Lexi patted my arm absently as she looked at something on her screen. "Vincent Kars is listed as director of research, bioengineering. That is interesting."

"It is? Why?"

"Well, it seems logical he'd lead the team that builds the inner workings of the prostheses. If he came all the way down to Excalibur Academy to talk to a patient, that might be significant."

"But what if he's not the person I saw? How can we be sure without seeing him in person?"

"You *will* see him in person. I'll give you something related to our work for BioLimbs to take him Monday after school. It's a job for an intern. It will also give you an opportunity for a face-to-face with Mr. Kars, whoever he is. I have a feeling that will be far more useful than hacking into the DMV at this point."

I reluctantly agreed. It was a sound approach, but I was disappointed I wasn't going to be hacking with her. "Okay. Makes sense."

By the time we wrapped things up, all the interns had left, including Wally. Lexi volunteered to give me a ride home. After we got in her car, a cherry-red Miata, I decided to take the opportunity to ask her some questions I'd been thinking about.

"Lexi, why is so hard for females in the tech industry? Right now, the field is only eighteen percent women, and it's declining by the year. Other than the usual sexist crap that happens at a lot of jobs, what's happening that is so awful it causes women to quit or leave?"

Lexi fell silent, taking a moment to collect her thoughts before she spoke. "I'm not going to sugarcoat it for you, Angel. I've only officially been in the field a few years, but on at least two dozen occasions—and that's a conservative estimate—I've had to move a man's hand from my thigh, back, or hair, and that's during an official meeting or a professional gathering. I've reported it each time it happens, but half the time, no one believes me. Coworkers have called me *sweetheart, honey,* and *little girl.* Men are openly shocked when I tell them I'm a hacker. We're called fake geek girls or wannabe engineers. I've personally been told I'm too emotional and I can't possibly think deeply enough on technical issues. I'm evaluated on personality and looks in ways men are not. It's a hostile environment for women, and I'm putting that mildly because I think you need to be prepared for that going in. You know my background. I'm an excellent programmer and coder, and I've published dozens of articles in respected peer publications. I'm often invited to speak on important and trending topics. But none of that stops jerks in the audience from trying to disrupt or disrespect me, all while disparaging my work, because I don't have a Y chromosome. I've received hate mail, disgusting suggestions about where I can stick my code, and comments on everything from my hair to my clothing. I ignore it because at twenty-six, I'm already near the top of my field. Why? Because I'm damn good at what I do."

For a full minute, I stared at her in awe. "Wow. Just wow. I'd like to say that if I hadn't already formed your fan club, I'd do it right now. But when you lay it out like that, I totally understand the exodus. That majorly sucks."

"Majorly." Lexi adjusted the rearview mirror and switched lanes. "Here's the kicker, though. Women are already rocking it so many areas of the tech field. For example, in the open-source software market, women have found that if they submit their work under their initials instead of their names, their code is accepted more often than men's."

"Really?

"Really. Because we are just as good, if not better, than our male counterparts. So how does change come about? Those eighteen percent of us who are sticking around—we're going to make it happen. Trust me, I'm not letting *anyone* stand in the way of my dreams. Coding and computers are my life. I love the challenge, the puzzles, and the fast-moving environment, not to mention the sheer enormity of how important the field is becoming in the development of the entire human race. I was born to be a coder, Angel. It's my passion, my gift—it's in my DNA. I'm not going to let some jerks derail me from what I was born to do."

"That was, by far, the most inspiring speech I've ever heard in my life."

"It wasn't a speech. Okay, maybe it was. Look, you and your female coworkers will help each other, and you'll figure out which of your male coworkers are giving you lip service and which ones will support you whether you're in the room or not. Remember, I've met two of my best friends—the Zimmerman twins—and my boyfriend in the industry. They're amazing guys and super supportive. Did you know that Slash was instrumental in helping to set up a diversity committee within the NSA to examine the agency's tech culture and make it more hospitable for women? He didn't even tell me. I found out from someone else."

"Slash is definitely a keeper," I said with feeling.

Her expression softened. "He is. But my point,

Angel, is that things will change if ordinary women, like you and me, are willing to stay on the front lines of the industry and fight the stereotypes to get the work done. The glass ceiling is ours to shatter. But you need to be ready for the fight. It won't be easy, and it won't be pretty. But I guarantee you, it'll be worth it."

With those words of wisdom, she dropped me off at home. I safely tucked away the manila envelope I would deliver to BioLimbs on Monday in my room. Since I had time before my mom got home, I would do some penetration testing to see what kind of defenses BioLimbs had. Not that I was planning on hacking, I just wanted to know. Oh, who was I kidding? I was totally going to hack as soon as I could.

I was so deep into examining the defenses at BioLimbs I didn't even hear my mom until she knocked on my door.

"Angel, are you in there?"

I jumped so violently, I nearly knocked my chair over. "Oh, hey, Mom. I'm here. Sorry, I was...focused. I'll be right out."

I quickly shut down the laptop and opened my door when my phone rang. It was Frankie.

"Hey, Angel. Guess what?"

"No idea. What?"

"I decided we need a name for our group."

"What group?"

"Us. The Scooby gang. You, me, and Wally. Except we need our own name and logo."

"What?"

"I considered the Lone Hackers, but I'm not a hacker. I came up with the Computer Busters, which is a wordplay on Ghostbusters, but we don't bust computers. So I went closer to home. Excalibur's mascot is the knight, right? Then I remembered that lecture you gave me on cracking and white hatting, and it gave me the perfect name for our group."

"Hey, that was *not* a lecture."

"So she says. Anyway, the name I came up with is the White Knights. The white is for the white-hatting part and the knights symbolize our connection to Excalibur. What do you think?"

She couldn't possibly be serious. "I'm going to go out on a limb here and say we *don't* need a name or a logo."

"Yes, we do," Frankie said firmly. "If we're going to be responsible for clearing Mr. Matthews, we'll need to be identified by name as the trio who saved the day. Now, about the logo. I've already made it. The White Knights are classy, smart, and cool."

"Don't you think you're getting ahead of yourself?"

"In this day and age of instant media? Never. Better to be prepared. I'm sending you a copy of the logo now. Let me know what you think."

Before I could say anything else, Frankie hung up. My phone instantly beeped, notifying me I had a text. I opened it up.

For a second I could only stare. The logo was... spectacular. Frankie had used her crazy, mad skills to create this simple and cool design of a white knight chess piece that looked both medieval and edgy. Even though I didn't want a name or a logo, I had to admit that girl had serious talent.

My phone dinged again with another text from Frankie.

So...what do you think?

You are wicked talented. It's prime.

Excellent. I will consider that as formal approval. You may now refer to me as the queen of digital graphics, or QDG for short.

I snorted. I had no idea how she did it, but she made me laugh…and, as this logo proved, she was incredibly skilled. I was lucky to have her as a friend.

That reminded me that Frankie and I had some unfinished business. Pushing aside my dread of talking about such things, I typed a message.

> Look, I may have said or done things that have hurt your feelings. If so, I'm sorry. If I'm wrong, just ignore this text.

After I pushed Send, I felt like maybe I'd been too hopeful on the last part. Still, the best-case scenario was she'd think I was crazy.

> You're not wrong, Angel.

I sighed, pressing my hand to my forehead. I'd figured as much. Still, I didn't like seeing myself and my screwups through other people's eyes. It wasn't a flattering picture.

> I'm sorry, Frankie. I'm not good at this friendship stuff. Will you forgive me?

> Of course. I already have. That's why we're still friends.

> Thank you. I'm going to try harder, I promise.

> I know you will. You're going to discover that having friends isn't that hard.

> Ugh! Speak for yourself!

She countered with a LOL and a weird emoji of a fox hugging a rabbit. I presumed that meant all was right with us.

I stuck my phone back in my pocket. It was pretty mind-boggling when I thought about it. I had a friend. I had *two* friends, if I counted Wally. And I did. I didn't know what I was doing right on the friendship front, but they were willing to hang in there with me. What did they see in me that I couldn't see in myself?

I had no rational explanation for it except sometimes the universe gave you just what you needed.

CHAPTER TWENTY-EIGHT

Angel Sinclair

The weekend passed quietly. I took stats for a football scrimmage game on Friday during which Excalibur destroyed Jefferson Tech forty-eight to seven. Colt had a stunning fifty-eight completions (a school record), zero interceptions, three touchdowns, and a total of 672 passing yards (another school record).

On the less exciting side of my weekend, I cleaned my room, did a boatload of homework, took two quizzes for my Georgetown courses, and had a babysitting gig for Mrs. Ross and her four-year-old daughter, Samantha, on Saturday night. I also did a lot of research on BioLimbs to see what I else could find out about the mysterious Mr. Kars and the company.

Monday morning, Wally and Frankie were waiting at my locker, just like always. We were becoming a regular trio. The crazy thing was, I wasn't minding it as much as I thought I would.

"We are almost full for the melee in terms of participants," Wally said proudly as I emptied the contents of my backpack into my locker. "Not surprisingly, the Trains, or the athletes' team, is already complete. I need a couple more guys for the Brains, but I'm not worried. Getting Colt onboard to captain the geeks was genius, if I do say so myself."

I slammed my locker shut and grabbed both Wally and Frankie by the arms, pulling them in close and lowering my voice. "I'm glad to hear that, but I've got something important to tell you." I gave them a quick update on what Lexi and I had discovered about BioLimbs on Friday and my assignment to deliver an envelope to Vincent Kars today after school.

"Are you sure he's the Vincent we're looking for?" Frankie whispered.

"No, I'm not sure, but if he's not, we'll rule him out. If he is, I'll have some questions for him." I did a double check over my shoulder to make sure we didn't have any eavesdroppers before I continued. "But I don't think I'm going to be wrong. I did a little, um, exploring late last night. Guys, there have been seven accidents involving the exact same prostheses that BioLimbs manufactures."

"Were they automobile accidents?" Frankie asked.

"No." I shook my head. "They were different kinds of accidents, but most resulted in serious injury, and one death."

"Death? What the heck?" Wally breathed. "Why haven't they pulled the prostheses yet?"

"They've haven't been able to tie the accidents to the prostheses," I said. "But I bet that's why they contacted X-Corp to see if they had a cyberpenetration. Only X-Corp didn't find one. Maybe that's not the problem. But they *are* worried that seven of their clients have had accidents, even if it can't be pinned directly to the prostheses."

"They should have pulled them anyway, just in

case," Frankie said indignantly. "Risking people's lives for money is not right."

"I'm not going to disagree with you, but that's not all I found out." I shifted on my feet and looked around to ensure our conversation remained private. "When I looked up the names of those seven people who had the accidents and cross-referenced them with the info Wally gathered, I found they had one thing in common."

Frankie's eyes widened. "What?"

"They were all American veterans who served in a particular region of Iraq."

"Mr. Matthews served in Iraq, too," Frankie said quietly.

"I know. There's something weird going on at BioLimbs. Can you guys go with me after school today to deliver the envelope?"

"I wouldn't miss it for the world," Wally said.

"I'm in, too," said Frankie. "If this company is doing bad things, we need to find out what it is."

"We will."

The bell rang, and we separated. I headed to math class and ran into Nic standing on the bottom step, waiting for me.

I did an immediate U-turn and headed for the other set of stairs, but he chased after me. "Angel, wait a minute. I want to talk to you."

"Go away, Nic."

"Just wanted you to know, I'm ahead of you in terms of current GPA."

I didn't have to ask how he knew that. He probably had hacked in and checked my every assignment, quiz grade, and teacher note. He could have changed any of my grades to suit his whim, but he knew I could do the same if I wanted to. Besides, he didn't want to beat me by cheating. Where would be the satisfaction in that?

"Good for you. Don't care."

"Yes, you do." He stepped in front of me, causing me to stop. He had a big smile on his face and his different-colored eyes gleamed when I looked at him. "Admit it. You want this as badly as I do."

I put my hands on my hips and frowned. I had no idea why he was so obsessed with my academic progress. "I don't, Nic. I *really* don't. I'm not playing a role in your creepy academic fantasy. I don't care if I'm valedictorian. Get a life and leave me out of yours."

I darted around him and down the corridor.

"This isn't over, Angel," he called.

I ignored him. I had to figure out what to do about that guy. He was starting to be a real problem. Unfortunately, for the time being, I had other, more pressing problems.

CHAPTER TWENTY-NINE

Angel Sinclair

W ally, Frankie, and I met in the parking lot after school and headed to BioLimbs. The main office was in Silver Spring, Maryland, about twenty minutes from the school.

When we arrived at BioLimbs, Wally pulled into a visitor spot. We sat in the car examining the office building. It was modern, sleek, and screamed money. A white sign with blue letters lit from behind perched over a covered entranceway to the building and said *BioLimbs.* I counted four floors.

"Cool design." Frankie rolled down the window and hung out it. "Modern with a hint of contemporary tech." She rolled up the window and climbed out of the car. "Come on. I want to get a look at the inside design."

We followed her to the front door and went inside. White marble floors and white walls gleamed with silver-tubed lighting. It was a little too much white for me, but Frankie whistled under her breath. "Sweet. Will you look at that?"

That, apparently, was the lobby in front of us. A long, white modular desk dominated the lobby. The waiting room consisted of white pod chairs around a circular coffee table made of clear glass. Only a splash of blue in the corner in the form of a waist-high blue sculpture of an hourglass broke up the whiteness.

A guy sitting behind the desk in a light-blue shirt and red tie rose. "Can I help you?"

I stepped forward. "Hi. My name is Angel Sinclair. I'm an intern from X-Corp. I have some papers for Mr. Vincent Kars."

"Is he expecting you?"

"I'm not sure. I'm just the intern. I was told I had to personally deliver the papers to him today."

"Personally?"

"Yes, sir."

"What's your name again?"

"Angel Sinclair."

He looked over Wally and Frankie. "And who are they?"

"That is Wally Harris, who also interns for X-Corp. Frances Chang is our assistant."

"Interns have assistants?"

"Yes." I didn't blink or change the expression on my face.

He looked me over and shrugged. He punched in a number on his phone, pressing the handset to his ear.

"Mr. Kars, Angel Sinclair and her two assistants from X-Corp are here to see you."

Frankie leaned over to whisper in my ear. "Just so we're clear, I am *not* your assistant."

"I know," I hissed back.

The guy talking on the phone was silent and then said, "I don't know. She says she has some papers for you and they must be delivered in person." He listened and then nodded. "Okay."

He hung up the phone and wrote something down on a paper. He looked up at us. "I need your driver's licenses, please."

Wally stepped forward, pulling his wallet out of his pocket. "I'm the only one with a driver's license."

"Will a student ID be okay?" Frankie asked.

Seeing as how he didn't have much choice, the receptionist took our IDs, scanned them, and returned the cards. I was relieved we were getting inside.

The guard asked us to wait in the pod chairs. We had fun spinning around in them until a woman dressed in a black skirt and white blouse retrieved us. Her blond hair was pulled back into a bun and she wore the reddest lipstick I'd ever seen. Or maybe it seemed like the reddest because everything else was so white.

She held out a hand. "Hello. I'm Nancy Reno, personal assistant to Mr. Kars."

She was stiff and unsmiling, like a robot. We all shook her hand—it was cold—before she led us to the elevator. When we got inside, Ms. Reno pushed the button for four and then stared straight ahead as if we didn't exist. The elevator music was electronic piano, which fit the decor but made me feel like I was inside a computer.

Ms. Reno led us down a sterile white corridor before stopping at a door. The doorplate read *Victor Kars, Director of Research*. I exchanged a nervous glance with Wally as the woman knocked on the door and a gruff voice indicated we should enter. Ms. Reno opened the door, and a man rose from behind a desk. Ms. Reno closed the door behind us and left as soon as we had entered.

My breath caught in my throat. It was the same guy I'd seen in Mr. Matthews's office, down to the black ring on the third finger of his right hand.

When his gaze fell upon me, he looked surprised.

"You? What are you doing here?"

I stepped forward. "You *do* recognize me. You were in Mr. Matthews's office on the first day of school. He spoke to you and said he was worried about something. You told him he was overreacting and that you'd take care of it."

"Okay." He spread his hands. "So what, and why are you here?"

I faltered. "So...you don't deny it?"

"Why would I deny it?"

Alarm coursed through me. "Because the police didn't know about it."

"Why would the police care about that?" His expression was one of confusion and frustration. Either he was a good actor or he genuinely didn't know what was going on.

I exchanged a concerned glance with Wally. My plan was going totally awry. "Don't you know what happened to Mr. Matthews?"

"No." Mr. Kars frowned. "What happened to Ryan?"

I gave him a brief rundown. When I finished, he sat down hard in his chair and ran his fingers through his hair. "Not Ryan. Oh, God, not again."

"Mr. Kars. Mr. Matthews was talking to you because of his prostheses, right?"

He hung his head, looking distressed. "Yes."

"He has the latest design made by BioLimbs. The one that uses IMES, right?"

He lifted his head and stared at me. "How do you know that? Why did you say you worked for X-Corp?"

"Because I do. I'm an intern and so is Wally. We're trying to help Mr. Matthews. I think there's something wrong with his prostheses. Something that caused him to have the accident. I don't think it was a coincidence that he was talking to you about it on the day of his accident."

"It's not the prostheses," Mr. Kars insisted. "Yes, Ryan was complaining of some unusual twitches the previous day, but it wasn't anything serious. We've done exhaustive sweeps of our software and hardware. We even hired X-Corp, as you know, to see if they could find an outside source, a cyberpenetration, that might have been interfering with the software. Nothing was found. If you work there, you can confirm that. We reset everything to default, and we're completely clean. The design is flawless. The problem is somewhere else."

"And yet accidents keep happening. Mr. Matthews isn't the first client with the new IMES prostheses to have an accident."

His dark eyes zeroed in on mine. There was shock, then anger. "How do you know that?"

I lifted my chin. "I'm resourceful."

We stared at each other for a long moment. Frankie and Wally were completely still next to me. It was so silent in the room I could hear myself breathing. Finally, Mr. Kars stood and leaned against a corner of his desk.

"We haven't issued any more of the new prostheses, just in case. But I swear, there is no malfunction in our hardware or design."

"But something is wrong somewhere," I insisted.

"What's wrong is that you're a kid and you already put this together. Now it's only a matter of time before this completely blows up. Investors will pull out, BioLimbs could face countless lawsuits, and all the advances BioLimbs has made to help veterans and amputees lead normal lives are going to disappear."

I thought about how Mr. Matthews had worn the prostheses for months and no one, including me, had ever noticed. He'd been given back his legs, and his life, because of the remarkable prostheses built by this company. Suddenly, I didn't know what was the right thing to do anymore.

I exhaled a deep breath. "We're going to figure this out, Mr. Kars. I promise you that."

CHAPTER THIRTY

Candace Kim

NSA Headquarters, Fort Meade, Maryland

Candace was leaving the director's weekly stand-up briefing when she saw Isaac angling through the departing staff toward her. He was probably going to complain that things were moving too slowly. She could count the ways she disliked him, starting with the perpetual smirk on his face.

As expected, he fell in step beside her. "What's new on the Avenger?" He looked over his shoulder to see who else might be in listening distance.

She kept walking. "Nothing new on our end. Have you made any progress going through the list of people he may have interacted with here at the agency?"

"I have a list, and I've even talked to people, some who remain at the agency and a few who are retired. I'm still working through it."

"Good. I went over the dossier you sent on Ethan Sinclair several times. If he's the Hidden Avenger, there's nothing in his record that might indicate why he left, and certainly not why he would have taken up such a career. I need more insight that might help us in our negotiations. He appears to be as much a mystery on paper as he is in cyberspace. How much interaction did you have with him back in the day?"

"Not much. He worked at the satellite office at King's Security. I wasn't there often. His reputation was that he was a loner. Kept to himself."

"Anything else?"

Isaac shrugged. "He always seemed a little odd to me. Brilliant, but odd. It was a long time ago, Candace. His motivations surely must have changed."

"Maybe. It's puzzling, though. His bio states he had a PhD in mathematics from MIT and was researching unbreakable new concepts in encryption. His performance reports suggest he was arguably the best in his field."

"That is certainly overstated." Isaac snorted in contempt. "He often took credit for the work of others."

Candace stopped in her tracks and turned to face Isaac. "Why do you say that?"

"Well, I don't know that definitively. I remember hearing rumors about it."

"It wasn't in his file."

"Not surprising. Who is going to write a rumor in a report?"

Candace studied him. She crossed her arms against her chest. "I want everything you have, Isaac. That includes rumor."

"Of course. I'm already on it."

"I need to know why he doesn't trust us. What does he want and why is he doing this? We must tread carefully. We don't want to spook him."

"We don't, indeed. I'll let you know when I'm ready with the information."

"Just make it soon." As he turned to leave, Candace shot out a hand, blocking his way.

"By the way, Ethan disappeared shortly after J.P. Lando, another of our analysts, died in a tragic boating accident in West Virginia. His file says they were working on the encryption project shortly before his accident. Do you think that had anything to do with him leaving? Might he be involved in that in some way, or could that have something to do with why he wants immunity protection?"

"I remember that accident." Isaac's expression was thoughtful. "I even went to Lando's funeral. But I don't remember the details. It was a long time ago. It's a potential angle, though. I'll check it out for you, but I don't think it's related."

"Just the same, would you shoot me Lando's file, please?"

"No sense in two of us spending time on it. I'll check it out for you."

"I appreciate the offer, but regardless, I'd like to have a look of my own."

Isaac smirked. "Fine. If you want to waste your time, go ahead. I'm not sure what you think you'll find."

"I'm not sure, either. It's just a hunch. And I always trust my hunches."

Isaac shrugged and walked away without another word. Candace watched him go, her feelings uneasy. He was hiding something. She hadn't worked her way up to the top of a super secretive agency without learning to read people. Something wasn't right with him, and she was going to find out what it was. Patience and determination were two of her greatest virtues. She'd figure it out soon enough.

CHAPTER THIRTY-ONE

Angel Sinclair

When I got home from BioLimbs, I paced the apartment trying to get my mind wrapped around everything. So much data, and none of it made sense in the big picture. I couldn't distinguish a pattern, a reason, or even a gut feeling.

I needed a break to rest my mind. The best cure for calming me—as odd as it sounded—was the search for my dad. I just knew that if he were around, he'd know how to make sense of this. According to my mom, he was a lot like me—analytical, logical, creative.

I sat down in front of my laptop. I'd just rested my fingers on the keyboard when my cell rang. I picked it up off my desk.

"Hey, Wally."

"Angel, you got a minute?"

"Sure. What's up?"

"Before you go all nuclear on me, I want to say up front that this isn't about BioLimbs, high-tech prostheses, or Mr. Matthews. It's about your dad. You can hear what I need to say or you can tell me to get lost and hang up. I'm giving you the option. But after I tell you, there is no going back."

It was like he'd hit me. I blinked, dazed, and then fought to get my thoughts in order. It must have taken me longer than I thought, because Wally spoke.

"Yo, Angel? You still there?"

My gut tightened as I fought to keep my voice steady, neutral. "What about my dad?"

He let out a breath, as if he'd been holding it. "Well, I've been doing some research on him—well, at least the company he was working for when he disappeared. King's Security."

"I know he worked at King's Security. Why are you doing this?"

He paused. "Because…you're my friend. Now, before you say it, I know you didn't ask me for help. I'll be the first to admit that sticking my nose where it doesn't belong is a bad habit of mine. But something about that police report didn't add up for me, either. It was too perfect. Too staged. It raised my hackles. Once that happens, I'm like a dog with a bone—latched on and not surrendering. You were on to something, Angel. I believe that."

I was half furious, half impressed by his audacity. At the same time, I couldn't express how much it meant to me to hear Wally say he believed me and trusted my hunch that the police hadn't gotten the full story.

"Anyway," he continued, "I think it had to be something he was doing at King's Security that either caused him to bolt or be forcibly removed. Unless he had a hidden second life. That, by the way, was going to be my next search avenue. But my first plan was to take a fresher, deeper look into King's Security."

I was stunned. "You think the police…lied about the company?"

"Maybe not lied, but definitely didn't pry. You are

far too trusting, kid. Let that be a lesson. Trust no one—or trust carefully. Always challenge the evidence and those who produce it. That doesn't mean I'm advocating chaos or anarchy, but there are no truths until you prove them so."

I truly didn't know what to say. I had mixed feelings about Wally messing in my personal life, while at the same time being utterly riveted by what he was saying. "Go on."

"I decided to *investigate* the company." Wally paused. "You know what I mean by investigate, right?"

Oh, I knew all right. Hacking. He'd hacked my dad's security company. I don't know why I'd never done it except...I hadn't thought there would be anything there to discover. I trusted the police report of the investigation into the company and the conclusion that my father hadn't been working on anything unusual before his disappearance. His meetings and visitors in the weeks before his disappearance had all been vetted and cleared. His colleagues were mystified as to why he'd go missing. What purpose would the police have for falsifying the report?

"What did you find?" My voice was surprisingly shaky.

He lowered his voice. "King's Security isn't who they say they are. They're not your run-of-the-mill security company."

"They're not?" My breath caught in my throat. "Then who are they?"

"The NSA."

Wally didn't want to talk any more about it on the phone, not that I blamed him. Besides, Frankie was coming over to help him make the powdered-sugar bullets for the Medieval Melee. We hung up, agreeing to speak privately later.

For a while, I sat, blindly staring at my computer and thinking. My father worked for the NSA? If so, why hadn't anyone mentioned that? Did my mom know? Was it a state secret or something?

My head was spinning, so I decided to relax on the bed for a few minutes. The next thing I knew, I woke up with my mom sitting beside me. It was dark in my room, but light spilled in from the hallway.

"Mom?" I said, sitting up in alarm. "What happened?"

She smoothed my hair down. "What happened is I came home from work to find you sound asleep. You've been burning the candle at both ends, so I let you sleep. Your dinner is in the fridge. Would you like me to warm it up?"

I rubbed my eyes and pushed the hair off my shoulders. "What time is it?"

"Nine o'clock."

"Nine o'clock?" My mouth dropped open. "I slept three hours?"

"You're exhausted." My mom put her hand on my shoulder. "Are you feeling okay, Angel? You seem so driven lately. I know you're taking this accident with Mr. Matthews very hard."

I struggled to sit up, then reached over and snapped on the lamp. Both my mom and I blinked in the harsh light.

I shielded my eyes for a moment. "I guess I was more tired than I thought."

She patted my arm. "I'm glad you got some rest."

I tugged on my blanket, pulling it up on my knees. "Mom, can I ask you a question? Did Dad work for the government?"

She looked at me curiously. "Why would you ask that?"

"I'm just wondering."

"No. Your dad worked for King's Security. You know that."

"He never worked for the NSA?"

Her eyes gave her away. Surprise, concern, but also...fear. My heart sank. She *was* hiding something from me.

"Angel, he worked for King's Security as an engineering analyst."

"Mom, I know you're not telling me something. Who was Dad?"

Her chin came up and her expression tightened. "He was a wonderful man who loved his family very much. He wouldn't want this for you—this obsession with finding him. I don't want this for you either. Please, drop it."

I twisted a corner of the blanket between my fingers and said nothing. I wouldn't lie to my mom.

After a moment, she sighed. "You're headed to college next year. Your whole life is in front of you. It's time to focus on what's ahead of you, not on what's behind, okay? It's time to move on."

I lifted my gaze. "Then why are you still wearing your wedding ring?"

"This is *not* about me. I'm asking you from the bottom of my heart to leave your father in the past."

"I can't," I finally said. "Mom, I can't and I won't."

She sighed, then stood and leaned over to kiss the top of my head. "You're a lot like your father. I'm always here if you need me, okay?"

I needed her now, to tell me the truth, to tell me what really happened to my father. But since that wasn't going to happen, I nodded. "Thanks."

A bit later I came out for dinner. We ate and talked

as if we'd never had the conversation about Dad. After we did the dishes together, Mom watched television while finished my homework and went to bed...again. Before I turned out the light, I checked my phone and email. Thankfully, I had no earth-shattering texts from either Wally or Frankie. I wasn't sure how much more I could take.

That night when I slept, I dreamed I was being chased by a shadowed figure of a man. When he ran into the light, it wasn't my father as I'd expected, just a horde of prosthetic legs. I woke gasping and unrested.

I needed answers, and fast.

CHAPTER THIRTY-TWO

Isaac Remington

Isaac got the alert when he was in his daily morning briefing. He excused himself from the meeting, left the building, and drove to the parking lot of a local Mexican restaurant before pulling out his burner phone and ringing his contact.

"What's so urgent?" he snapped as soon as his call was answered.

"Sorry, sir. A few hours ago, a penetration attempt was made at one of our satellite offices, King's Security. It's where the Avenger worked before he disappeared. The hack was traced back to Wallace Harris, one of the classmates of the daughter and the kid responsible for the DoD hack."

Frustration and rage swept through him. "Who the heck *are* these kids?"

"No worries, sir. The penetration was unsuccessful, but Harris deduced enough information from the attempt to identify the agency. A subsequent phone call from Harris to the girl confirms he informed her of the association. She has not yet attempted her own penetration or taken any other steps to follow up on this discovery. But this means she is now aware of a possible association of her father to the agency."

Isaac's initial dismay faded, and his mouth stretched into a smile. "Good. That may work for us. Is the honeypot ready to go?"

"Yes. We uploaded the bogus content last night. That was the hardest part—finding unclassified information that appears to be relevant, but not too helpful. We don't want her suspicious."

"Given how thorough she seems to be, it shouldn't take too long for her to find the bread crumbs that will lead her to the pot."

"I hope you're right."

"I always am."

CHAPTER THIRTY-THREE

Angel Sinclair

Unfortunately for me, things went from bad to worse at school.

Wally and Frankie were waiting by my locker as usual. Frankie's hair was styled in two braids and dotted with green and white beads. I surprised myself by barely thinking twice about it.

"How many powdered-sugar bullets were you guys able to make last night?" I asked, spinning the combination lock. "I'm in for helping tonight as needed."

"No need." Frankie held up her hands, as did Wally. They were stained red. "We finished. Two hundred and forty-two bullets. Half red, half gray. Wally and I are a great team."

I was impressed. "How long did it take you?"

"About five hours. I ate dinner at Wally's and he brought me home at ten. His family is so nice. Now my parents—and his—think we're dating since we're together so often. I let them think that, because it's better than telling them the alternative."

She had a point. What *would* they tell their parents—"Sorry, Mom and Dad, we aren't really dating, we're busy hacking into police departments, hospitals, and tech companies to save our vice principal"?

I lifted my hands. "It is what it is."

She smiled. "Exactly."

Frankie continually surprised me. I don't think I'd ever met anyone so…easygoing. Did anything ever upset her?

Wally rubbed his shoulder. "Well, I hate to be a downer, but I feel it's my duty to point out that I checked the nothingbutthetruth.com website last night."

I let out a loud sigh. "Now what?"

"This." He took out his cell phone and pulled up the website. The lead story's bold headline read *Teenagers Look for Clues at BioLimbs for Answers to Vice Principal's Accident.*

My mouth dropped open in shock. "*What?* Are you kidding me?"

"I wish."

I quickly scanned the article. It mentioned Wally, me, and Frankie by name, mentioning we'd gone to BioLimbs to try to pin the blame for the accident on the company instead of Mr. Matthews. It wasn't far from the truth, but how was this possible?

"Who knew we went there?" My mind was racing. "Who's spying on us?"

"I don't know." Wally stuck the phone back in his pocket. "This totally sucks, though, and it's not going to help Mr. Matthews's case at all."

Red-hot anger flooded me. This had to stop. I clenched my jaw. "When did the article go up, Wally?"

"I'm not sure. I noticed it after one o'clock last night. What are we going to do, Angel?"

"I'm going to bring it down. Right now."

Frankie's eyes widened. "But…we have class."

"I'm skipping. Wally, give me the keys to your car."

An alarmed expression crossed his face. "Why? You don't even have a driver's license."

"I'm not going to drive your car. I'm going to sit in it and do some work."

It took Wally a minute to get there. "You're going to hack in my car?"

"Yes."

Wally leaned back against the lockers. "It won't stay down, Angel."

"I know, and I don't care. But it will last at least seven hours while the owner of the website is in school. And it will serve as a warning."

"Owner?" Wally looked puzzled. "You know who the owner of the website is?"

"There is only one person this could be," I said, narrowing my eyes. "Nic Nerezza."

When I'm determined, it's amazing how quickly and efficiently I can get things done. I'd have to break into the school system later and reset my absence as being present, but that wouldn't be a problem. I was more interested in seeing how quickly my handiwork— bringing down the website—was noticed.

It happened faster than I expected.

Nic ran into me when I was on my way to lunch. "You just did something really stupid." He was furious, his different-colored eyes flashing with pure hate. I had no idea what I'd ever done to this guy to deserve this kind of malice. "How dare you."

"How dare I what?"

"I know it was you. You took the website down."

"What website?" I hoped my expression looked innocent. "I don't know what you're talking about."

He jabbed a finger at me. "It won't stay down. It'll be back up by dinner."

I lifted my shoulders in a show of nonchalance. But inside anger started to burn hot. "I'm flattered you think me capable of bringing down a website. You made my day."

Nic's eyes narrowed. He was so angry red spots had appeared on his cheeks. "How did you know it was mine?"

I figured my cheeks had red spots of their own. "I don't know what you're referring to, but if it's a website that spouts lies, misinformation, and loads of crap, it's easy to conclude it would have *your* fingerprints all over it."

He leaned toward me, literally seething. "You can't stop me. I can play this game better than you."

"It's not a game, Nic. It's a person's life. It's time to stop this deranged competition you think we're having. I'm willing to offer a truce."

He blinked, his expression wary. "Such as?"

"You want to be valedictorian? Fine. It's yours. I abdicate."

He laughed in disbelief. "You expect me to believe that? You want it more than me."

"No, I don't. Honestly, I'm not even trying. If I gave my academics even one-tenth of my effort, you'd be blown to kingdom come. But I'm willing to continue the pretense and even ease back to let you slip past, if you do something for me in return."

His eyes narrowed. "What?"

"Take down your stupid website and keep it down. Stop stalking my friends and me. That's it. Pretty simple."

"What kind of deal is that?" He spread his hands. "You think I'd go for that? I know what this is all about. You're scared."

"I don't have time for this. Please, stop already. It's pathetic and beyond sad. I already said you could be valedictorian."

"You don't have to give it to me. I'll earn it. You can forget about your stupid deal."

He stormed away, slamming a fist against a half-open locker and causing it to bang shut and then pop open again.

Wow. I sure did have a way with people.

CHAPTER THIRTY-FOUR

Angel Sinclair

I was shaking with anger by the time I got my lunch and sat at the table. Frankie and Wally were already eating.

"You're dope. No, better than dope." Wally wagged a french fry at me. "You are *the* geek princess. Even I'm amazed by what you did, and I'm an excellent hacker. You'll have to spill how you did it."

"That's a discussion for another time. What's important is that Nic knows it was me. He just confronted me about it in the hallway. He's beyond pissed."

"How did he know it was you?" Frankie asked in astonishment. "Do you hackers have a weird kind of telepathy?"

"No, Frankie. It's a feeling I got when I reviewed the code, not to mention the content. Nic has a style. I have a style. After giving it some thought, I knew it was Nic, just as he knew it was me. This whole stupid obsession he has with me and wanting to be smarter is dragging Mr. Matthews down. It must stop. Now."

"I agree. But how?" Wally spun his fork in the

206

middle of what sort of looked like spaghetti. "He'll have the website up again by this evening."

"I know." The anger, effort, and mental drive drained out of me. I was exhausted—mentally and physically. I hadn't stopped Nic, but I'd given him fair warning, which was more than he'd ever done for me. "But now he's going to have to take more precautions, be more on guard. That's going to take time. Time we need to figure out how to help Mr. Matthews."

Frankie stabbed some canned green beans. "Well, when I was in the office this morning, Ms. Eder told Headmistress Swanson that she's going to visit him after school."

I sat up straight. "We have to talk to him first."

"Why?"

"Because she'll ask him if he's guilty. If he says yes, she'll fire him. She'll *have* to fire him."

"But he already told the police he did it."

"He can't be held accountable for what he said when he was under the influence of narcotics. At least, I hope not. We all know he didn't do it on purpose. Who's with me?"

"I'm in, of course," Frankie said, eating the rest of the beans off her fork. "My mom never expects me home after school these days anyway. Especially now that I'm dating Wally."

"You're *not* dating Wally," I said. "You're fictitiously dating Wally."

"Whatever." Frankie shrugged.

"I'm cool with fictitious dating." Wally grinned. "It's the most dating I've ever done before. It looks like we're going to the hospital after school."

"Not *after* school," I said. "*Before* school ends. We must get there before Headmistress Swanson. We'll leave before the last class of the day starts."

Wally and Frankie looked at me as if I'd grown two

heads. I got their shock. They weren't the skipping-school kind of students. I wasn't, either. Today would be the first day I'd ever skipped a class in my life, and now I was going to make it three classes in one day.

Who had I become?

Frankie studied me. "You want me to skip PE?"

"Yes."

She considered and then shrugged. "Okay, I can be a rebel. Wally, you're coming, too, right?"

"If you're there, babe, I'm in, too."

I winced. "Guys, knock it off."

They started laughing, but Wally pointed his finger at me. "I'm giving you a heads-up. If we get in trouble, we're blaming it on you."

"Fine. I'll take one for the team."

We split up, with Wally going one way and Frankie and I heading down the same hallway.

"Frankie, can I ask you a question?" I suddenly stopped, causing Frankie to pass me and then turn around to look at me curiously.

"Sure. Go ahead."

I fidgeted with the strap of my backpack. "You're not *really* dating Wally as part of the fake-dating thing, are you?" I winced as the words came out. Maybe she'd tell me it was none of my business. This friend thing was getting more complicated by the minute.

She stared at me, puzzled. "Angel, are you asking me if I like Wally in a romantic way?"

"Yes!" I blew out a breath. "Wow. You make it sound so simple when you say it like that. I ask because I'm not good at figuring out nonverbal stuff like that. Are you pretending to date or are you pretending to pretend because you secretly like each other? It's too confusing for me to process. If you're really a couple, could you let me know? I can still pretend it's fake, if that would appropriate."

She blinked and then laughed. "Oh, for heaven's sake. We are just friends, Angel. Why? Do you like Wally?"

"Of course I like Wally. I mean, not in a romantic way. He doesn't feel that way about me, either. But he's a great guy."

"He is. I'm glad we're all friends."

"Me, too."

Now that the supreme awkwardness of that discussion was over, I had one less thing to be anxious about, although skipping school was a pretty big deal for someone like me. Even though the decision had been made, I was nervous for the rest of the day. Even Colt sensed something was wrong in chemistry.

"Angel, is everything all right?" he whispered during the lecture. "You seem edgy."

I almost jumped out of my seat. I hadn't heard a word the teacher had said. For a moment, I thought he'd called on me. But Colt was just asking about my well-being, so my heart calmed a bit.

"I'm fine. Thanks for asking. I'm thinking...about stuff."

He didn't talk to me much after that, which was fine with me. I wasn't sure I'd be able to carry on much of a conversation anyway. As soon as the bell rang, I bolted out of the classroom. Colt probably thought I'd lost my mind. Maybe I had.

I met Frankie and Wally at my locker as planned. Wally looked anxious. "I hope my mom doesn't find out I skipped. I'll get in a lot of trouble."

"It's for a good cause," Frankie reassured him. She looked at me. "Right, Angel?"

"Right." I had a twinge of worry that I was dragging them to the dark side. But in the scheme of things, it was important. We slipped out one of the school's side doors and almost ran to Wally's car. If guilt could kill, all three of us would be dead.

Once we were on the way to the hospital, I gave them the entire replay of my conversation with Nic before lunch.

"That guy is a total weasel." Wally shook his head in disgust.

"An *evil* weasel is more like it," I said, then paused as something occurred to me. "Hey, why aren't you in the running for valedictorian, Wally? You're smarter than Nic."

"I've got a C in woodworking. Power tools are kicking my butt. Thank God PE is pass or fail."

"No kidding," I said with heartfelt conviction. "Why didn't you take photography or astronomy or something?"

"I already took them. I wanted to take another math class, but my dad made me take woodworking. Said a man needs to know how to properly use a drill and other tools. Unfortunately, the tools are owning me. It is *not* a match made in heaven."

I felt a twinge of sympathy. Gwen was the power-tool user in our family, but I could get by as needed. But having to take a class on it? The thought made me shudder.

Wally found a parking space and we walked to the hospital. We went directly to the ICU but were told by the nurse on duty that Mr. Matthews had been moved to another floor. Before we left, I asked how Anna, the woman who had been hit with the car, was doing.

"She's stabilized and has been moved to the same floor. The doctors are optimistic."

"Oh, that's great," I said with relief.

We took the elevator up two more floors and approached the nurses' station. The young guy at the desk in scrubs walked us down the hall to his room. This time all three of us were permitted to go in.

The nurse took a quick peek, then waved us in. "You're lucky. He's awake."

Mr. Matthews was propped in a hospital bed with lots of machines hooked up to him. He was pale, and the circles under his eyes looked like small bruises. He had a bandage on one side of the top of his head. But his eyes were open, alert, and clearly surprised to see us.

He noticed me first. "Angel?"

"Hey, Mr. Matthews. How are you?"

"I'm...alive. Wally Harris? Frances? What brings you kids here"—he glanced at the large clock on the wall next to the mounted television—"during school hours?" His eyes narrowed. He might have been in a hospital bed, but he still radiated authority.

I gulped. "I'm sorry. They're here because of me. We wanted to talk to you before Headmistress Swanson met with you."

He frowned. "Bonnie is coming here?"

"Yes. But you can't tell her you hit that woman on purpose with your car, because she will fire you from your job and we need you there."

He let out a sigh and placed a hand on the part of his head with the bandage. All the cords connected to that arm followed. "Look, this is complicated. I appreciate your support, but you shouldn't be here."

"They're going to charge you with assault with a deadly weapon," I blurted out. "They're building their case right now."

He stared at me for a moment. "How do you know that?"

I raised my chin. "I just do. Why did you tell them you hit her on purpose? We know you didn't."

He closed his eyes. "I didn't tell them I did it *on purpose*. I didn't. But I did hit her. It's all a bit fuzzy. I remember slamming on the gas. I...don't know why. I tried to stop, but it all happened too fast. I saw the woman and tried to swerve, but I hit her anyway. Luckily, I angled the car into a wall of a parking lot, so no one else got hurt."

"But why?" Wally asked. "Why did you press on the gas?"

"I don't know."

"Does this have anything to do with the reason you were talking with Vincent Kars the day of the accident?" I asked.

"You heard our conversation?"

"Not much, but enough to know you were worried. But I didn't know you had prostheses at the time." I glanced over at his legs plugged into the outlet. It didn't freak me out anymore, but Frankie gave a loud gasp when she followed my gaze and spotted them.

"Only the staff knew. It was to protect my privacy, that's all."

"That's how you stopped the bleachers with your foot and it didn't hurt," Frankie exclaimed.

"Yes."

"Mr. Matthews, what were you worried about when you were talking to Mr. Kars?" I asked.

"That's not any of your business."

"Please. It's important. You're the eighth veteran to have an accident."

I'd surprised him. "What? Where did you get that information?"

"Where I get all my information—the Internet. I know not all accidents are the same, but the only thing you all have in common, other than your military service in Iraq, is that you all have prostheses created at BioLimbs."

To my astonishment, he laughed. "You're blaming my leg for pressing on the gas? That's not possible. I alone control my prostheses, Angel."

"What are you saying? You *wanted* to hit that woman with your car?"

"Of course not. I don't know what happened."

"Then at least entertain that it's a possibility the signal was interrupted or mixed up."

"It's not a possibility. Nothing happens if the signal is interrupted or jumbled. I'm the only person connected to those limbs. If the signal is interrupted, I simply can't move it. It works off *my* brain waves. Interrupting or manipulating the signal certainly can't make me press my foot on the gas."

"Are you sure about that?"

He considered. "Are you?"

"No, I'm not sure. Not yet. We found Mr. Kars. I gave his name to the police, although at the time I talked to them, I didn't know his last name or what he does."

"You tracked Vincent down?"

"Yes. We had a lot of questions for him."

"Kids, I'm touched by your faith in me. Really. But this is on me. I've got to figure it out."

"How are you going to do that from the hospital?" I asked.

"Yeah, we can help," Frankie interjected. "We're *going* to help. We know you're a good guy, Mr. Matthews."

"This from the student who met me once?" He looked amused.

"Twice, actually. One in the school interview and once in the gym. What can I say? I have spot-on instincts about people. Plus, you saved me. I owe you."

Wally spoke up. "By the way, the toxicology report came in a few hours ago. You're clean."

Mr. Matthews narrowed his eyes. "How in the heck did you get access to that report, Mr. Harris?"

Wally's cheeks reddened. "Um, that's a very good question. Would you believe I'm also quite resourceful, like Angel?"

He sighed but said nothing.

"I'm on your side, Mr. Matthews," Wally said quietly. "We all are."

Mr. Matthews lifted his hands. "Why are you kids doing this?"

"Because we know you're innocent," I said. "You've helped us, and now we want to help you. Please, Mr. Matthews, let us do what we can. Will you answer a few questions for me?"

After a moment, he relented. "I guess I can answer a couple of questions."

It was a small victory, but I'd take it. "When did you get your prostheses—the IMES ones you have now?"

"About six months ago. I don't think the prostheses are the problem here."

"Just covering all bases. You said you don't know why you pressed on the gas. If you didn't do it intentionally, then there must be some explanation. What was the situation you were discussing with Mr. Kars?"

"I was having some uncomfortable sensations. Almost like small electric jolts. It caused my legs to twitch uncomfortably and at unexpected times. I was mostly afraid of a fall or hitting my head. But that's a far cry from someone intentionally manipulating my brain to jam my foot on the gas and keep it there. The truth is that other than the weird shocks the week before the accident, the prostheses have been flawless. A lifesaver. I'm not convinced the problem lies with them."

I glanced across the room at his legs. "They have to be charged, right? Maybe it's nothing to do with the software. Could it be an electrical problem?"

"Vincent said they already checked that. They found no electrical problems."

"How long do the prostheses hold a charge?"

"Fourteen hours."

I blinked. "That's amazing. How often do they have to be serviced or tweaked?"

"This is a pilot program, so we were required to come in twice a week for the first four months, and now once a week for adjustments."

"The IMES is a software, right?"

"Right."

I considered other possibilities, my mind sorting through and discarding possibilities. "It's *got* to be something with the software," I muttered.

"The answer always has to do with software when you're involved, Angel," Mr. Matthews said with a trace of amusement.

"True." I smiled. "And I'm almost always right. This time, however, it's more of a gut feeling. How do the upgrades happen?"

"At the beginning of the program, we had to go in for the upgrades. Now I can upgrade it myself through a special app on my phone."

That interested me. "Can I see the app?"

"I don't know where my phone is. Probably confiscated by the police."

"Okay. I'll figure that out on my own."

Wally leaned forward. "We're running a fund-raiser for you tomorrow night. Headmistress Swanson said we can use the stadium for an impromptu Medieval Melee. Hopefully the entire school will come and donate a lot of money to help you out."

"I made posters," Frankie volunteered. "And put out the word on social media."

Mr. Matthews's expression was total astonishment. "You kids did that? For me?" We nodded, and he swallowed. "I'm touched by your concern. But I'm going to sort this out."

"And we're going to help," I said firmly. "Just do us a favor and don't admit to anything when Headmistress

Swanson gets here, okay? Let us do our work first, okay?"

His lips twitched, and for a moment, there might have been a familiar twinkle in his eye. "I'll see how long I can hold out against the headmistress."

CHAPTER THIRTY-FIVE

Angel Sinclair

T rue to his word, Nic had the website back up and running by dinnertime. Unfortunately, he'd also updated the website, which now held a sensational headline: *Important Announcement Coming! Will Shock Community and Excalibur Academy to Its Core.*

Ugh. That guy was a serious piece of work.

As I suspected, a quick probe indicated Nic had significantly switched up his defenses. It was a hack I didn't want to spend time on right now. I had homework, a paper, and a quiz to study for, not to mention that I had several threads I wanted to pull on my dad given Wally's NSA revelation.

But first things first.

BioLimbs had designed the prostheses to accept software and firmware updates to allow for any bugs and fixes, so the version upgrade of the software could be distributed to enhance performance and reliability. Mr. Kars had said they couldn't find any issues with the software or hardware controlling the limbs. Lexi said X-Corp had checked it out and confirmed that.

In my opinion, that meant it was clean.

There was a lot to consider. Mr. Matthews said there was no way to make the limb do anything he didn't want it to do, but what if he were wrong? What if someone was hacking in and controlling the limbs? The mind-boggling question of *why* would have to wait, because without the *how*, it wouldn't be worth visiting yet.

I began to pace, trying to work it out. If it were a hack, they had to get in somehow. But a hack of this magnitude *had* to go through the software or the hardware.

No matter how many ways I looked at it, I didn't have an answer. I hated that. A lot. Because no answer meant Mr. Matthews was guilty.

Two hours wasn't enough sleep for a growing girl. I dragged my butt out of bed and gulped two ibuprofen tablets to alleviate the raging headache. I'd driven myself crazy scouring the web for any insightful information on BioLimbs, IMES, and answers to Mr. Matthews's predicament. I learned more than I ever wanted to know, but nothing seemed to lend itself to an explanation of what was happening. Eventually, I'd turned to chasing down leads on my dad to give myself a mental break.

Although I trusted Wally's hacking skills, I decided to probe King's Security to see what I could find for myself. To my astonishment, I'd found a hole in the company's security and had waltzed right in. It seemed shocking that the NSA could be so careless, but I considered it a stroke of luck. It took me under twenty minutes to find several files mentioning my father.

It looked like Wally was right after all. Somehow, my dad was connected to the NSA. But how and why?

I copied, took them all, and got out. I'd started reading but finally stopped when the letters started to bleed together. When my alarm went off, I was barely able to drag myself out of bed. I tried to avoid a direct look at my mom in case she noticed the gigantic dark circles under my eyes. Unfortunately, my mom has a sixth sense about things like that. I'd just sat down at the table when she spoke.

"Angel, did you get enough sleep last night? You look exhausted."

"I'm good, Mom." I shoveled a spoonful of cereal into my mouth. "Studied late."

"How late?"

"Uh, I lost track of time."

"You'll go to bed early tonight."

"The fund-raiser for Mr. Matthews is tonight," I reminded her.

"Then you'll take a nap before you head out."

"What?" I lifted my head sharply. "Mom! I'm not five. I'm *not* coming home after school to take a nap like a preschooler."

"Oh, yes, you are, young lady. The fund-raiser doesn't start until seven thirty. You'll come home first and take a nap before you get sick. I'll drive you to school about six thirty when I get off work. It's either that or you aren't going. Understood?"

Her jaw was set. I'd never win. "Fine," I huffed. "I'll take a stupid nap."

"Good." Happy she'd won, she ruffled my hair and then pressed a kiss on top of my head. "Don't get me wrong. I'm glad you are participating in school events. You don't know how happy that makes me. I just want you to stay healthy while doing it."

I wanted to assure her this was a onetime thing, but

that would only trigger another lecture, so I kept my mouth shut.

When I arrived at school, I met Frankie and Wally at my locker.

"Are we ready for tonight?" I asked.

"Ready as we'll ever be," Wally answered.

"I hung up all the posters and put out the news on my social media," Frankie offered. "I also got four other students to help us collect donations."

I leaned back against my locker. "I have a small problem, guys. I can't help after school. I'm under strict orders to go home first. I was up most of the night hacking and my mom nailed me on it. Not the hacking part, thank goodness, just the lack of sleep thing. She's going to drive me back to school when she gets off work. Is that okay?"

"Fine with me," Frankie said, shrugging. "We have enough volunteers to handle the setup. The players have already paid and Wally got one of the students to referee. But even better, Wally's got a secret."

I looked at Wally. "Spill."

He puffed out his chest and grinned. "I contacted the local television stations. Guess what? We'll have live coverage from two of them. I played the wounded-American-hero-turned-school-administrator-needs-our-support card and they took the bait. We're on!"

"Sweet!" Frankie grinned. "We'll be on television."

"Well, not us, exactly. But the game will."

Now I felt guilty that other than getting Colt to play, I'd done squat to get this fund-raiser off the ground.

"I hope it raises a boatload of money for Mr. Matthews," Wally said.

"It will," Frankie assured him. "It's going to be epic."

Frankie dashed off to her class, while Wally and I walked down the hall together. I sincerely hoped the topic would keep me engaged and conscious.

Before we parted ways, I pulled on his arm, yanking him against some lockers. "I need to talk to you for a minute," I said. "It's important."

He looked slightly alarmed. "What's wrong?"

"I did some, um, work on the King's Security site myself last night. You were right. My dad either worked for or was associated with the NSA."

He looked at me, astounded. "You hacked the site *after* I told you it was NSA? Are you nuts?"

"Don't worry. I was careful—*more* than careful. I found a hole, a security lapse. I waltzed right in."

Wally shook his head vigorously. "No way. There was no hole. I swear. I probed it thoroughly. I would have seen it."

"You must have missed it."

"I *didn't* miss anything." He frowned. "What if it was a trap?"

"Wally, I'm not stupid. I know what a trap looks like."

"We're talking about the NSA! You don't know squat."

I bristled. "I took extra precautions. I got inside and found documents about my father. I didn't have time to go through it all yet. But I'm going to find out the truth. I wasn't traced or tagged. No worries."

"Right. You hack the NSA and tell me not to worry." Wally blew out a breath. "Angel, is this worth it? What if your father *is* dead? Are you ready for that?"

I met his gaze evenly. "My father has been dead to me my whole life. Confirming it won't change anything."

He shook his head. "Are you sure about that?"

"I need the truth, Wally."

"Okay. I hope you're satisfied with what you find."

I didn't see him again until Red Teaming. Mr. Franklin started the class by asking us what we'd learned by researching the intersection of cybersecurity and artificial intelligence.

Wen Hai raised his hand. "After researching the work of Gustav Monteray and Omar Haider, I discovered brain-computer interfacing, or BCI for short. It's the hot new marriage between biotechnology and artificial intelligence. This involves a lot of the work these two guys are doing. In fact, it opens lots of possibilities for hackers to break into things like insulin pumps and pacemakers. Did you know that Dick Cheney, the forty-sixth vice president of the US, had his pacemaker disabled because of the hacking risk?"

"No way," Brandon breathed.

"Way," Wen Hai countered.

"Come on. BCI isn't new," Wally countered. "Doctors have been using it for years, and hackers have been exploiting it for about as long." He looked at Mr. Franklin. "Not that I know that from personal experience or anything."

"Okay, but BCI is evolving fast," Wen Hai insisted. "There are a lot of new technical developments."

"Like what?" I asked, leaning forward on my desk. My sleepiness temporarily vanished. A quick look at my peers indicated they were equally as interested.

"Yes, Wen Hai, please enlighten us," Mr. Franklin added. The way he said it, I had a feeling he already knew, but wanted to let his student speak.

"Well, doctors and scientists are implanting microchips into the brain to improve memory function, remove depression, control neurological diseases, and other stuff like that," Wen Hai explained. "Artificial retinas have been engineered and inserted into the eye to help people see. Special implants in the ears can help deaf people hear. The software interacts directly with the brain, so everything that happens is fluid and natural."

"Whoa," Piper said. "That is way cool."

Mr. Franklin tapped his chin. "So, class, where does the technology end and the human begin? Or do they become indistinguishable at some point? Can technology supersede the brain to become its own form of artificial intelligence?"

"To me, that's a secondary question." I blew out a breath. "Wen Hai touched on it. From a cybersecurity point of view—which is why we're all in this class—the most important information to come from this discussion is regardless of how sophisticated the technology is or how it merges, if it requires hardware and software, it's hackable. That means there's going to be a big demand for anti-mind-hacking technology someday. This will be huge for the field of cybersecurity. That's why you brought it up, Mr. Franklin, isn't it?"

Mr. Franklin nodded, clearly pleased by my answer. "It is, indeed, Angel. Well done, class. For your homework, I want you to delve deeper into the implications of Mr. Monteray and Mr. Haider's research."

Unfortunately, the rest of my day wasn't as exciting. Lunch wasn't edible, so by chemistry I was tired, cranky, and hungry. I barely greeted Colt and didn't even look at him once.

"Are you okay?" Colt whispered while the teacher was writing a long formula on the board. "You don't look well."

"I'm fine," I whispered back in an irritable tone.

"You've been acting strange the last couple of days."

I sighed. "I have a lot on my mind. Besides, the melee is tonight."

"It should go off without a hitch. Is everything ready?"

"I think so. Wally and Frankie finished making all

the powdered-sugar bullets. They have volunteers ready to set up the field after school."

"No need to be worried."

"Easy for you to say. I don't like large crowds."

"Oh. Okay, I get that. What's your role in this thing?"

"I have to carry around the money bucket and convince people to put cash in it." I tapped my pencil on the notebook. "That means I'll have to talk to people. Sort of. Not my favorite thing."

"No wonder you're worried," Colt said somberly.

The way he said it, tongue in cheek, made me smile. "Are you making fun of me?"

"Teasing, a little."

I shifted in my chair. "Aren't you nervous at all about being the captain of the Brains? That's going to be a challenge in itself."

"I'm not worried. I like challenges."

"I'm impressed. Nerves of steel. Don't let all the television cameras distract you."

"*What* television cameras?" The sudden sharp tone of his voice startled me. He looked at me, his expression angry and weirdly...betrayed.

I fumbled to process his sudden change of mood. "Wally got a few of the local television stations to cover the melee. Hopefully that means more people will come and contribute to the cause."

"You said this would be contained to the school. I asked you specifically."

I stared at him. He looked...pissed. "Well, yeah, it is. Sort of."

"Television stations covering this event is *not* 'sort of,' Angel. That makes this exhibition game a lot more high profile. Not happy right now."

I looked at him, baffled. I had no idea why he was so upset. But before I could ask him what was wrong, Mr.

Jackson resumed his lecture. We didn't have a chance to talk any more. When the bell rang, Colt grabbed his stuff without another word or even looking at me.

What the heck was going on?

I rubbed my temples. Apparently, I was a dork. I wasn't interpreting anyone's signal right. Not that it had ever been easy for me. Maybe my mom was right. I needed a nap to recharge my brain because, right now, nothing made sense.

When school finished, I took the bus home and headed straight for bed.

CHAPTER THIRTY-SIX

Isaac Remington

Isaac was staring at his last burner phone, waiting for it to ring. He was going to have to make another Target run. He was also going to have to stop eating at this Mexican restaurant. His stomach was in knots, and he couldn't put all the blame on the food or the hot sauce. This situation was slipping out of his control. He had an uncomfortable feeling the Hidden Avenger was hunting him instead of the other way around. It was absurd, yet it unnerved him. When his phone finally vibrated, he answered with annoyance, sure it was going to bring more bad news.

"What is it?" he snapped.

"Honeypot accessed. All went according to plan."

"Finally," he huffed, relaxing marginally. It was about time things started going his way. "She got the info we planted on her father?"

"Yeah, and she was fast getting in and getting out, too. She knows her stuff. She's got a real future with us, if she wants it."

"Are you that much of an idiot? The last thing we

need right now is another idealist who doesn't understand how the real world works."

"I won't disagree with you on that. But her skills are worthy."

"I don't care about her skills or her future. I need her father." Isaac ran his fingers through his hair. "Do you think she got suspicious? Was it too easy?"

"I'll be honest, I worried about that. I was monitoring her in real time. She found the info quickly and grabbed it, but before she left, she looked around like she wanted to be sure she wasn't being set up. Did I mention she's *real* good? The apple didn't fall far from the tree with this one."

"Do you think she suspected it was bogus data?"

"Well, it's not *all* bogus. I was getting worried as she prowled the folders. I think she was looking for something that would corroborate that she had access to real information that we would otherwise share. To lead her on, I dropped in a file ahead of where she was going that I knew she couldn't resist looking at. That should convince her everything is aboveboard if she attempts to corroborate."

"I didn't authorize that. What did you give her?"

"A list of names, phone numbers, and addresses of real people so she can confirm they exist and have a relationship with the agency."

"Are you kidding me? Which list? You didn't give her the actual agency directory, did you?"

"Of course not. I'm not stupid. Just the Research Directorate's personnel roster. I had it at hand. She stopped looking immediately after finding it and slipped back out of the system."

Isaac's stomach churned worse. "Let me get this straight. You gave her our department names, addresses, and phone numbers—including yours and mine?"

"It was a spur-of-the-moment kind of thing. I had a feeling she would require something authentic if she were to swallow any of it. If she's able to verify some information, she'll be more likely to believe the parts that are fabricated. It's a calculated risk, but one I felt comfortable taking. Don't worry. She won't have a clue who we are."

Isaac clenched his teeth. "She'd better not."

CHAPTER THIRTY-SEVEN

Angel Sinclair

My phone rang. I groped for it, then bolted to a sitting position. Crap. I'd overslept.

"Mom?" My voice sounded scratchy.

"I'm on my way. Be out front in two minutes and I'll drop you off at the school for the game. Did you get your nap?"

Boy, did I ever. I glanced at the clock. I'd overslept by at least two hours. That meant I hadn't eaten or done the laundry. I yanked open my dresser. I had only one clean bra and a single pair of undies. I wasn't as lucky in the rest-of-the-clothes department. I'd have to make do with a pair of jeans that had a ketchup stain on the right thigh and a white T-shirt I never wore because of the stupid saying on it—*Hedgehogs. Why Don't They Just Share the Hedge?* I grabbed a sweatshirt on the way out to account for the cooler evenings, but mostly to hide the T-shirt.

My mom was already outside when I got down to the front of the complex. She frowned as I climbed in and buckled my seat belt. "Really, Angel? You're wearing that?"

"I didn't have a chance to do my laundry. I overslept."

"You don't have even one clean pair of jeans?"

"Not even one."

"Why didn't you do your laundry last night like I suggested?"

"Mom, I was studying, remember? I don't want to talk about my clothes, okay? Be glad I'm getting out."

"I *am* glad. But I thought since you're going to be on television, you would like to look nice."

"I'm *not* going to be on television, thank God. I'm going to be in the crowd holding a bucket and asking for money. This is *not* about me or how I look. I'm helping Wally behind the scenes. That's it."

"You could have at least combed your hair."

"*Mom!*"

"Okay, okay. I'm stopping now."

Mom dropped me off in front of the school after contributing a twenty-dollar bill for Mr. Matthews's fund, which I crammed into the pocket of my jeans. I followed the crowd of kids headed behind the school to the football field. I found Wally on the fifty-yard line directing the drama club students setting up the melee obstacles, which were basically beat-up medieval-looking props.

"Glad you could make it," Wally commented wryly when I came running up. He gave me a once-over. "You dressed up. Is that a ketchup stain on your jeans?"

"I overslept and didn't have time to do my laundry."

"That's obvious."

I glared at him. "What's wrong with everyone today? No one ever cared how I dressed before."

"That's because I've only seen you in your school uniform. I'm not familiar with your casual look. If I'm honest, it needs work."

I folded my arms against my chest. "Can we drop the issue of my clothes? Don't worry, Wally. Despite my appearance, I'll get you the money for Mr. Matthews."

"You'd better. Your bucket is over there."

I looked over his shoulder at a bucket decorated with green glitter swords and a sign that said, *Help Mr. Matthews. Donate Something Worthy of King Arthur!* Frankie had done a nice job with them.

Wally ran off and began talking to everyone, directing the show like a general. A chubby, curly-haired, thick-glasses-and-no-spiffy-uniform-or-cool-hat Napoléon, but a leader, nonetheless. I couldn't help but be secretly impressed.

The stands were full and more people were coming. The teams were walking around, talking and huddling—probably reviewing last-minute strategies. Wally ran over and yelled something at the Trains, who were easily identified by their chest bumping and random, loud bellows of unfocused emotions.

Ugh. Jocks.

As required by the rules, all the participants wore white T-shirts and a gray or red ball cap, depending on their team, and held tubular marshmallow blasters. Everyone was wearing safety goggles, either on the top of their heads or hanging around their necks. When the game started, all players had to cover their eyes or be disqualified. The drama club had already positioned the two swords mounted in stone replicas at either end of the field. One sword had a gray scarf tied around the handle and the other a red scarf. A red train was on a sign behind the sword in stone with the red scarf. A gray brain was on the other sign.

Wally walked back to me, studying my expression. "What's wrong?"

"Nothing. I can't believe you pulled this off. You're amazing, Wally."

"Thank you. Between you and me, I was barely able to get enough people on the Brains team. If it hadn't been for you co-opting Colt to be captain of the Brains, we wouldn't have had enough. As it is, the Trains are pissed Colt is bailing on them."

"It was nice of Colt to agree to help us out," I agreed. Then I remembered his anger in chemistry class and looked around, wondering if I had time to ask him about it. I didn't see him on the field yet.

Wally waved a hand at someone on the Brains team and then turned to me again. "I don't know what kind of hold you have on Colt, but I appreciate it."

My cheeks heated. "I don't have *any* hold on him. He wants to help Mr. Matthews, okay?"

"If that's your story, I'm onboard." Wally leaned over toward me and lowered his voice. "Did you see who's captain of the Trains? None other than your best friend, Mary Herman."

I glanced at the other end zone, where a sea of red caps was currently jostling around. "This could get ugly."

"You think? Mary is the one to beat. No question."

A kid in a referee shirt, carrying a clipboard and with a whistle around his neck, strolled by. "Who's that?" I asked.

"Cameron Locke. He's not at the top of the brain chain, but he's no jock, either. A neutral party, and therefore as decent a referee as I could get."

"As neutral as you can be knowing that if the jocks lose, Mary Herman is coming after you first."

"Keep that quiet," Wally hissed. "I can't afford to lose Cameron at this stage. But given the physical prowess of the Trains, I will say with great sincerity that those Brains who lay down their lives to help Mr. Matthews will never be forgotten."

"Better them than me."

"I wholeheartedly agree, but privately, of course. As the mastermind of this operation, I must maintain neutrality."

I looked around. "Have you seen Colt?"

"I thought *you* were in charge of Colt."

"I'm not in charge of anybody. I'm barely in charge of myself."

Mark Shinsky of the Brains trotted over, standing in front of me with his hands on his hips. "Hey, where's McCarrell—our fearless leader?"

I lifted my hands. "Why does everyone think I know?"

"Wally said you two were an item."

"*Wally!*" My face turned scarlet as I glared at him.

Wally spread his hands in an innocent gesture. "What goes on between two consenting individuals is none of my business. I don't want to know the details."

I whirled on Mark. "Colt and I are *not* together. We're lab partners in chemistry. That's it."

"Like I care. Just get your boyfriend here. Game time is in fifteen minutes. The Brains are getting nervous."

Wally stuck a finger in my chest. "Take care of it. The television crew just arrived. Be right back." He rushed over to two guys who were standing on the sidelines, one of them balancing a heavy camera on his shoulder.

I took my phone out of my pocket and texted Colt.

Where are you?

I waited but got no answer. After a few minutes had passed with no response, I called. The phone went right to his voice mail. I left a message asking him where he was and telling him to come to the school as soon as possible.

More minutes ticked past, and no Colt.

Panic began to bloom in my stomach. Cheering arose and I looked over. The jocks, or the Trains—presumably because they intended to steamroll the Brains—had co-opted the assistance of the cheerleaders, as Wally had predicted. They were in full uniform, shaking their pom-poms and just about everything else.

Great.

Where the heck was Colt?

Wally rushed back to me. "We are T-minus seven minutes until game time. Any word from Colt?"

I checked my phone. "No."

"What are you going to do?"

"Me?"

"This was your one and only responsibility."

"I…don't know."

Mark jogged over to us. "Where's Colt?"

I lifted my hands. "No idea."

"Well, without him, we're short one person. We might as well forfeit. We can't play if we're short one person, and who the heck is going to volunteer in his place? Without him, we'll be creamed."

This was turning into a disaster. I felt like I might throw up. Why hadn't Colt shown?

Patty Trent, her hair swept back into a long, sleek ponytail, marched over to us. Until she stood right next to me, I'd never known how short the cheerleaders' skirts were. Wally must not have noticed that before, either, because he was having a hard time keeping his eyes on her face.

Patty smiled at him. "Wally, are we going to start the game now? We want to know when we can start our opening cheer sequence."

"Ah…ah…" he stammered. He couldn't seem to form a coherent thought. She'd probably never spoken to him directly before. Now that she had, he was acting as if he were stuck in a loop, calculating the infinitesimally small probability that she would ever go out with him.

I elbowed him in the gut, rebooting his central processor. "We're still waiting for Colt, Patty."

"Really?" She laughed, her eyes narrowing into amused and nasty slits. "Come on, Angel. Did you seriously think Colt would show for you? Please. You're either more stupid than I thought or truly delusional. He's not coming. So, either start the game or forfeit."

Wally exchanged a worried glance with me. I swallowed hard. I had no idea what to say.

"We'll forfeit," Mark said quickly after taking one look at my face. "Without Colt, we'll get killed."

The crowd had started to get restless. I could hear catcalls and people shouting for us to get the game under way.

OMG. Patty was right. I'd been stupid to think Colt would do this for me. I'd let everyone down, but worst of all, I'd failed Mr. Matthews. My cheeks burned with shame and, not surprisingly, anger.

Colt played me. Why?

I balled my fists against my side. No way was I going to let Colt ruin the fund-raiser.

"No forfeit." I pulled my hair back in a ponytail with the rubber tie around my wrist and grabbed Mark's marshmallow popper. "I'll take Colt's place." Then in a moment of inspiration, I added, "We have not yet begun to fight!"

Wally's mouth dropped open in shock. "Are you out of your mind?"

"Apparently so." I turned to Mark. "Come on, dude. Let's do this."

CHAPTER THIRTY-EIGHT

Angel Sinclair

Mark didn't budge. Instead his eyes widened in a holy-crap-we-are-in-a-lot-of-trouble way. "Whoa. Wait. *You* want to fill in for Colt? Do you even know how to use that?" He pointed to the marshmallow shooter that I now held upside down.

I turned it right side up and flipped it in my hand like I was a fancy gunslinger. "Sure, I know how to use it. How hard can it be?" It suddenly exploded in my hands. Gray confectioners' sugar sprayed across Patty Trent's perfect chest and chin.

She screamed and swiped at her face. It only served to smear the powder around more. Her face and cheerleader outfit suddenly looked like the inside of an ashtray. Patty began shouting and stomping around.

"You!" she shrieked, pointing at me. "I'm ruined."

The crowd roared in laughter and clapped as if this had been a planned part of the show.

Patty glared at me. If looks could kill, I'd have been dead a hundred times over. No question—I'd made another enemy for life…or at least for the rest of my senior year.

Fine. She could get in line behind all the others. Ugh.

"You did that on purpose," she said to me between clenched teeth.

I had to try hard not to smile. "I didn't. But perhaps you and I should take a bow anyway. I think the crowd expects it."

I gave a flourished bow, and the crowd roared again. After one more murderous glare at me, Patty stalked off toward the sidelines. I took a breath and turned to Wally. "Tell Cameron to give us three minutes, then start the game."

"Can I talk to you privately?" Wally yanked on my arm, pulling me away from Mark. "Are you insane? Need I remind you that Mary Herman is on the other team? Not to mention you don't even know how to use that popper."

"It's not rocket science," I said, but I held the popper a bit more gingerly. "We're out of options, Wally. I don't know why Colt didn't show."

Wally looked at the determined expression on my face and sighed. "Fine. It's your funeral. Take off your sweatshirt."

"Excuse me?"

"A white T-shirt has to be showing."

I hated the hedgehog shirt, but I didn't have any choice. At least it was white. I tugged off the sweatshirt and tossed it to him.

He took one look at my shirt and shook his head. "You're a hot mess today."

"Shut up and let's do this."

He tossed me a gray cap and I put it on, brim backward. I turned to Mark, and we jogged over to the rest of the Brains.

"Um, why is *she* here?" David Smithson asked. I had him in my English and PE classes. Super smart guy, but no filter. I liked him for that, except for right now.

A quick glance at my teammates confirmed there wasn't a single girl, other than me, present. That only went to show you that women *were* a lot smarter than men, since none of us—other than me—had signed up for this disaster about to happen.

"Colt's a no-show." Mark tossed me safety goggles. "She's filling in for him."

"*What?*" David exclaimed. "We get Angel Sinclair instead of Colt McCarrell? Is this a joke? I didn't sign up for total extermination."

There was a lot of muttering. The entire crew seemed seconds from laying down arms and walking away in forfeit. If they did that, we'd have to refund the players' money, no one in the crowd would donate, and Mr. Matthews would have nothing.

I groped for something to keep them there. "Wait. I have a strategy."

The skeptical glances that came my way almost made me walk away with them, but I steeled myself and lifted my chin. "The way to win in the Medieval Melee is to get the other team's sword out of the stone, right? So the typical plan is to go on the offense and try to get past them or shoot your way through them until you can steal their sword. Let's face it. They are bigger, faster, and stronger than us. That's not a good strategy. But what if we give them only a few targets to shoot at? In other words, we don't play offense, we play defense only. We move and evade, but we don't try to press ahead. We dig in and wait. It'll take them a lot longer to get to our sword, which gives us a better chance of picking them off one by one when they come for it."

"Yeah, but they'll still get through—it will only be a matter of time," one of the guys said. "If we don't get their sword, we can't win. So what's the point of prolonging the agony?"

"The point is patience. See that box over to the right? What if one of us works our way under it and hides?" I motioned to it with my head. "The person in the box doesn't shoot or move—just stays hidden and lets the enemy pass. When they realize we aren't pressing forward to threaten their sword, it's logical they will leave their sword mostly, or possibly even entirely, unprotected. When we're down to only one or two defenders, someone shouts a code word to let the person under the box know it's time to go for the sword. Even if there's an enemy defender protecting the sword, the odds of one against one are at least doable."

"That's the dumbest strategy I've ever heard," David said. "You can't hide under a box for the whole game."

"You can," I argued. "There's nothing in the rules that says you can't. You can't leave the field, but so long as the box stays on the field, it's fair."

To my relief, none of the Brains had left yet. Either I'd confused them too much with my so-called strategy or they were still trying to figure it out when Cameron blew his whistle as his first official act as referee.

"Game is officially started," he yelled through a megaphone. "Teams, take your positions and go."

Someone tossed Mark a popper, and he caught it with one hand. "Well, it's not like we have time to develop a better strategy." He adjusted his safety goggles over his eyes and gripped his popper and ammunition bag. "You heard her. Fall back and protect the sword. Angel, since the box was your idea, you do it."

"*What?* No, I don't want to get under the box. I'm claustrophobic."

"You also can't shoot worth a crap." He shoved an ammunition bag in my hands. "Besides, you're the smallest. Make your way over there and get under the stupid box before you accidentally shoot one of us."

"Fine. What's the code word so I know when to come out?"

"How about *Xena*? You're going to need to be like her if we have any prayer of winning this."

"Xena?"

"You know, the warrior princess. She always saves the day and looks hot while doing it. So save the day, okay? Unless you've got a better code word to offer. In my opinion, we're going to need a lot more than you under a box to win this thing."

I was about to offer some pithy comeback when Mark ducked. A bullet with powdered sugar whizzed past his ear, slamming into the ground and spraying red dust everywhere.

"Get down," he shouted at me.

"Aagh!" I yelped as another sugar bullet passed over my head.

I dashed toward the biggest obstacle I could find, a large wooden panel. I quickly slid the goggles over my eyes and dared a quick peek around the panel. I didn't see anyone. The Trains were also hiding behind their obstacles, plotting their takeover. My glance confirmed the box I had identified to hide under was about twenty-five feet in front of me.

I hunched down behind the panel, my heart pounding. I had no freaking clue what I was doing except I had to get to that box quickly. If I waited too long, the Trains would be there. I held my popper like I knew what I was doing, although I wasn't even sure how to fire it properly, and dashed around the panel toward the box. A couple of bullets were shot my way, but for once in my life, being small worked in my favor. They all shot too high, and when I ran in a half crouch, they couldn't hit me. I made it safely behind the box, struggling to catch my breath because I was shaking from nerves.

There was a sudden barrage of popping and shouting occurring on the left side of the field. Mark and a few of the others were trying to draw attention away from me. The screaming and yelling from the crowd heightened, but I couldn't understand any of what was going on. Their words were more like a swell of noise that ebbed and flowed but had no actual meaning.

No time to waste. I carefully lifted one corner of the box. Again, my small size was an advantage, because the box lifted only slightly as I wiggled under it.

My claustrophobia kicked in the second I was in the box. It wasn't as dark as I'd expected, but it was closed. Plus, I was vulnerable to anyone who discovered I was in there. They would only have to kick the box over and I was toast. I'd never even know they were coming.

Kids were shouting things, but it was hard to make out what was going on. I hoped that held true for the Trains as well. It wouldn't be long before they realized our strategy of holding back and not pressing forward with wild abandon. The crowd was going nuts now; the roar was loud. Strategically, I'd made a serious error. The box muffled sound a lot more than I expected. The screaming on the field and from the crowd didn't help me hear better, either.

I froze when a thump hit the outside of the box. It was from the Train side, so I figured it was an enemy player. I quietly lifted my popper in case they pushed the box over. But after a long minute—maybe the longest minute of my life—the box stayed intact, and there was no more thumping. I relaxed my guard slightly, hoping whoever it was had moved on.

I decided it would be a better strategy to minimize my exposure by reducing the distance I had to run to make it to the sword as much as possible. That meant scooting the box toward enemy territory as stealthily as possible. Hopefully, no one would detect the motion of the box while they were running around and shooting at people.

Little by little, I started to move. I moved to my hands and knees and began to crawl, with the strap of the marshmallow gun in my teeth. I slid the box in tiny increments toward the direction of the enemy sword. I stopped every few seconds to listen. The farther I got, the more confident I felt that if the Trains had left someone behind to defend, they would surely have seen me by now. However, if they *hadn't* left anyone to guard the sword, I had to move fast since that meant the Brains were now outnumbered.

The noise was getting fainter, so I assumed the action was getting hotter and heavier around our sword. That couldn't be good. I had no idea how long the Brains could hold out.

I had to move quicker or abandon my sanctuary.

The crowd seemed to be screaming louder now, or maybe it was my breath whistling out between my teeth as I clenched the strap. I was too far away from my team now to hear a code word. My entire team could be screaming *Xena* at me and I wouldn't know it.

Enough time had passed. I needed to go for it. I stopped crawling, got into a crouch, and gripped the popper with my hands.

It was do-or-die time. Probably die, but I didn't want to dwell on that when I needed every ounce of courage to get the heck out of the box.

Before I lost my nerve, I threw off the box and started running toward the enemy sword. To my enormous relief, there wasn't a single defender at the sword. The screaming from the crowd was deafening now, but I didn't dare slow down to figure out what was happening at the other end of the field. I dropped my popper and ran straight for the sword, grabbing the handle with both hands and yanking on it. It was harder than I thought to pull the stupid thing out. As I pulled, I glanced across the field. Mary Herman stood over our sword, pulling it out.

Holy Excalibur!

It was a race to determine who crossed the midfield first with sword in hand to win.

CHAPTER THIRTY-NINE

Angel Sinclair

etermined, I pulled at the sword with all my might. To my relief, the sword slipped out of the fake rock and into my hands. I turned to dash toward the midfield when I was pulled up short. A piece of my T-shirt was caught in the rock.

No way was that going to slow me down.

Gritting my teeth, I yanked hard. My T-shirt ripped off me with a sickening sound as cool air enveloped my torso. I ran with everything I had toward the midfield in nothing more than my bra and jeans. I could hear the crowd screaming in frenzy. My teammates were shrieking and my heart thundering. Everything seemed to be moving in slow motion no matter how fast I pumped my legs.

It was going to be close. I was faster than Mary, but the sword was heavier than I'd expected. Mary was stronger. We barreled toward each other, much like two medieval jousters ready to collide in a spectacular boom.

Then something miraculous happened. Mary stumbled and went down.

I was going to win it! The geeks were going to take down the jocks. I summoned every last ounce of strength and pumped toward the finish line when...

Splat!

For a moment, I didn't comprehend what had happened. I faltered as I looked down at the front of my bra and the huge red splatter of powdered sugar on the left boob of my—oh, dear God, this couldn't be happening—Hello Kitty bra. I stumbled to a stop. Mary was down on one knee, holding a popper I hadn't known she had. When she fell, she must have picked up a popper from the ground and shot me. Or had she had an extra popper all along? Did it matter?

A smirk blossomed across Mary's face as she stood, picked up the Brains' sword and strolled across the midfield. Cameron blew his whistle, signaling the end of the game. The Trains rushed toward her, whooping and shouting while I stood there, covered in red powdered sugar and no shirt, still holding the sword and not quite sure what the heck had just happened.

Mary untangled herself from her teammates and walked over to me. "Nice bra. Hello Kitty? What are you, ten years old? Did you really think you could beat me?"

Before I could say a word, she was swamped by her teammates, who were whooping, yelling, and slapping her on the back. Wally ran up to me, out of breath, and handed me the shreds of my T-shirt, which I pulled over my head.

"Heck of a game, Angel." He slapped me on the back. "You almost beat the jocks, and without the help of Colt McCarrell. An absolutely respectable showing."

I was still dazed. "I didn't see her other popper."

"She picked one off the ground and shot you when she realized she wasn't going to beat you. Lucky for her there was a bullet left. Hey, is that a cat on your bra?"

I yanked the T-shirt closed the best I could, but it still gaped. It was a losing battle…just like the game.

"Keep your eyes up here, okay?" I pointed to my face.

Wally grinned. "Sure. Whatever you say."

Mark and some of the other members of my team came over and patted me on the shoulder. "Not a bad performance, Angel," Mark said. "The strategy, as crazy as it was, almost worked. Tough ending."

The fact that my teammates didn't hate me made me feel a little better, even though we'd lost.

Frankie dashed toward us, holding two buckets filled with bills and coins. "That was so exciting, Angel. I almost had a heart attack. People in the stands were completely losing it, screaming their heads off. What a fantastic game. People were practically throwing money in the bucket, they were so thrilled. We made a decent haul even if you weren't helping us collect. By the way, I *love* your bra. Hello Kitty. Who knew? I never would have guessed you to be into that level of fashion."

"I am *not* into fashion." My cheeks flushed. "Can we please stop talking about my bra? My aunt Dorothy gave it to me for Christmas and I didn't have another clean one for today. I didn't know it was going on display."

"I wish I could borrow it, but it looks too small."

"Frankie!"

"Sorry. Just thinking aloud."

I half-heartedly shook hands with the other team—except Mary Herman, who had apparently deemed it beneath her to shake my hand—and mumbled, "Good game." A couple of the jocks slapped me hard on the back with their congratulations, almost knocking me over.

I just wanted this day over and out of my memory. Forever.

CHAPTER FORTY

Angel Sinclair

The next two days at school were mostly a blur. Somehow, I survived the agonizing loss to the jocks and the meows that followed me wherever I went. After the first few mortifying hours, I managed to tune it out. Frankie and Wally tried to cheer me up, but it didn't help much. Wally was ecstatic with the money we'd raised and obsessed with figuring out how to apply his marketing genius to increase those funds even more.

I was happy with the haul for Mr. Matthews, but they didn't seem to understand the depth of my mortification. Numerous photos of me in that bra, taken from every imaginable angle, were being circulated with abandon around all of cyberspace. Colt was notably absent from school both days, and no one seemed to know what happened to him.

Not that I cared one single iota.

My nights were spent looking through X-Corp's cybersecurity analysis of BioLimbs as well as the BioLimbs site itself. I exhaustively reviewed the notes and screen shots I'd taken when Lexi and I investigated the company server and logs. A little after midnight on Saturday, I came across something I hadn't seen before in BioLimbs' app installation software. I checked and rechecked, but I didn't like what I saw. I needed a second opinion. I would have asked Lexi, but I wasn't supposed to be in the system on my own, so instead, I shot a text to Wally asking him to call me when he woke up.

I finally fell into bed about five o'clock. Before I fell asleep, it occurred to me I hadn't corresponded with any of my online gaming friends in ages. No one had messaged me, asking where I'd gone or why I hadn't played for a while. I'd never gone this long without gaming or needing to check in with my online friends.

My mom, not knowing of my late night, woke me up at nine before she left to go to work for a few hours. A quick check indicated neither Wally not Frankie had tried to call, text, or email me yet. They had probably both gotten a decent amount of sleep. I dragged my butt out of bed and was eating cereal bleary-eyed when the doorbell rang.

Mr. Toodles went nuts barking. I looked through the peephole. Colt stood there, dressed in his varsity letter jacket.

Crap.

I turned around and backed up against the door. My exhaustion vanished. What was he doing here?

He rang the bell again. "Open the door, Angel. I know you're in there. Your mom just left for work. She told me you were inside."

"Go away."

"Please. I want to talk."

"I don't want to talk. I'm in my pajamas."

"Get dressed or get a robe. I'll wait."

"I told you, I don't want to talk to you."

"Then I'll bang on your door until I wake up all the neighbors. Seeing as how it is Saturday morning, I'm sure that won't make them happy. Look, I'm asking for a few minutes of your time. Please."

I peeked through the door again. Colt had a look of determination on his face. He wasn't going anywhere. I could ignore him, but there was a strong possibility he would follow through and bang, if not wait out there until my mom came home. Then she'd make me invite him in and probably listen to the entire conversation.

Ugh.

"Fine. You'll have two minutes."

"I'll make it work."

I ran back to my room, pulled on a T-shirt and jeans, and ran a brush through my rat's nest hair. There wasn't anything I could do about the dark circles under my eyes. Sighing, I left my feet bare.

When I returned to the door and peered out the peephole, Colt was still there, patiently waiting. Inhaling a deep breath, I pulled open the door.

He quickly stepped inside, like he was afraid I might change my mind. I might have, so it was a good move.

"Thanks for hearing me out, Angel."

I closed the door and stood in the entranceway, crossing my arms against my chest. I wasn't going to invite him in any farther.

"What do you want?"

"To apologize. I'm sorry I couldn't make it to the melee."

"You couldn't text me to let me know?"

"I was…busy."

"So busy you couldn't find five seconds to text or call? For two days?"

"It's taken me that long to work up the courage to come here." He ran his fingers through his hair, a pained expression on his face. "I wanted to tell you in person. I shouldn't have agreed to participate in the first place."

"I'm not going to argue with that. But the night of

the event, after having made a commitment, is *not* the time to come to this realization."

"I know. I'm sorry." His expression was miserable. "I wanted to help you because I like Mr. Matthews. I like you, too. But then you said there were going to be television cameras and...I couldn't do it."

"Why should that matter?"

"It shouldn't, but it does. I'm apologizing, Angel."

I looked at him incredulously. "That's it? I'm sorry? No explanation? After I was humiliated in front of the entire school."

"I didn't know you'd fill in for me." He looked at his shoes. "You think I'm a jerk, right?"

"Pretty much."

"Well, I guess that's better than knowing the truth. Look, I've got to go. I wanted you to know I feel terrible about this. I wish this hadn't happened."

"I wish so, too."

He opened the door and exited, leaving me confused, embarrassed, and mystified. He came over to apologize but refused to explain his behavior?

Jerk, first-class.

I narrowed my eyes. He might have made a fool out of me, but he'd also made me curious. Big mistake.

Time to do what I always did when I wanted answers. I went to my computer.

It took me less than two hours to discover most all there was to know about Colt McCarrell.

A surprisingly easy hack into the records of St. Michael's Catholic High School in nearby Adelphi, Maryland—his school before abruptly transferring to Excalibur—indicated Colt had been a straight-A student, quarterback on the varsity team with the school record for most touchdown passes (even though he was just a sophomore!), and the recipient of St. Michael's Catholic High School's most prestigious citizenship award, the Golden Leaf.

The school's freaking golden boy.

So why had his parents yanked him out of that school and enrolled him at Excalibur Academy when he was doing so well at St. Michael's? And why had Colt said Mr. Matthews had been instrumental in getting him into Excalibur? With an academic and personal achievement record like his, why would getting into another private school be a problem?

The answers I needed were not evident in his school records at St. Michael's. Other than a departure date noted in the records of October 16 and a transfer of his school records to Excalibur on the eighteenth, I had no other information to go on. Which meant there was something else, somewhere else, that caused him to leave the school.

I did a quick check on the website. The principal at St. Michael's was Sister Mary Jean O'Connell. I'd never hacked a nun before, and I admit I felt nervous—not to mention guilty—about it. While I didn't believe in holy thunderbolts and all, the possibility still made the back of my neck itch.

It didn't take me long to get into her email. I started a week before October 16 and skimmed through the subject lines. I came to a screeching halt on October 14 at an email with the subject "Colt McCarrell."

I read that email in its entirety, and then the two follow-up emails. After reading them all, I sat back in my chair, my hand on my head in disbelief.

"Holy crap," I murmured. "So *that's* why you didn't show, Colt."

CHAPTER FORTY-ONE

Angel Sinclair

While I was hacking into Colt's old school, Frankie had texted me asking what was up. I quickly texted her back.

Can you meet me at the library in an hour and a half?

I've got to go shopping with my mom, but I'll have her drop me off when we're done.

Perfect. See you then.

Wally texted a few minutes after that, and I asked him the same thing. He said he was free—his social calendar was *never* filled. Ha. He'd meet me at the library.

After my mom got home from work and changed, she drove me to the library after I told her I was meeting Wally and Frankie there.

"I think it is so nice that you are getting out more and spending time with your friends, even if it is in the library," she said. "I'm proud of you for working so hard." She beamed with happiness. I felt guilty since the real reason for going was to hack, not hang out with my friends.

I smiled half-heartedly. "Yeah, Mom, it's great."

When she dropped me off, I promised to call her if I needed a ride home. Thankfully, the library was mostly empty, so I snagged a private study room and set up my laptop before Wally walked in.

"Well, it's official. You're now viral. In case you didn't know, Susie Manover—Mary Herman's BFF—posted a video of you getting splatted in your Hello Kitty bra on YouTube. As of last check, it had six thousand and two hits."

"*What?*" I stared at him in horror. "Six *thousand* hits of me in a Hello Kitty bra? Are you kidding?"

"I wish." Wally scowled. "I'm sorry for your humiliation. Mary and Susie are such losers. Look, I'm totally in for helping you hack into YouTube and bringing those videos down. I thought that's why you wanted me here today."

"No, it isn't, but thanks, Wally." His offer made me feel better. "They'd only put them right back up, and we've got more important things to worry about. But I appreciate you having my back."

"Any time." He pulled his laptop out of his backpack and began setting it up. "Ever hear from Colt?"

"Yes." I blew out a frustrated breath. "But I don't want to talk about it, okay?"

"Sure. I hope he had a good excuse."

"He didn't."

"Figured as much. So, if we aren't hacking YouTube or devising a scheme to ruin Mary's and Susie's lives, what are we doing here?"

"Hacking, but with a different target." I flexed my fingers. "I want to show you something. Malicious code. You interested?"

"Oh, baby, you had me at *malicious.*"

I rolled my eyes. "Listen carefully. I'm tired and I don't want to make a mistake. Remember how Mr. Kars told us that BioLimbs had designed the prostheses to accept software and firmware updates to allow for bug fixes and version upgrades?"

"Yes, but Mr. Kars and Lexi both said the software and hardware were clean. They've both been over it ad nauseam."

"Right. But what about the app?"

"What about it? Lexi said she'd checked it and it was clean, too."

"Yes, she checked the app and the installer. Both were clean...the times she checked it. Lexi and I were working inside BioLimbs when I was at X-Corp, so I know how to get in their system. Last night when I checked it, the installer had something there that wasn't there before."

"On the installer?" When I nodded, he thought for a moment. "That would certainly be an excellent place to hide malicious code. Not that I've ever hidden malicious code, mind you. Well, not often. Not that I'm admitting anything."

I rolled my eyes. "Seeing as how I've never worked with actual malicious code before, I'd like a second opinion."

"Of course. Are we safe here examining it at the library using public Wi-Fi?"

"Not really. But it's the safest we've got, and by that, I mean that it'll be hard for anyone to trace this to us. Naturally, I'll take precautions. Give me a few minutes to set up, okay?"

"Okay."

Wally played around on his laptop until I was ready. When I felt like I'd taken enough security measures, I slipped inside the BioLimbs system.

"Wally, come look," I said. I tapped on my screen. "Here."

He studied the code for a long moment. "Okay, I see nothing out of the ordinary."

"Exactly." I opened another window and pulled up a screenshot of the same code I'd taken last night. "Now, look at this."

"Whoa." He stared at my monitor, stunned. "What is in that string of code right there?"

"Good question. Someone wiped it clean this morning."

Wally grabbed a notebook and began scribbling the code down. "I've never seen anything like it. I'm not sure whether to be appalled or turned on."

"What's important here is that I don't think it's disrupting the signal between the program and the limb. It's...doing something else."

"Agreed. But what?"

"I know you're going to think I'm nuts, but I think it's instructions to the brain. I know we talked about this possibility earlier, but I'm leaning toward this not being science fiction, but a new reality."

"What?" Wally's face was ashen in disbelief. "No way."

"Way," I insisted. "Look at it, Wally. It's some kind of instruction."

"Okay, I concede, it's instructions. But to the brain? That's not yet possible. You can't hijack someone's brain with code. Not yet, anyway."

"Says who? Don't you remember our lesson in Red Teaming on artificial intelligence?"

"*That* was a theoretical discussion in school. This is real life. We can't hack organic yet. You know that. We're not there in terms of technology."

"Says who? We're just kids in high school. We don't know every advance being made in the field of artificial intelligence. Especially not those being made in secret. It's not that out there, Wally. You know I'm right."

"What I know is this kind of thing is way beyond us. We're talking superadvanced. Where are the trials, experiments, papers, ethical discussions, and so on? I've never read anything that leads me to believe we are this far along, except for a few theoretical cases, developed mostly by Monteray and Haider. Do you think we're at the point we can hijack a brain and instruct a person to do things against their will?"

"That's *exactly* what I think. If someone is hurting people with this technology, we can be assured it hasn't been vetted ethically or medically. And it's not targeting *any* people, Wally. These are veterans. American veterans. All eight of the people who had accidents wore BioLimbs prostheses and served in the US military in Iraq. I don't think that's a coincidence. Besides, BioLimbs works with all kinds of people, not just veterans, so whoever is hacking these devices is specifically targeting US servicemen and -women."

Wally sighed and studied the code some more. "That's an incredibly frightening thought."

"I agree, but I'm not making this up. The code speaks for itself."

Wally bent over my laptop, blew out a breath. "Who would do something sick like this?"

I leaned back in my chair. "I don't know. But we've got to tell Mr. Kars what we've found. They need to recall those prostheses right away."

CHAPTER FORTY-TWO

Angel Sinclair

Frankie arrived just as I left a message for Vincent Kars on his personal cell phone. I hoped he didn't ask how I'd obtained his number. I left a message asking him to call me, adding it was urgent.

While we waited for him to call back, we updated Frankie on the developments. She leaned back in her chair, listening quietly. Today she wore a red-and-black-checked flannel shirt with dark leggings, ankle boots, and two braids wound with red yarn. She looked like a cross between a lumberjack and a cat toy.

"Okay, you guys have to slow down. I barely understood any of that." Frankie made a swooping motion with her hand. "As far as I understand it, someone with an ax to grind with the US military is hacking the brains of veterans who have prostheses made by BioLimbs. Right?"

"Right," I said. "Whoever is doing this has not only mad cracking skills, but an expertise with AI and/or biotechnology. This isn't the work of a simple hacker.

There aren't many people in the world who could pull this kind of thing off."

"Agreed," Wally said. "Which should narrow our field of suspects. What do we know about the malicious code itself so far?"

"Well, the veterans use the updating app and, thereby, the installation program, when they are instructed to do so by someone at BioLimbs. Each person's prostheses are unique. So, if the cracker wanted to target someone specific, he or she would wait until the person received instructions to install the upgrade before planting the code."

"He's wiping the code after each installation to hide the evidence," Wally mused.

"Yeah. No evidence left behind. But that's where he plants it. We have to wait for him to set up another attack, then we stop it."

"How does he know when each veteran is instructed to update the software?" Frankie asked.

"He has to be monitoring the targets somehow," Wally said. "Spying or tapping their phones. Or maybe he planted a listening device in their cars or houses. All of which means this is premeditated and carefully planned."

"It wouldn't be that hard." I considered the possibilities. "It would also explain how only those servicemen and -women who served in Iraq and have prostheses made by BioLimbs are being targeted. BioLimbs serves dozens of veterans, but only those who served in Iraq during a specific time span have been the victims of these accidents. That is not a coincidence. It's significant, but I don't know why."

The sound of my cell ringing startled me. I grabbed it out of my pocket and looked at the caller.

"It's Mr. Kars," I said to Wally before punching the Accept button. "Hello, Mr. Kars?"

"Ms. Sinclair?"

"Yes, it's me. Thank you for calling back. I've got some important information to tell you about...well, you know, the problem."

"I'm going to stop you right there. There is *no* problem. I don't want you to call me again. I believe you are a very intelligent but misguided young woman. BioLimbs is handling this matter internally."

"What? But we found—"

"There is *no* problem. I do not wish to hear from you again. We are no longer working with X-Corp. Our connection is hereby terminated." He hung up.

I stared at the phone is disbelief. "I can't believe it. He hung up on me. He didn't even let me explain. He says they are no longer working with X-Corp."

"What?" Frankie gasped.

"If he had given me three minutes of his time, I could have told him exactly where the malicious code is located." My thoughts spun in disbelief.

Frankie looked between Wally and me. "What are we going to do now?"

"Can you reach Lexi?" Wally suggested.

"I can try." I dialed Lexi's number. When she didn't pick up, I left her a message to call back when she had a chance. I added that it was about BioLimbs and urgent, in the hope she'd make a return call to me a priority.

I leaned back in my chair and tried to still my thoughts. In the meantime, what could we do? We were three high school kids who knew squat about how to deal with a mysterious cracker who was apparently trying to control the prostheses of American veterans.

What would Lexi do?

Then...just like that, I knew. I'd set a trap.

The more I thought about it, the more I liked the idea. If we could uncover the identity of the cracker, it would help us determine the motive and the next steps to take to stop the hacking.

I looked up at Wally. "I've got an idea."

"I'm glad you do, because I'm coming up blank. What have you got?"

"We're going to catch the cracker ourselves." I looked between Wally and Frankie. "But I'm going to need both of your help to pull it off."

Wally's eyes flashed with interest. "You've certainly got my full attention."

"Mine, too," Frankie added. "Although I'm not sure what I can contribute."

"A lot," I assured her. "Wally, are you in?"

Wally gave me a small salute. "I am. What do you have in mind?"

Grinning, I leaned over my keyboard and showed them.

CHAPTER FORTY-THREE

Angel Sinclair

"A mirror app?" Wally breathed after I'd outlined my plan. "Are you crazy? Wait, don't answer that. I already know you are if you're considering this."

"I'm fully aware this is a dangerous proposition, but it's the easiest way to trap him at this point," I said calmly.

"What's a mirror app?" Frankie asked.

"It's an exact replica of the original app, including the installation component, but it's just that…a mirror," I explained. "The hacker thinks he's hacking the actual app, when in reality he's hacking a fake app—one I created to mirror the actual one."

"How does that trap him?" she asked.

"I'll tag him. I should be able to pinpoint his location, and it will give me the chance to watch the hacking in real time. That could provide important clues to his or her identity as well. It's not a perfect solution, but it gives us a fighting chance."

"What makes you think he'll be going in to modify the program?" Wally asked.

"I don't think he's finished with the code that's currently in there. He's got his next target in the crosshairs, but he's got to refine it. We're going to stop him."

"How?" Frankie leaned on the table, her brows scrunched together.

"Because he'll be making those modifications in the fake app only. None of these instructions will go to anyone's actual app."

"But what if someone from BioLimbs has to make legitimate updates?" Wally asked.

"I'll see it and make sure they get where they need to go," I said with confidence. "Trust me."

"Think about it a bit longer, Angel. This is a seriously dangerous proposition," Wally said, blowing out a breath. "You do know this is illegal, right? If BioLimbs finds out what you're doing, they could press charges. You could go to jail."

"Hacking is illegal in whatever format it happens. I know, Wally. I'm willing to take the risk. This is on me, guys, but I need your help."

Frankie surprised me by putting her hand on the table, palm up. "If we're talking about saving a life, or lives, I'm in."

Wally looked at me for a long moment and then laid his hand on top of Frankie's. "I guess sometimes doing the right thing is dangerous."

I nodded and laid my hand on top of theirs. "One for all and all for one, then. Now let's get to work."

It took nearly five and half hours, including a break for lunch at a nearby deli, before we were finished. Our parents were delirious with the thought that we were working so hard on a Saturday, presumably on homework. No one asked for specifics, so we didn't volunteer any.

The final product made the time spent worth it. My

neck, back, and wrists ached, but Wally and I had successfully set a trap. A clever one, if I did say so myself. We'd created a mirror site. Anyone outside BioLimbs would have to enter through our site to get to the program where the malicious code was hidden. Our site was filled with all kinds of tracking and tracers, so I would know everything about the person who infiltrated. Now Frankie was adding the final visual touches to our site to make everything look legitimate.

I looked over her shoulder for the umpteenth time and whistled at her progress. "How did you create that so fast?"

"How do you write a string of code so fast?" She didn't lift her gaze from the monitor.

"Practice?" I considered. "Trial and error?"

"Precisely. Plus, I'm copying someone else's design. That makes it a lot faster than creating something original."

"Seriously, Frankie, when you talk like that, it totally turns me on," Wally said. "Can you make fake IDs, too? If so, I may have to marry you."

I rolled my eyes. "Don't distract her, Wally."

"I'm not distracting her. I'm praising her wicked skill. It's different."

"In the room, you know." Frankie paused, flexing her fingers. "Yes, Wally, I can make fake IDs. Not that I'm in that business. I have no intention of going to jail, this particular hack notwithstanding. But I may have made one or two in my past. I'm pretty certain I could do a decent job given enough time and access to the graphics I'd need."

"Sweet," Wally said, peering over her other shoulder. "No wonder your posters are so good. I bow to your skill."

"You may call me QDG. Bowing is allowed. More potato chips would be better."

"QDG?" Wally asked.

"Queen of digital graphics," I explained. "Just go with it."

After a few more minutes, Frankie pushed back from my laptop. "Done. Is this good enough?"

I slid into the vacated seat. "Is it good enough? Frankie, it's sheer perfection. I'm totally impressed. Amazing work, White Knights. Let me finish this off and we'll call it a day. A long day."

I wrote a bit more code and asked for Wally's review. He tweaked one section and we were done.

I closed my laptop. "Okay, that's it. The trap is officially set. I will receive an alert if it's sprung. From there on, it is a matter of tracing back the steps until we find our perpetrator."

"So we wait?" Frankie asked.

"Welcome to my world," I said. "We wait."

Frankie stood, stretched. "Can I be the first to say it feels like I'm in the Scooby gang, except we have Wally's beat-up car instead of the groovy van? We're hunting a hacker and saving our vice principal. Totally ace."

"My car is not beat-up," Wally protested. "It's got character, remember?"

"Oh, right," Frankie said.

"Just so everybody knows, this is not going to be as simple as pulling a plastic mask off the bad guy," I warned, but I smiled anyway. "But yeah, this mystery-solving thing is pretty cool."

Frankie grinned. "If we had to assign Scooby-like roles...Angel gets to be Velma, no contest. You're totally the brain of this operation."

"Hey," Wally protested. "I have a brain, too."

Frankie pretended she didn't hear him. "I'm definitely not Daphne-like, although I do have my own style of fashion. However, I'm good at making friends, so I'm more like a female version of Shaggy."

Wally narrowed his eyes at her. "I swear, Frankie, if you say I'm the dog, I'm never driving you anywhere again."

Frankie and I both laughed. We slung our laptop bags over our shoulders and headed out of the library.

"Now that we have a logo, I think the White Knights should also have a theme song," Frankie said.

I stopped in my tracks. "No. Just no. No theme song. I'm putting my foot down on this one."

"Seriously? You need to loosen up, Angel," Frankie pouted. "Have some fun."

"Hey, we just spent the day hacking. What do you mean I don't know how to have fun?"

"See?" Frankie sighed dramatically. "Point made."

After we pigged out on ice cream—my treat—Wally drove us home. He dropped me off first and then took Frankie home.

My mom was watching television when I came in. "That was a lot of studying. Ready for dinner?"

"Not really. I just ate ice cream. I kind of have a stomachache."

"Oh. I was thinking about going to see Mr. Matthews at the hospital, anyway. Want to come with me?"

"No, thanks. But if he's awake, tell him I said hi."

She stood and kissed the top of my head. "Sure will. See you in a bit."

After she left, I went to my room, set up my laptop, and checked the mirror app. Untouched so far.

Now I had some alone time, there were two things I wanted to do. First, check on Nic's website and see if he'd unveiled a new, shocking lie. Second, I needed to follow up on some leads regarding my dad. I wanted to go through some of the material I'd downloaded from my hack into King's Security.

I pulled up Nic's website and my phone dinged, indicating a text. I stood and dug it out of my pocket. It was Colt.

Are you home?

I stared at the words, surprised he still wanted to talk to me and wondering why he cared if I were home or not. I'd been so busy I hadn't even had time to process the things I'd found out about him and his reasons for leaving St. Michael's. Now I wished I hadn't looked and didn't know. But I did. I'd crossed a line, and now there was no going back.

I perched on the edge of my bed and tapped my phone.

I'm home.

Do you have time to talk? Can I call you, please?

I didn't want to, but I had to face this sometime. Guilt had already started to make my stomach churn.

Okay.

A few seconds later, my phone rang. I inhaled a deep breath.

"Hello."

"Hi, Angel. Thanks for taking my call. I wasn't sure you would."

"I wasn't sure I would, either."

Silence stretched on before he finally spoke. "I owe you an explanation."

"No. You really don't. Let's forget the whole thing, okay? This is on me."

"This isn't on you."

"Fine. End of conversation. Goodbye."

"Angel, will you listen, please? This is hard enough for me as it is."

I closed my eyes. "I'm listening."

Colt was silent for so long I thought he'd hung up. I looked at my phone, but we were still connected.

Finally, he spoke. "I want you to know something about me."

"Colt, you don't have to tell me anything."

"I know. But I *want* you to know." He fell silent again, and I could feel how difficult this was for him, which made the guilt twist my stomach up even more.

"You don't have to say it," I blurted out. "I...already know. I found out online." The confession spilled out. Shame, guilt, misery, and embarrassment swept over me.

I waited for him to say something...anything, but there was only silence. The analog clock on the wall my mom had bought when I was six ticked loudly. I braced myself, knowing I deserved every terrible word he was going to say.

"Mad computer skills," he finally said. "I should have expected that. Did you hack into my former school as well?"

My cheeks heated. "I'm sorry, Colt. Curiosity and a burning need to get to the bottom of every mystery is my worst fault. Yes, I went places I shouldn't have. But I didn't tell anyone what I found. I promise you that."

Again, dead freaking silence. Embarrassment swept through me, hot and fierce. For the first time in my life, I was faced directly with the feelings of a person whose privacy had been hacked. Whose privacy I'd invaded. Although I hadn't shared any of the information with anyone else, it didn't absolve me.

Right now, I didn't like myself very much.

"I made a terrible mistake, Colt. I had no right. My pride was hurt and I was mad. I should have never violated your privacy."

"No, you shouldn't have."

My shame deepened. "Not that it excuses me whatsoever, but I was so mad you didn't show. I let my anger get the better of me."

"I had no idea you would step in for me—take charge of the Brains. That was crazy…and brave."

"It was sheer desperation. I was completely humiliated in front of the entire school and now, most of cyberspace, losing my shirt—literally—in the process of losing the game. Then you showed up and offered some lame apology. That only made it worse, you know."

"It wasn't one of my finer moments," he admitted.

"I'm really sorry, Colt. This has been a painful lesson for me. I was terribly, horribly wrong to do what I did."

"I'm sorry, too."

I was trying to figure out what to say next when I glanced at my open laptop. Nic's sleazy website had been updated.

The headline, screaming in all caps, read *EXCALIBUR'S STAR QUARTERBACK IS GAY!*

CHAPTER FORTY-FOUR

Angel Sinclair

The breath whooshed out of me as if someone had punched me in the gut. I stood horrified, staring in disbelief at the headline.

"Angel?" Colt said. "Are you still there?"

I couldn't speak. How did Nic know? It had to be my fault. Nic was obsessed with me, following my every move, and I'd led him straight to Colt.

OMG.

I found my voice. "Colt, do you know a guy named Nic Nerezza?"

"Is he that creepy guy with dark hair, weird eyes, and a smug attitude?"

"That's him. What you might not know about him is that he's the one running the disgusting website nothingbutthetruth.com."

Colt snorted. "You mean the one that spouts everything *but* the truth? The one printing all that crap about Mr. Matthews?"

"That's the one. And now…" I gulped. "I'm so sorry. I don't know how to say this. Before you called, I was

269

on his website trying to figure out whether it was worth the hack to try to take it down again—"

"Whoa, wait. You hacked that website, too? And brought it down?"

"Well, yes, but *that* was for a good cause. I brought it down briefly. Nic is a pretty experienced hacker himself, so I can't keep it down permanently."

"Okay, first, I'm totally floored you did that. Second, why are you sorry?"

I hesitated. "Because you're the new headline, Colt."

"What?"

"I swear I didn't tell him. I didn't tell anyone."

I could hear Colt moving, then typing, presumably pulling up the website himself. Then silence.

"I…don't know how he found out." My words ran together. "I think I might have inadvertently led him to you. Nic is obsessed with me, or at least with trying to best me academically. He might have been cyberstalking me. I should have taken special precautions. I feel sick."

I'd never, *ever* felt like this about hacking before. This wasn't why I hacked. This wasn't me. And yet…I'd invaded his privacy, learned things about him that were none of my business.

Finally, Colt spoke. "I believe you, Angel." His voice sounded weary, glum. "Apparently, as you discovered, the information is not that hard to uncover if you're determined to find it."

"I feel awful, Colt. Worse than awful."

"Not much to be done about it at this point," he said. "The cat's out of the bag, so to say. Again."

"That's why you had to leave St. Michael's? They found out you're gay? I mean, who cares?"

"They care. The school has a morality clause as part of their school charter. I made a mistake by confiding in a teacher about my orientation. That teacher betrayed my trust. I could have stayed at St. Michael's if I'd

renounced my orientation and agreed to undergo special counseling. That's what my parents wanted me to do. I admit I considered it. I had a lot of friends at St. Michael's, excellent grades, and contributed to several athletic teams. But I'll be honest. I couldn't do it—the therapy, the counseling. I just wanted to be who I am."

I was silent for a minute, absorbing the sadness in his voice. "I had no idea a school could do that."

"Private religious institutions can. The reasoning is fair—if the student doesn't respect the beliefs of the school or the church, or lives in a manner that openly rejects those beliefs, the school has the right to expel the student. In my case, after I refused counseling, they let me withdraw instead of being expelled. I appreciated that, at least."

"That's just...awful, Colt. What about your parents? Did they know you're gay?"

"I thought they suspected, but I was wrong. It took them completely by surprise. They had no idea. They were devastated, of course. My orientation is something they don't understand and can't easily accept, given their beliefs and upbringing. It's going to take us time. But they've supported me anyway, the best they can. I appreciate that. It's not easy for any of us, but we're working through it."

"Does Mr. Matthews know?"

"Yeah, he's friends with my dad from the Marines. He knows, as does Headmistress Swanson. Mr. Matthews made the transition from St. Michael's easy for us as a family. He wasn't judgmental at all, which surprised my dad, I think. It's also why I wanted to support you and your efforts to help him. I hadn't intended to come out at Excalibur, because I'm trying to make things easier for my parents until I go to college. I thought I could manage two more years so long as I didn't have to lie about who I am. I'd started

271

to believe I could fly under the radar and make it to graduation. Then, when you said there were going to be television and camera crews at the melee, I panicked. I didn't want that kind of exposure in case someone recognized me. Then kids would start talking, and I'd be outed all over again. Excalibur parents would start talking to my parents, and we'd go through the same public hell."

I blew out a breath. "Holy crap. I had no idea. I thought you were just blowing me off. What about you being Excalibur's star quarterback? Wouldn't kids from other schools see you and realized where you moved?"

"We don't play Catholic schools, which is the only reason I agreed to be on Excalibur's team. That, and I really like playing football."

"Wow. This is *so* not fair."

"No, it's not," he agreed. "Regardless, my life is about to turn into a living nightmare at high school. Again."

Helplessness, shame, and regret swamped me. This was *my* fault, and I didn't have a clue how to help him. Still, I had to do something, offer the one thing I had at my disposal.

"I feel like a million apologizes from me aren't going to be enough." I paused and then said what I needed to say. "So, I'll offer the one thing that might make a small difference—from here on out, I'm going to have your back, Colt. To be honest, I think you'll find a lot of students at Excalibur won't care what the heck your orientation is as long as you're a good guy, an even better lab partner...and maybe a half-decent quarterback and/or pitcher."

He chuckled. "That may be the nicest thing anyone ever said to me."

"Don't get used to it," I warned. "I don't normally do nice."

"Oh, no worries, Angel. Your secret is safe with me."

I smiled for the first time in the conversation and leaned back in my chair. "Why are people so unfair?"

"It is what it is."

"I know *exactly* what this is, Colt. It's war. Nic Nerezza is going down. And this time, I'm not backing off until he's finished for good."

CHAPTER FORTY-FIVE

Angel Sinclair

Less than four minutes after I hung up with Colt, Wally called me. "Red alert. We have an emergency. Have you seen Nic's website?"

"I'm looking at it now."

"Can you believe it?" He let out a loud sigh. "Nic is such a tool. Like Colt McCarrell would be gay. Seriously? Next thing you know, Nic will be telling everyone *I'm* gay. Just because I've never dated a girl, kissed a girl, or barely talked to a girl—other than you and Frankie, it doesn't mean I'm gay."

"Wally, I don't *care* who's gay." I gritted my teeth. "Will you zip it and listen? We must stop Nic and his toxic website once and for all. I can't waste time bringing it down because he'll bring it right back up. We'll have to do something else to shut him down. Something that will discredit him and his website for good."

"I'm totally onboard with that, of course, but what do you have in mind? And what about the trap for the cracker? That's why I called."

"Let me worry about the trap. I've got another task for you. We need to figure out a plan to deal with Nic. What's your schedule look like tomorrow afternoon?"

"Must you ask? My social schedule is always an empty book."

"Good. Come over at one o'clock sharp and bring your laptop. Oh, and can you see if Frankie is available to come, too?"

"What? First I'm your chauffeur, and now I'm your secretary? This better be worth it, because I'm looking forward to some serious hacking."

My eyes strayed back to Nic's website and the screaming headline. "Me, too, Wally. Me, too."

CHAPTER FORTY-SIX

Isaac Remington

"We've got a problem."

Isaac held the burner phone in one hand and had the other hand on the steering wheel. He had a raging headache. The last thing he needed right now was a problem.

"What is it? I just spent an uncomfortable hour on a Saturday in Candace's office answering and evading questions about the investigation. She refuses to let me into the negotiations."

"Does she suspect anything?"

"I doubt it. She's keeping me abreast of everything. She wants to be in control so she can take all the credit, if she brings him in."

"That's unfortunate."

"I know. She kept harping on Lando's accident. She claimed her gut told her it was related somehow and she was going to get to the bottom of it."

Silence, and then the person on the other end of the phone spoke. "She'd better be careful. Accidents can happen to anyone."

Isaac rubbed his temple. "The fact she's personally

invested in finding the Hidden Avenger and handling all negotiations is inopportune, to say the least. Still, she had to be pacified, so I did my best. Unfortunately, the woman has a nose for evasion, and it took a lot of hard work to pull it off."

"I bet."

"So, what's the problem?" Isaac was exhausted and wanted nothing more than a quiet dinner, a bath, and a glass of brandy. Instead, he had to deal with a new problem.

"The daughter has a special connection."

Isaac blinked and slowed the car to stop at a light. "What kind of connection?"

"She has an internship at a cybersecurity firm called X-Corp."

"Why should I care about that?"

"Her mentor is Lexi Carmichael."

The name was familiar, but Isaac still couldn't make the connection. "Who is she?"

"The live-in girlfriend of the new director of the Information Assurance Directorate."

"Our IAD?"

"The one and only."

Isaac closed his eyes. "Slash?" He did not want—could not afford—to have Slash snooping around the operation. He posed a significant danger if he were to find out about the core group.

"Yes. Slash."

"That's not good. Do everything you can to keep her out of things. I want to be notified immediately if there is any involvement of her or IAD."

"Of course."

The car behind Isaac honked impatiently. He opened his eyes, moving his car forward. He felt rage rising and clenched one hand on the steering wheel, somehow managing to keep the anger in check. "I cannot emphasize how important it is that IAD does *not* become involved in this, especially Slash. Is that understood?"

"Yes, sir."

"Keep observing the daughter. I still believe she's the key to finding him."

CHAPTER FORTY-SEVEN

Angel Sinclair

The trap alarm went off at 8:42 the next morning, waking me from a deep sleep. I must have been having a nightmare, because my cheeks were wet when I awoke and bolted to my laptop. I slipped into the chair, my fingers flying across the keyboard even as my brain was still waking up.

Someone had entered the mirror app and was already coding. My heart pounded as I studied the string of code he was writing, confirming I'd caught the perpetrator red-handed. I opened another window and started my trace. As far as I could tell, the cracker had no idea I was there or he was in a mirror site. After a few minutes, I located his IP address. I couldn't get an exact address without a court order, but I had enough. A quick search indicated was using a block IP address owned by the Smithsonian. Although I couldn't be sure, my best guess would be that the perpetrator was sitting in the new cybercafé in the Air and Space Museum, because any decent hacker would want the speed. It was only forty minutes away from my apartment.

"Holy crap," I murmured. "The cracker is right in my backyard."

I sent a group text to Wally and Frankie letting them know the cracker had sprung the trap and his location was right here in DC. My plan to bring down Nic's website had just gotten pushed to the back burner in terms of immediacy.

Frankie called me immediately. "What? The cracker is at the Smithsonian? Right now? This is so exciting. It's like a James Bond/Jason Bourne/Scooby-Doo episode all rolled into one."

I resisted commenting. Not like I had a ready response. "It's going to take some time for him to finish coding—a few hours, at least. If he's in the café, we'll find him. If he's a Smithsonian employee, we're in a harder place. It's not like we can go knocking on office doors. But I don't think he's a museum employee. That's a gut feeling. I think he's there to use the Wi-Fi."

"Did Lexi call you back yet?"

"No." I blew out a breath. "But it hasn't even been twenty-four hours since I called her. She could be on assignment or something. Regardless, I don't think we can wait to do it."

"Do what?" Frankie asked.

"Catch the cracker, of course."

Less than an hour later, Wally and Frankie were both at my apartment. My mom couldn't have been more thrilled, thinking we were going to the Smithsonian to work on a school project. She'd even provided some homemade brownies to fortify us before she headed out to meet a friend for coffee and a movie.

"You have mad cooking skills, Mrs. S," Frankie said.

She'd dyed pink streaks into her hair and wore matching pink leggings and a short-sleeved black tunic. Silver earrings with pink stones wound up her lobes. She looked like a cute Asian flamingo. "You'll have to share the recipe."

My mom didn't bat an eye at the outfit, so maybe it was just me.

"You're so sweet, Frankie." My mom slung her purse over her shoulder. "There are more brownies in the jar on the counter if you want to take some with you."

After my mom left, I stood in front of the gang.

"Are you ready?" I asked. "We all know there might be danger involved. Possibly even physical danger."

Wally crossed his arms against his chest. "Ha! I spit in the eye of danger."

"Of course I'm in," Frankie said. "The White Knights are on the case."

Wally drove to museum, where we spent another fifteen minutes driving around until we found an open space at a parking meter. It was a pretty Sunday afternoon, still warm for September.

As we walked toward the entrance, Wally filled us in on the history of the museum. "Did you know there are two National Air and Space Museums?"

"I did," I said.

"Did you know the museum started in 1876 when a group of kites was acquired from the Chinese Imperial Commission."

"The museum started with a kite?" I glanced at him in surprise. "Really?"

"Really."

"Sometimes I wonder about all the trivial facts locked inside your head," Frankie said. "You're a walking encyclopedia."

"If that's your way of saying I'm brilliant, I accept the compliment." Wally grinned at her, and she laughed.

We had to check our backpacks and computers through the magnetometer. We headed straight for the sleek, new cybercafé tucked into the corner of the upper floor. The museum was crowded, as always, but we found a table in the corner facing both the entrance and exit. As I glanced around, there were a lot of people, most with computers, naturally.

We pulled our laptops out and plugged them into a nearby outlet.

"How are we going to find who it is?" Frankie asked in a low voice as her computer booted up. "It could be anyone in the café."

"It could," I whispered. "But I'll figure it out. Let me make sure he's still in the app coding. It's only been about an hour and half since he, or she, tripped the alarm. I sincerely doubt that's enough time to finish the hack."

Wally and Frankie began staring at everyone in the room until I told them to stop.

"Can you be a little less obvious?" I snapped.

"Sorry," Frankie mumbled.

It only took me a few minutes to confirm the hacker was still at work right here at the museum somewhere. "He's still here," I hissed. "And the odds are high he's working right here in the café. We have to check it out."

Wally gulped, staring at his screen. "This was a lot more fun when it was theoretical."

"Walk around the room and take selfies of each other," I instructed them. "Be casual, but try to get a look at everyone's screen. Wally, it's up to you. You know what to look for."

"Yeah, I know." Grimly, he stood, grabbing his phone in one hand and Frankie's arm in the other. "Come on, Cinderella. Smile pretty."

They started going around the room taking pictures. They did it right, two teenage kids having fun, posing for pictures. I took some notes and watched the cracker work online. He typed steadily away, which meant whoever we were looking for would be intent on his work. Focused, working, hacking.

I pushed the lid of my laptop down and scanned the room. Wally and Frankie were on the left side of the café laughing, joking, and taking more photos. There were plenty of people working on their laptops, but where was my cracker?

I ruled out several people right away because they were either not focused on their computers or weren't engaged enough to be involved in a crack. I also eliminated, for now, those working on a computer who were there with other people. The person I was looking for would almost certainly be solo.

There were a few guys on the right side of the room who seemed deeply involved in their work. It didn't mean they were hackers, but I wanted Wally to get a better look at them. When Wally glanced my way, I tipped my head to that corner.

He got the message. He began steering Frankie in that direction. They took a couple more pictures over in that area before Wally abruptly walked back to me. Frankie followed, clearly confused.

"What's going on?" I hissed as he sat down.

"We don't have to look anymore," Wally said, his face serious. "I know who the hacker is."

CHAPTER FORTY-EIGHT

Angel Sinclair

M y eyes widened. "You saw his screen?" I asked excitedly.

"Not exactly."

Frankie plopped into her chair. "Thank goodness that's done. No offense, Wally, but my mouth is tired from fake smiling."

Wally didn't answer and started typing on his laptop while I watched him, mystified. After a minute, he angled his laptop toward me.

"Omar Haider."

The screen filled, showing a man with dark hair and a dark mustache. I looked between the picture and Wally. "The guy we are talking about at school in Red Teaming?"

"The one and only."

Frankie peered at his screen over my shoulder. "Who is Omar Hairless?"

Wally snorted. "Haider. He's one of the architects of a bioengineering artificial intelligence research study."

I stared at Wally in disbelief. "Haider is here? In Washington?"

"Not just here, but *here*, sitting right over there hacking." Wally lowered his voice. "I got a good look at his face and his screen." He held up his phone. "Even snapped a photo, too. I recognized him from the paper today."

My head was spinning. "What paper?"

Wally tapped some more keys and pulled up the front page of the *Washington Post*. In the lower left corner was a picture of two men smiling and shaking hands. I scanned the article attached to the picture. I read the headline aloud. "'Iraq's New Cybersecurity Guru Pledges Cooperation With Director of US Cyber Command.'" Looking over at the corner, I tried to make out Haider, but he was too far away to see clearly. "Are you saying Omar Haider is here on some kind of diplomatic mission to pledge cyber-cooperation with the US?"

"That's what I'm saying," Wally said.

"But why would he want to hack prostheses?"

"Why, indeed?" Wally answered. "But I guarantee you this is our guy. Let's see if we can find out what his deal is."

While Wally started his background investigation on Omar Haider, I watched the hack. The more I watched the things the cracker was doing—stuff I'd never imagined, let alone seen—the more I thought Wally might be on to something.

"This guy is incredible," I murmured. "Wizard level."

"He fits the profile." Wally looked up from his monitor. "Omar Haider was born in Baghdad to a well-off family. His father is an engineer and currently employed at the Ministry of Health in an unknown position. No info on the mother. He has—make that *had*—one older brother, named Adir. More on that later. Despite wars, conflicts, government changes, coups, and so on, Omar managed to graduate with an undergraduate degree in computer studies from the University of Baghdad and went on to get a master's of computer engineering at EPITA, which is a privately endowed technical educational institution right outside Paris. That's probably where he met Gustav Monteray and they launched their research. Haider's first job once he was back in Iraq was with the Ministry of Communications, where it looks like he was basically delegated to be the IT guy. Which means he was probably the only guy who knew anything about computers. He survived all the government changes and it looks like he got elected to form a cybersecurity framework for Iraq."

"Iraq doesn't have a cybersecurity plan?" I asked in surprise.

"Nope. They don't even have a government agency responsible for cybersecurity. Apparently, Haider is in Washington, in an official capacity, attending a three-day comprehensive cybersecurity building program, which he hopes to recreate in Iraq."

"So why in the world would he hack the prostheses of American veterans?" Frankie asked, her eyes wide. "You think he's like a cyberterrorist or something?"

"No." Wally shook his head, pushing his fingers through his hair. "I don't think it's terrorism. I don't think it's a political statement, either. I think it's personal."

That surprised me. "Personal? Why?" Another glance at my screen indicated the cracker was still deep into the hack. We hackers referred to that place as "the zone." Under most circumstances, that meant we had a bit more time while he worked things out. But this wasn't most circumstances, and Omar Haider wasn't any run-of-the-mill hacker.

"Because American soldiers killed his brother, Adir."

Frankie and I both gasped.

"*What?*" Frankie clapped her hand over her mouth and peered over Wally's shoulder at the screen. "What happened?"

"Friendly fire. It was an accident."

I blew out a breath. "That's terrible. Look, I'm contacting Lexi again. Regardless of Mr. Haider's motive, if it's him doing the hacking, we can't let anyone else to get hurt or killed. It stops right now...with us."

I grabbed my phone and started texting Lexi, briefly outlining our suspicions and letting her know we were with Haider at the Smithsonian. I pushed Send and set my phone down.

"Do you know anything else about Mr. Haider?" I asked Wally.

"I've only scanned open sources so far, but get this. His father's job at the Ministry of Health...he's not just an engineer. He's a *bioengineer.*"

"That's bad," I murmured. "If Haider is inside BioLimbs' system, he has access to proprietary information. He could steal it and pass it to his father."

"That's a real possibility," Wally said seriously. "It's called industrial spying. That would be an ideal setup for him. He could steal technical information *and* exact revenge on his brother's killers."

"Was Mr. Matthews involved in the friendly fire incident where Adir Haider was killed?" Frankie asked.

"I don't know." Wally lifted his hands. "Those specific details are not for public consumption. It would require a much deeper hack into the Department of Defense. Sorry, but I'm not going there from here. But I'm betting he was."

My phone dinged, indicating I had a text message. I snatched it off the table. "It's from Lexi."

> Sorry. I've been out of the country. We know about Mr. Haider. Will explain later. We are coming to the museum. Please do everything you can to stall him until we get there. However, do NOT put yourselves in danger. If he leaves, do NOT follow him. Understood?

I handed my phone to Wally and Frankie so they could read it. "Time for the Scooby gang to get real," Frankie whispered.

I glanced at my screen, and my heart skipped a beat. "Guys, he's finishing up with the hack."

"What?" Panic flashed in Wally's eyes as he handed me back my phone. "What are we going to do? How are we supposed to stall him?"

I stuck my phone in my pocket. My mind raced. I had absolutely no clue.

"We could spill something on him," Frankie suggested. "Make him clean up. That takes time."

"That won't get him to stick around," Wally protested. "That will only make him leave sooner."

"I have an idea," I said. "You stay here, Wally. Frankie and I are going to go fangirl over him."

"Say again." Frankie crinkled her brow. "I'm going to do *what?*"

"Fangirl. Follow my lead."

"Are you crazy?" Wally hissed. "This guy is trying to murder people. Don't go near him."

I looked over at him. Haider had already closed his laptop. I shoved my own computer into the bag. "No time to argue. Just do what I say. Pack up, everyone." I slung my laptop strap over my shoulder and looked at Frankie. "Act normal, okay?"

"I *always* act normal except when I'm nervous, which I am right now. You, however, are the tightest-wound fangirl I've ever seen."

She was right, but I didn't answer since we were almost to Omar Haider's table. My heart hammered so hard in my chest, I was afraid I might pass out. He glanced up at us. Surprise and then wariness flashed in his eyes. "Can I help you young ladies with something?"

"Excuse me, but are you Omar Haider?" I said, hoping I sounded like an awestruck fan. "I saw your picture in the *Washington Post.* We're studying your research at my high school. I go to a school for kids who are gifted in science and technology." My words came out in a horrid squeak because a.) I was freaking terrified, b.) I hated talking to strangers—well, people in general, and c.) I was facing a murderer.

Maybe because I was genuinely nervous, he seemed to relax. He leaned back in his chair, crossing his legs. "Yes, I am Omar Haider. You are high school students?"

"Yes. Your work on artificial intelligence and bioengineering is amazing. Seriously cool."

"It's pretty advanced material."

"We're discussing the overall implications of your research on cybersecurity."

"Interesting that American schools are examining my research." He looked at us thoughtfully.

"Yeah," Frankie added with enthusiasm. "Your work is fascinating. That thingy you did with the...um...computer was amazing."

It took everything I had not to smack Frankie on the back of the head. Thingy? He'd never believe we were gifted students.

"Anyway, Mr. Haider, we wondered if you had time to give us your latest thoughts on AI and cybersecurity," I said. "I could share it with the class."

He sipped his coffee, studied us. "Actually, I'm sorry. I have an appointment. I must go now."

"Oh, no! That's too bad. Way too bad." My blood

pressure jumped. "Maybe you could give us a brief summary."

"I'm afraid not. It was nice to meet you, girls." He slid his laptop into his bag.

"Wait. Would you mind if we got our picture with you first?" I asked. Before he could answer in the negative, I whipped out my phone and ran behind him. "We'll take a couple of selfies. Right, Frankie? Won't that be cool to show everybody at school?"

"Totally cool." She rushed over beside me, and we bent down with Omar's head between us. I pretended to fuss with the angle and light until I sensed his impatience. I snapped a couple and then looked at Frankie behind his back with panic in my expression. We couldn't let him leave yet.

She read my desperation and moved around to the front of him. "Well, it's been great to meet you, Mr. Laider."

"Haider," I coughed.

"Right." She stuck her hand out and, in the process, knocked his coffee cup into his lap. Omar jumped up with a yelp while Frankie gasped in shock.

"Oh, I am *so* sorry." She grabbed a couple of napkins and started to dab him. "I'm such a klutz."

He stepped back, shaking the coffee off his hands. "It's okay. I'll go clean it off."

"We'll wait here with your stuff," I volunteered.

He wiped his hands on a dry spot on his pants. He started to leave and then, after a moment's thought, he grabbed his laptop bag. "I'll be right back for my jacket."

He headed to the bathroom. As soon as he was out of sight, I motioned to Wally to follow him. Wally vigorously shook his head no, looking scared. I glared at him until he got up and headed reluctantly to the bathroom.

I turned to Frankie. "Way to stall."

She was still mopping up the coffee from the table. "Well, he was already leaving. We didn't have anything to lose. Sorry. I had to think on my feet."

I rubbed my temples. "It was better than what I could come up with, which was zip."

Two minutes later, my phone dinged. It was a frantic message from Wally.

> He's on to us! He went to bathroom, but not coming back for jacket. He's pushing the Down button for elevator.

I quickly texted back.

> Stay with him, Wally. Do NOT let him out of your sight.

I shoved the phone in my pocket and jumped up. "Haider is at the elevator. Hurry." I snatched his jacket as we raced to the elevator, our laptop bags banging against our thighs.

Unfortunately, the elevator had already arrived, and Omar was on it.

"Wait!" I shouted. "Mr. Haider. You forgot your jacket."

It was too late. We screeched to a halt as the elevator doors closed. The last thing I saw was Wally's face, as white as a sheet, standing alone in the elevator with a killer.

CHAPTER FORTY-NINE

Angel Sinclair

"**C**ome on!" I shouted at Frankie, whirling around and racing down the corridor toward the escalator. I grabbed the handrail and swung onto the moving steps, taking two at a time and startling a couple of tourists as I pushed past.

I could see the elevator moving. I wasn't going to make it in time to intercept Omar, not to mention, I had no plan in mind how to keep him in the museum, especially if he suspected we were up to something. I also had no illusions that Wally could stop him after seeing the deathly pallor of his face when the elevator closed.

I could barely breathe as I flew down the steps. I was halfway down the escalator when the elevator door opened. Omar stepped out. Thank all the stars above, Wally also walked out behind him, alive and apparently unharmed.

Omar took a few steps, and Wally dutifully followed. At that moment, disaster struck. Omar whirled around to face Wally, grabbing him by the collar of his shirt and saying something to him.

Wally was so startled he almost collapsed. My heart leaped to my throat as I jumped down the last three steps on the escalator and raced toward them without a clear idea of what was next. I was about fifty feet from them when suddenly Wally saved the day.

He hurled. When I say hurl, I'm being literal. He sprayed Omar right in the chest as if he were holding a hose.

Omar cursed and released Wally, taking a step back. I skidded to a halt about fifteen feet away, torn between saving Wally and being grossed out by the barf fest. Frankie came up behind me. She put a hand on my shoulder, breathing hard. "Thanks for waiting for me."

"Angel!"

I spun around. That voice was familiar. "Lexi!"

Lexi ran toward me, waving a hand. Right beside her were Slash, two guys in dark suits, and a Smithsonian security guard. Omar didn't even try to run. He stood there in disbelief, dripping in Wally's puke.

Wally dropped to his knees, still shaking, but at least he wasn't throwing up anymore. Lexi stopped next to me as Slash and the two guys in suits surrounded Omar and started to speak to him quietly. The security guard helped Wally to his feet, and a couple of other security guards started a protective perimeter around us, keeping curious tourists away.

"What the heck were you doing?" Lexi asked me with a frown. "What part of *do not* follow him didn't you understand?"

"We weren't going to follow him, but then he bolted. Didn't even come back for his jacket." I was still holding it. "I think he knew something wasn't right. He tried to slip out. I told Wally to get in the elevator with him. I don't know what I was thinking. I didn't want him to get away."

"I'm glad you're okay. Just so you know, Gwen would have had my head on a platter if anything had happened to you. Between you and me, your sister kind scares me when she gets all fired up."

"Join the club." We shared a smile, imagining Gwen, all five foot three of her, scolding us. "What took you guys so long?"

"What do you think? Traffic. Even on a Sunday, it took us longer than expected to reach the head of security at the museum and explain our suspicions. They'd just gone on alert at the exits. I spotted you right away, racing across the room with a look of sheer panic on your face."

"He had Wally by the collar." My heart jumped again, remembering it. I calmed myself by looking at Wally and realizing that, while shaken, he was alive.

"Yeah, I saw that, too," Lexi said. "He looks okay now. Who's your friend here?"

Frankie was staring at Slash from across the room with her mouth open. I rudely elbowed her in the stomach, and she grunted in surprise.

"Lexi, meet Frankie. Frankie is my...friend and one-third of the White Knights."

Lexi raised an eyebrow. "White Knights?"

"Yeah, we formed a group, well, a cybersecurity posse. Using white-hat hacking methods, we save the day with our brains and"—I spread my hand out toward Wally—"vomit, as required."

Lexi lifted an eyebrow, then shook Frankie's hand. "Nice to meet you, Frankie. Someone once told me an agent uses whatever tools are at hand. You kids did a good job. We've got a lot to talk about. Let's get Wally cleaned up and go somewhere we can debrief in private."

"Did she say *agent* and *debrief* in the same sentence?" Frankie whispered to me. "That's *so* James Bond-like."

I patted her on the shoulder. "It could mean the White Knights are moving up from the Scooby game."

"Well, there's only one thing to say to that," Frankie said, grinning. "Jinkies."

CHAPTER FIFTY

Angel Sinclair

S lash and the two guys in suits escorted Omar and his laptop out of the museum. Omar loudly insisted on seeing representatives from the Iraqi Embassy. Wally cleaned up in the bathroom while Lexi spoke with the director of security at the museum. He confirmed he had spoken to both the DC police chief and the deputy director of the NSA and we were good to go. He seemed anxious to get us out of the museum, as if the cloak-and-dagger stuff had somehow tainted his establishment.

Not that any of it was our fault—at least, not exactly.

All three of us called our parents, and they spoke briefly with Lexi. She promised she would get us home safely and provide the details of our evening. For now, we'd been witnesses in a federal investigation, so we needed to be interviewed before we could go home. I thought my mom would completely freak out, but she didn't. Wally's and Frankie's parents, while surprised, were both mostly calm, although naturally concerned, while Lexi updated them on events. Before we could leave, however, Wally had to turn over his car keys to another agent, who promised to get the car home in one piece.

We piled into a black sedan with one of the agents driving and Lexi in the front seat. The three of us sat in the back.

"Where are going?" Frankie looked out the window as we stopped in front of a guarded underground parking garage.

"The NSA," Lexi answered. "One of their satellite offices, at least."

"Are we in trouble?" I asked.

"No." But the fact that she didn't offer more information worried me.

"Just so we're all clear—I don't think I can withstand waterboarding," Wally said. "I have a low threshold for pain."

"Waterboarding is CIA territory." Lexi sounded amused. "But no worries. I'll make sure there's no torture involved. Just answer their questions honestly, okay? You'll be fine."

"I'm going to tell them that you said that. Your word carries weight, right?"

"Right."

We pulled into the garage and parked. The driver opened our door so we could climb out. We went up two floors to what I assumed was the lobby. A man dressed in a suit and tie sat behind a desk and asked us to sign in by pressing our palms on a pad, then signing our names into an electronic book. After we did that, we walked through a magnetometer to make sure we weren't carrying weapons and through a door with frosted glass that buzzed to allow us entry. The agent who'd driven us didn't go in with us, but sat down in a waiting area. Lexi guided us to an elevator and pushed a button for the third floor.

When we got off the elevator, two female agents were waiting. One took Frankie to the left and the other led Wally down a long hallway to the right.

I looked at Lexi. "What about me?"

"There's someone special who wants to talk to you."

I followed her down the hallway in the opposite direction of where Wally and Frankie had gone. She stopped at the second door on the left and knocked. After a moment, she looked up at a camera mounted on the wall and waved. The door buzzed open, and we walked in.

Sitting at a long wooden conference table was Slash.

I took two steps forward. "What's going to happen to Omar Haider?"

Slash leaned back in his chair and smiled. Wow, his smile made him look so friendly and approachable. "That remains to be seen. He's being questioned as I speak."

"Then why am I here?"

"There are a lot of people who want to know how you found him."

"I…I don't want to go to jail. I just wanted to help Mr. Matthews."

Slash's expression softened. "I know. It's okay, Angel. I'm not going to let anything happen to you. You're *not* going to jail. You have my word on that."

"No offense, but can I get that in writing?"

"Of course." He pulled a notebook toward him and wrote something on a piece of paper, signing his name with a flourish. He pulled it out of the notebook and slid it over to Lexi. She read it, initialed it, and then passed it to me.

"There, you have both of our promises," Lexi said.

I studied the note in silence. "So, I'm safe? Really? No jail, no matter what I say?"

"No jail. No record. No nothing. Just honesty." Slash

motioned to the chair next to him, so I sat after I folded up the note and stuck it in my jeans. Lexi came around the table and took the chair on the other side of him.

"His word is good, Angel," she said. "Mine is, too. You trust me, right?"

"Seeing as how I am the president and founder of the Lexi Carmichael fan club, I think you already know the answer."

She winced when I mentioned the fan club, but managed a smile. "Remember how you helped Slash and me with that important mission in Egypt? We trusted you to do good work, so now I'm asking you to trust us, okay? We need you to walk us through the entire thing. How did you connect this to Omar Haider? Start at the beginning and don't leave anything out, including the hacking."

I told them, starting with the first day of my senior year at Excalibur and the bleacher that rolled onto Mr. Matthews's foot. I only stopped twice—once to go to the bathroom and once to drink half of the bottle of water that Lexi brought me. On several occasions, Slash opened the laptop on the table and had me walk him though my hacks on BioLimbs and the app and how I'd found the malware.

"So, you set a trap of this magnitude using the Wi-Fi of a public library?" Slash asked with a raise of an eyebrow.

"It was only the starting point. I'm not stupid. I hopped around plenty. I didn't want it traced back to me and my house in case something went wrong."

"You're going to need a few more lessons on cyberevasion," he said.

"Cool." I wiggled my fingers. "I'm ready when you are."

Lexi leaned back in her chair. "You know, I'm going to see if BioLimbs wants to hire us to beef up their security. If a fifteen-year-old can hack in…"

"Hello. Almost sixteen here," I interjected. "And Vincent Kars told me BioLimbs was no longer working with X-Corp."

"They are singing a different tune since you uncovered the malware."

"Really?" I looked at Lexi in surprise. "You told them?"

"Of course I told them. Even better, I showed them. That was creative thinking about the update software for the app, Angel. Mr. Kars was embarrassed—not to mention ashamed—for not listening to you."

"I don't know what to say. Thank you."

"You're welcome. You deserve the accolades for logical, solid thinking. And for perseverance."

Slash dipped his head in agreement. "She's right. But I do have another question for you, Angel. Who set up the mirror site? Not the coding, but the graphics and design? It was spectacular work."

"That was Frankie. She's got an amazing eye—an artist's eye. She can spot the tiniest detail and replicate it from just one look. She sees the smallest discrepancy in everything from architecture to clothing. It's pretty amazing."

"It is, indeed." Slash shut the laptop. "You've got a bright future in front of you, Angel. You're resourceful and smart, but even better, you're innovative and you accepted help when you needed it. You'll be a valuable resource in today's cyberworld."

"I will?" I perked up. "You think I'm innovative?"

He nodded. "I do."

Lexi leaned across the table, looking at me with steady eyes. "I do, too. So, as a result, I'll give you one more important piece of advice when considering your future in this industry. Always be a rebel. Stand up for yourself and your ideas. Change the environment, don't conform to it."

I nodded, a lump forming in my throat. She'd passed

on the mantra to me. Coder to coder. It was a milestone for me—a significant moment.

Lexi truly was my heroine, my mentor, and now perhaps even my friend.

Slash gave Lexi an affectionate glance—one she totally missed—before he stood. I scrambled to my feet, too.

"Wait. What now?" I asked. "What happens to Omar Haider?"

"We'll figure out what we need to do to take care of the situation," Slash said. "You go back to school and focus on that excellent future of yours. Besides, there's a certain vice principal who will be returning to school soon who will likely need your and your friends' support."

"Mr. Matthews," I breathed. "Will the police drop the charges in light of what we found?"

"I think that's a very likely scenario. Give us a few days to work through this, but I have a feeling things will be back to normal sooner than you think."

"Oh, thank you!" I impulsively hugged him. He smelled good, like leather, soap, and the faint scent of aftershave. "You guys are amazing."

He patted me on the back and then exchanged a smile with Lexi. "You and your White Knights turned out to be an impressive set of cyberdetectives. Let me know if I can help you in any way."

Any way?

I froze as it suddenly occurred to me. Slash worked for the NSA. Maybe he could help me find out if my dad worked for the NSA, and if so, what had happened to him.

The request hovered on my tongue. I just had to ask him.

I clamped my mouth shut. I couldn't ask him. Not yet. I liked Slash, but I wasn't sure who to trust. I didn't have enough information yet. Wally was right. I had to be careful.

But there *was* something else Slash could help me with. "Well, Slash, there's this one little thing…"

He lifted an eyebrow and listened carefully while I told him. When I finished, he nodded. "Consider it done."

"Really? Oh, you're ace. More than ace." I couldn't stop the smile that stretched across my face. "I can't wait to tell Wally and Frankie."

Slash put an arm around Lexi's shoulders, and she leaned into him comfortably. They fit well together, probably better than she realized.

"I'll bet they'll be happy to hear it," she said. "Looks like you've made some pretty nice friends with the White Knights."

I grinned. "Yeah, Wally and Frankie are pretty cool." I paused and then shook my head. "Oh, who am I kidding? They're amazing."

She smiled. "You know, Angel, I was once a lot like you. I reveled in solitude. I loved it…or at least I thought I did." She glanced up at Slash, who had an amused and affectionate expression on his face. "Anyway, I used to think I didn't need other people in my life to make me happy. I was content being alone. But after a while, solitude can start to feel a bit like a cage. In my case, it was a friend—no, *friends*—who unlocked that cage for me. I'll be honest, I didn't come out easily, and there were a lot of painful bumps on the road. But things got better. In the end, it's been worth the effort, a hundredfold."

She and Slash exchanged a long glance that made me envious of what they had—what they'd built. Maybe I *did* want something, or *someone*, like that someday. I agreed the first step out of my cage had been shaky. But Lexi was right.

It had also been worth it.

CHAPTER FIFTY-ONE

Angel Sinclair

t turned out I couldn't tell Frankie and Wally what Lexi and Slash said. A driver, a different one than the one who had taken us to the NSA building, took me home. I didn't see Wally and Frankie, and the driver didn't know where they were when I asked.

My mom was waiting up for me. Although she'd sounded calm earlier on the phone with the agent, she was a lot more worried than I expected. She started crying the minute I walked in the door and fussed over me like I was four years old. Gwen was there, too, and that helped calm things down because she told Mom to stop freaking out.

Despite the measure of support from my sister, neither of them would let me rest until I told them what happened. Although I was exhausted, I gave them a shortened version.

"So, you aren't in trouble?" my mother asked when I finished.

"No, Mom. I helped bring down a serious hacker. Plus, I have a written guarantee of immunity from Slash himself." I fished the wrinkled note out of my jeans pocket and handed it to Gwen. "Slash and Lexi personally thanked me. He thinks the charges against Mr. Matthews will be dropped."

"That's great, Angel," Gwen said. "It's incredible what you've done."

My mom looked at me through red-rimmed eyes. "So, all that time you were hacking when I thought you were making friends?"

"That's the thing, Mom. I did make friends. Good friends. Friends I can trust."

Gwen's face softened. "See, I told you it wasn't so hard."

"Speak for yourself. For me, making friends involved trapping an attempted murderer, hacking into multiple sites, and a scary interrogation by the NSA. What's not hard about that?"

"Smart aleck." But she gave me a hug anyway.

Later, in my bedroom, I was too wound up to sleep. I needed to relax, so I went to my go-to activity—the search for my dad. I sat in front of my computer and thought about all the things I knew about my dad's disappearance. Had he worked for the NSA? And if so, did it have something to do with his disappearance? On my desktop were the files I'd collected from King's Security—still unread. I wanted to read it all, but not tonight. I needed a fresh head to do that. Tomorrow would come soon enough.

Swinging my cursor away from the King's Security files, I pulled up my latest find from MIT's database— my dad's thesis, "Asymmetrical Cryptography: Authentication and Encryption."

I wasn't sure how much of it I'd understand or if it, too, might have played into his disappearance. It would, at the very least, get me a step farther into his head. I had a feeling that's where I needed to be if

I ever had a chance of finding out what happened to him.

I leaned back in my chair, clicked on the document, and started reading.

CHAPTER FIFTY-TWO

Candace Kim

NSA Headquarters, Fort Meade, Maryland

Candace spent a full forty minutes reading Slash's report about the three high school kids who had brought down an Iraqi hacker. When she finished, she took off her reading glasses, picked up the phone, and punched in the numbers.

"IAD."

"Slash? This is Candace Kim from NSOC."

"Hello, Candace. What can I do for you?"

"I finished reading your report on the Haider incident. It's unbelievable. Three high school kids brought him down?"

"Not just any kids. Three extremely talented kids."

Candace considered her next sentence, chose her words carefully. "One of them...Angel Sinclair. Did you know her father was once one of ours?"

"I'm aware."

"We think he's the Hidden Avenger. His name is Ethan Sinclair. We're presently in an active investigation regarding him that involves NSOC, Jim Avers in operations and Isaac Remington in the Research Directorate. You've heard of the Hidden Avenger, of course?"

"Of course. Why the sudden interest?"

"He recently made contact with us through CISB, who passed it up to Jim, who sent it up the chain to me."

"Has the director been advised of the situation?"

"He has."

Slash paused. "Why wasn't IAD informed?"

Candace picked up a pencil and tapped it on her desk. "That's on me. I'm trying to keep this tight to the chest, because something is off about this situation. I'm not sure who to trust."

"So why call me?"

"I trust you."

Slash was silent for a moment. "What's off about the situation?"

"It's hard to say. I've got a feeling there's more to this situation than meets the eye."

"Start at the beginning. Why did he come to us?"

"Apparently, he intercepted chatter from a terrorist group via the ShadowCrypt encryption key that indicates they may be planning something at the Super Bowl. He's offering us information on it so we can shut it down."

Slash's voice hardened. "In exchange for what?"

"Immunity and protection for his family."

"His family's in danger?"

"I don't know. Negotiations are excruciatingly slow. He doesn't trust us."

"Then why did he come to us?"

"Good question. We're still trying to figure that out, as well as what he wants the immunity for. Also, Isaac worked with him years ago. He said the connection was minimal, but I think there's something else there. He's not saying."

Slash didn't speak for a long moment. "What else?"

"Well, since the girl has a personal connection to you and Ms. Carmichael, I thought perhaps one of you might be able to persuade her or her mother to help us find out if they know anything about her father's disappearance."

There was a long stretch of silence before he spoke. "You want me to question a schoolgirl about a father she's never met and determine if she knows something the NSA, the FBI, and the CIA haven't been able to discover?"

Candace sighed. "I know it sounds ridiculous. But if Ethan is scared or desperate, he may try to contact her or the mother. So far, the mother isn't talking. We can't protect his family if we don't know what we're protecting them from. I'm trying to see if we can learn anything new to move the investigation forward."

Slash paused again and finally spoke. "I'll look into it."

Without saying goodbye, he hung up. Slash had never been the chatty type, but Candace didn't mind. She wasn't one for small talk, either. Slash was very good at what he did—the youngest IAD director in NSA history—with a fine mind and wicked skill behind the keyboard. She'd spoken the truth when she said she trusted him. She'd done what she needed and enlisted his help. That's as far as she could take it.

Unfortunately, it didn't bring her any closer to answers. She still had no idea what the Hidden Avenger wanted and why. She had a growing certainty that an important part of the unknown issue resided in the same building as she did.

CHAPTER FIFTY-THREE

Angel Sinclair

When I arrived at school bright and early on Monday morning, I wasn't surprised to spot both Wally and Frankie waiting at my locker. Frankie's dark hair was wound into two Princess Leia buns and streaked with green. She had a big smile on her face. I couldn't believe how wonderful it was to see them. I gave them both fist bumps, but Frankie and Wally pulled me in for a group hug. I didn't even mind.

Much.

"I'm so glad you didn't get arrested, Angel," Frankie said. "I would have visited you in prison if you did, though."

"Gee, thanks." I untangled myself from her embrace. "I'm glad to see you survived your interrogation, too."

"They gave me Coke and snacks. It wasn't that hard. Agent Simone asked me a few questions. I didn't know what you guys were doing on the computer, so I'm sure I had the least to offer. However, it did sound kind of James Bond-like when I described the stakeout in the museum café. I mean, let's take a moment to think about

309

it. Wally was trapped in the elevator with a possible murderer, and we chased after them by basically jumping down the escalator to the rescue. Do you think if a movie was made Selena Gomez would play me?"

"You're half Chinese, Frankie."

"I know, but she's pretty."

"You're prettier."

"You think so?"

"I *know* so."

"Speaking of pretty, I didn't mind my questioning, either," Wally piped up. "Rhonda Coswell, the agent who questioned me, was so hot I almost burned up. Seriously, if I were a couple years older, I would have gone for it. The whole questioning session ended way too soon, if you ask me. I could have withstood another six hours alone in a room with her."

I imagined what poor Agent Coswell had gone through with her debrief of Wally and tried not to laugh. "Oh, please, Wally." Still, I smiled as I spun the combination on my locker and pulled out my books.

"You heard that Mr. Matthews is going home from the hospital in a few days, right?" Frankie asked. "Ms. Eder was talking about it in the office this morning."

"Really?" I pulled out my math book and notebook. "The police aren't going to charge him?"

"Not yet, at least," Wally said. "They need to review the new evidence. My guess is they won't charge him at all based on what we know."

"That is the most excellent thing I've heard in a long time. Is he well enough to go home?"

"Apparently so." Wally grinned. "Given the influx of cash from our fund-raiser, he can afford a visiting nurse for a while to help him out."

"Sweet."

The bell rang, so the three of us separated. I was nodding off during a lecture about multivariable calculations when an announcement came over the loudspeaker.

"Angel Sinclair. Please report to the office."

Everyone's heads swiveled toward me as I stood. Ms. Horowitz handed me a slip, and I headed to the office wondering what was up. When I got there, Mrs. Eder and Headmistress Swanson were talking with a dark-haired woman in a pink top and black skirt.

"Angel," Headmistress Swanson said. "This is Miranda Bai. She's one of the marketing coordinators for Hello Kitty. She'd like to speak to you."

"Marketing coordinator?" I took a step back. "Hello Kitty? Look, if this is about the bra—"

"Yes, it's about the bra." She smiled and held out a hand for me to shake. "I saw the video."

"Oh." I reluctantly shook her hand then crossed my arms against my chest. Ms. Bai had a Hello Kitty purse slung over her wrist. "Ah, about that. It wasn't planned and…"

"It's okay. We at Hello Kitty *love* it. The footage is raw and real. You were caught in a true moment, for a good cause, and while wearing your Hello Kitty bra. We can't make this stuff up."

"But…my team lost and my bra got splattered with powdered sugar."

"Winning doesn't matter. It's the story—high school students band together to support their vice principal, an honored US veteran who was injured in an automobile accident. I couldn't have written a better script. It's perfect. To cut to the chase, we'd like your permission to use your likeness and story in a marketing campaign for the company. In return, we'll make a generous five-thousand-dollar contribution to the fund for your vice principal."

"Five thousand dollars?" I stared at her, stunned. "For me getting splattered in a bra?"

"A *Hello Kitty* bra."

"That's it? I don't have to do anything else? Just agree to let you use my likeness and our story in a marketing campaign."

"That's it. It's only for a limited time, and if we wanted to continue with the marketing strategy, we'd renegotiate the deal with you. Anyway, here is the agreement. Take it home, review it with your parents, your lawyers, whoever, and let us know."

I gave up trying to understand. After a few minutes, Ms. Bai left, and I was left holding a manila envelope with the information.

"That's it," Headmistress Swanson said with a smile. "I'm officially assigning you as the head of any future fund-raisers for this school."

"Just so we're clear, I'm not wearing that bra again."

She laughed. "Deal."

I floated back to class on a strange cloud of happiness—until I returned to my locker before lunch. Nic was there waiting for me. He leaned against the lockers, his arms crossed against his chest, looking furious as usual.

Just like that, my happiness cloud evaporated. I ignored him, but he got in my face, blocking the way to my locker. "You're going to pay for what you did, Angel. I'm never going to forget it."

I sighed. "What did I do this time?"

"They came to my house. The frigging NSA. They talked to my parents. They took my computer equipment. They claimed I was a cyberbully."

"You *are* a bully, Nic. Cyber and otherwise."

"I had to issue an apology on the website and now I'm facing disciplinary action at the school. You did this to get me out of the way so you could be valedictorian."

"You're the one that put up that stupid website and talked trash about people. I didn't have to do much."

"I'm not going to let you get away with this. You'll get yours. I promise you that."

Ugh.

"Aren't you tired of threats yet?" I brushed past him and opened my locker. "Why can't you turn over a new leaf and leave me and my friends alone?"

Nic grabbed my arm. "You're lucky I didn't push harder."

It took me a minute before I understood what he was referring to. My mouth dropped open. "It was you. *You* pushed the bleachers on me and Frankie."

His fingers tightened on my arm. "I don't know what you are talking about."

"You're certifiable, Nic. You could have *killed* Frankie and me. And for what? Because of some deranged desire to be valedictorian? What's *wrong* with you? Why do you hate me so much?"

"It was only supposed to be a warning. I didn't know your new friend would be there, too, and you'd be dumb enough to stay behind to try to save her. Seriously? You'd risk your life for someone you didn't even know? You're never going to make it in the real world, let alone in cybersecurity. You're going to get crushed. You'd better watch your step, because we aren't finished here. Not by a long shot." He released me with a hard shove and strode down the hall toward the office.

I had to steady myself against the lockers for a minute. That kid was living at the corner of deranged and completely unhinged. Finally, I collected myself and headed to lunch.

Enough was enough.

From this moment on, Nic Nerezza was in my past.

CHAPTER FIFTY-FOUR

Angel Sinclair

W e had a new lunch buddy at our table.

"Hey, Angel." Colt flashed his impossibly white teeth at me. "I saved you a spot." He patted the bench next to him, so I set my tray on the table and sat down. Frankie sat across from us. She was eating what might have been an egg salad sandwich, but I couldn't be sure. She took a bite and waved at me with her pinkie.

Wally sat next to her, eating chicken nuggets. Something seemed different about him. He sat up straighter and seemed more...confident. He'd found his groove. I guess facing danger did change people. I suddenly didn't want to tell them what Nic had told me about pushing the bleachers on Frankie and me. It wasn't like I could prove it, anyway. And right now, everyone looked so happy, so content, I didn't want to spoil the mood.

"Where were you?" Frankie asked, her mouth full of steamed carrots.

"I was talking with Nic in the hallway," I announced.

"Slash held to his promise. Operation Shutdown is a success. The NSA visited Nic last night, and he had to issue an apology to everyone he slighted on the website—that was an order from his parents. They're also investigating his hacking history. After a bit, I'm sure the website will go down for good. Nic is facing disciplinary action with the school, too."

Colt gave me a high five. "Great work, Angel. He won't hurt anyone again."

"Well, I wouldn't count on that. He all but threatened me and anyone associated with me."

Wally paused with his fork near his mouth. "He suspected you had something to do with the takedown?"

"He *knows* it was me. I'm not sorry for that. I'm only sorry it was too late to stop his vitriol about Colt."

"Hey, I don't care, and apparently, no one at Excalibur does, either," Colt said. "I'm beyond surprised since I officially came out. Everyone's been so cool and compassionate, even the football team. I didn't expect that level of support. My parents are a lot more relaxed about it this time around, too. This is a great school—it's the right place for me. Don't sweat it, guys. Nic did me a favor. I'm not going to be anyone else but me from now on."

"Score one for the good guys," I said with a smile. "It's about time."

CHAPTER FIFTY-FIVE

Angel Sinclair

After school on Monday, Mom took me to see Mr. Matthews in the hospital. He was sitting up and reading a book. Color infused his cheeks, and his eyes lit up as he saw us come in.

"You've got visitors," the nurse announced cheerfully.

My mom acted first, walking over to carefully give Mr. Matthews a hug. "Ryan, I'm so glad you're doing better."

He took her hand, squeezed it. "It's all the good news I'm getting. You've got a heck of a daughter there."

"I most certainly do."

I couldn't help the goofy smile that stretched across my face. "I'm glad everything worked out, Mr. Matthews, and you'll be coming back to school as soon as you're better."

"I'm looking forward to it." The familiar sparkle was back in his eyes. "Between you and me—the hospital food and entertainment are sorely lacking, although the nurses have all been stellar." His expression turned more serious. "What you kids did for me was amazing. I'm not certain I even know the whole story yet."

"There'll be plenty of time to tell you all about it," I assured him. "But Frankie and Wally want to be present when it happens."

"I bet they do."

For the next half hour, Mom and I sat in the visitor chairs, chatting with Mr. Matthews about everything from school to sports. Eventually, my mom excused herself to use the bathroom.

After she left, Mr. Matthews studied me thoughtfully before he spoke. "Thank you, Angel."

"No, thank *you*, Mr. Matthews. Even though you're not exactly one of my teachers, you've taught me more than everyone else put together. You've been patient and kind, yet you've always stayed one step ahead to motivate and inspire me to do better. That's what a great teacher does. That's what an amazing *leader* does."

He smiled. "You've risen to every occasion. You are meant for great things in this life, Angel Sinclair."

I met his smile with one of my own. "You know, Mr. Matthews, I used to wish you were my dad. But now I feel lucky you're my teacher."

CHAPTER FIFTY-SIX
Slash

When Lieutenant General Maxwell Norton, director of the NSA, personally opened the door to his office and ushered him in, Slash felt as though he were being treated as a favored son. Norton slapped him on the back and offered him coffee, which he declined, but he did take the seat across from the general, who balanced a mug of steaming-hot coffee on his hand.

Slash had played many roles in his life—operative, spy, hacker, analyst. He'd done things he never wanted to think about again. But for some reason, it was here, in the director's office, that he felt so keenly at home. For reasons he did not yet understand, this was where he belonged, where he understood the rules of the game and how to play to win. He respected Norton and his method of doing business. Norton was a solid guy—intelligent, straightforward, and tough as nails. His silver hair was cropped close to his head in a military haircut, and he took no prisoners when he spoke. Direct, blunt, and brutally honest.

"Did we catch Haider red-handed?" Norton finally asked him.

Slash nodded. "His laptop was hot. We traced him to everything. He was directly responsible for all the accidents that happened to the veterans, including the one death. We're still unraveling it and determining whether it was state sponsored."

"How did he do it?"

"He hacked a brain-computer interface that a tech company, BioLimbs, developed for use with prostheses. Basically, he intercepted electrical signals that were being transmitted from the patient's brain to the bioelectronic sensors in their affected limbs. He hacked their prosthetics via the software update app on the patients' phones, then installed a back door that allowed him to instruct them to do whatever he wanted."

"How would he know when to instruct them to harm themselves or others? Was he surveilling them?"

"I think so. He was certainly surveilling Ryan Matthews. We found a hidden camera in his car. We'll investigate the others, but I'm confident we'll find the same."

Norton let out an uneasy breath, frowning. "So, you're saying he could have made anyone with prostheses do whatever he wanted?"

"Yes, given more time for trial and refinement. Obviously, this has become an area of great potential threat."

"Hacking brains. Good Lord, what's next? I trust we're on it."

"We are, sir."

Norton set his coffee mug on his knee. "And Haider was caught by a couple of kids?"

"Three exceptionally bright and innovative high school kids calling themselves the White Knights. That's why I asked to speak with you today. I think they're excellent candidates for the Underage Training Operative Program. They are all seniors in high school, eligible for entrance—upon nomination, of course."

"You want to nominate them for UTOP?" Norton snorted, shaking his head. "Come on, Slash. I've seen their files. They're not typical spy school candidates. They don't have the athletic skills we need—they're bookish. Can any of them fire a gun, wield a weapon? I also doubt they'd have the emotional or social skills to withstand the psychological testing. They'd wash out in the first few days."

Slash was silent for a moment as he considered how best to present his case. He finally spoke, pressing his fingers together in a steeple.

"Sir, when you asked me to become the youngest director of IAD in NSA history, one of the requests you made of me was to bring the agency in line with the needs of and threats to our country today. As part of that younger generation, I see things a bit differently than most in the current management. What I see is precisely what you just said. These kids are *not* the typical candidates for UTOP. Physical skills are no longer as important as they used to be. We need tech-savvy spies. These are new times. Two of these kids have mad hacking skills—in fact, they possess more sophisticated, creative, and nuanced skills than I've seen among most adult candidates for the job. In my opinion, they would be tremendous assets in the field as agents. The third student has a wicked eye for detail and design, which she's capable of utilizing quickly and digitally. She's got exceptional raw talent in an area of great need. All three represent important components of the future of protecting both this agency and our country. They're *exactly* who we need on the front lines. I'm not asking for them to be shoo-ins to the school or be given any special consideration. I'm asking only that they're given a chance to prove their worth in their own unique ways. I think you may be surprised."

Norton studied him for a long moment. "What about the girl...Angel Sinclair? The matter with her father could be a problem."

"*If* he's the Avenger. I think there is more to the story than we know."

"The investigation is continuing?"

"So I understand. I'm happy to assist as required."

"It may come to that. My upcoming retirement has unleashed an inordinate amount of ambition and people jockeying for my job. I'm concerned it might interfere with the Avenger investigation."

"As the newest director, I'm not looking to take your job. My focus on the Avenger can be singular and discreet, if you need me, sir."

Norton sighed, rubbing his chin. His eyes looked tired. "I'll keep that in mind. Slash, do you really think those kids are what we need in this agency?"

"Yes, sir, I do."

Norton took a sip of his coffee, thinking. Slash remained quiet. Although he felt strongly about his request—and was certain Lexi would, too—this wasn't their decision to make.

After a minute of wrestling with the idea, Norton spoke. "All right, your request is granted. Invite them, but be advised, they must pass the trials on their own. Let's see what the White Knights have to offer."

Slash stood and shook Norton's hand. "Let's see, indeed."

CHAPTER FIFTY-SEVEN

Angel Sinclair

When Mom and I got home from the hospital, I sliced a thick piece of banana bread and headed into the bedroom to open my laptop. Once it booted up, I leaned back in the chair and clicked on my email.

I was about to take a bite of the bread when I froze. The subject line on an email caught my eye. I didn't recognize the address, but I remained riveted just the same.

"Your Father"

I'm an experienced hacker, and there were a million reasons why I shouldn't have clicked on the email. But at this moment, none of them mattered. I couldn't have stopped myself even if I'd wanted to.

I opened the email and held my breath as I scanned the contents. There were two sentences, and it wasn't signed.

> You are being monitored by criminal elements within the NSA. Do not attempt to contact your father.

I dropped the banana bread onto the plate. My entire world narrowed to the two sentences on my screen. My gaze narrowed so tightly I could see the pixels that made up the letters. My heart was thundering in my chest and I felt dizzy. I wasn't even sure I was breathing.

All my life, I'd longed to know...and now I did.

My father was still alive.

More from Julie Moffett

The White Knights series continues with **Knight Moves** and **One-Knight Stand**. Check Julie's website at http://www.juliemoffett.com/ to check for availability or send her an email via her Contact page to ask!

Julie Moffett   Julie Moffett

Check out the
Lexi Carmichael Mystery Series!
Get Your Geek On!

Julie's Bio

JULIE MOFFETT is a best-selling author who writes in the genres of mystery, historical romance, and paranormal romance. She has won numerous awards, including the 2014 Mystery & Mayhem Award for Best YA/New Adult Mystery, the prestigious 2014 HOLT Award for Best Novel with Romantic Elements, a HOLT Merit Award for Best Novel by a Virginia Author (twice!), the 2016 Award of Excellence, a PRISM Award for Best Romantic Time Travel *and* Best of the Best Paranormal Books of 2002, and the 2011 EPIC Award for Best Action/Adventure Novel. She has also garnered additional nominations for the Booksellers' Best Award, the Daphne du Maurier Award, and the Gayle Wilson Award of Excellence.

Julie is a military brat (Air Force) and has traveled extensively. Her more exciting exploits include attending high school in Okinawa, Japan; backpacking around Europe and Scandinavia for several months; a year-long college graduate study in Warsaw, Poland; and a wonderful trip to Scotland and Ireland, where she fell in love with castles, kilts, and brogues.

Julie has a BA in political science and Russian language from Colorado College, an MA in international affairs from the George Washington University in Washington, DC, and an MEd from Liberty University. She has worked as a proposal writer, editor, journalist, teacher, librarian, and researcher. Julie speaks Russian and Polish and has two sons.

Sign up for Julie's occasional newsletter (if you haven't done it already) and automatically be entered to win prizes like Kindles, free books, and geeky swag: www.juliemoffett.com.

Watch the book trailer for Julie's series:
http://bit.ly/2jFBsiq

Follow Julie on BookBub and be the first to know about her discounted and free books:
https://www.bookbub.com/authors/julie-moffett

Facebook: facebook.com/JulieMoffettAuthor

Twitter: twitter.com/JMoffettAuthor

Instagram: instagram.com/julie_moffett/

Julie's Facebook Fan Page (run by fans):
http://bit.ly/1NNBTuq